Fishing, Festivities & Fatalities

Mary Seifert

Books by Mary Seifert

Maverick, Movies, & Murder
Rescue, Rogues, & Renegade
Tinsel, Trials, & Traitors
Santa, Snowflakes, & Strychnine
Fishing, Festivities, & Fatalities

Visit Mary's website and get a free recipe collection!
Scan the QR code

Fishing, Festivities & Fatalities

Katie & Maverick Cozy Mysteries, Book 5

Mary Seifert

Secret Staircase Books

Fishing, Festivities, & Fatalities
Published by Secret Staircase Books, an imprint of
Columbine Publishing Group, LLC
PO Box 416, Angel Fire, NM 87710

Book layout and design by Secret Staircase Books
Cover images © Deeboldrick, Mitya Chernov, Chernetskaya,
Photographerlondon, Richard Nelson
First trade paperback edition: March, 2023
First e-book edition: March, 2023

* * *

Publisher's Cataloging-in-Publication Data

Seifert, Mary
Fishing, Festivities, & Fatalities / by Mary Seifert.
p. cm.
ISBN 978-1649141262 (paperback)
ISBN 978-1649141279 (e-book)

1. Katie Wilk (Fictitious character). 2. Minnesota—Fiction. 3.
Amateur sleuths—Fiction. 4. Women sleuths—Fiction. 5. Dogs in
fiction. 6. Christmas fiction. I. Title

Katie & Maverick Cozy Mystery Series : Book 5.
Siefert, Mary, Katie & Maverick cozy mysteries.

BISAC : FICTION / Mystery & Detective.
813/.54

ACKNOWLEDGEMENTS

Katie Wilk and Maverick have found a home and I want to extend my unending gratitude to Stephanie Dewey and Lee Ellison for their help making this extraordinary experience a reality. Thanks to my beta readers, Susan, Sandra, Isobel, Paula, and Marcia, for polishing the words to a high shine. Thank you to those dear to my heart who have provided encouragement, answers, unfailing support, inspiration, and advice along the way: John, Kindra, Adam, Danica, Mitch, Charles, Thomas, Jack, and Leo. I couldn't have done it without you. I so appreciate my readers and cheerleaders: Dennis Okland, Randy Betts, Patty Gehlen, Colleen Okland, Jenifer Leitch, Evy Hatjistilianos, Deb Van Buren, and Ruth Neely; fact checkers Luke Seifert, Jim Ellingson, Tom Peterson, and Curt Mottinger; my book buddies: Dr. Amy Ellingson, Sandra Unger, Dr. Joan Christianson, Eve Blomquist, and Maria Hughes; and anyone else who had a hand in this writing.

A huge thank you to Kathryn Marie Karlman for winning the bid and allowing me to use her birthday and nickname for a character.

Thanks to all who take time to read. You are the best. If you like what you read, please leave a review on your bookseller's webpage or on your favorite media site and spread the word.

"The beauty of chess is it can be whatever you want it to be. It transcends language, age, race, religion, politics, gender, and socioeconomic background. Whatever your circumstances, anyone can enjoy a good fight to the death over the chess board."

—*Simon William*

CHAPTER ONE

My last class vacated in such a frenzy when the final bell rang, my students sucked the air out of the classroom. Antsy all week, winter break had come just in time. Teenagers looked forward to a visit from St. Nick and so did I.

I stowed my books and homework pages in my briefcase and carted it to the math office, humming *Jingle Bells*. The teachers shared classrooms but each of us had our own space in the main office. I cleared the top of my desk and polished the chrome handles, wasting time until I felt I could confidently leave without drawing attention to myself. As the newest addition to the math staff, I hadn't wanted to be the first to leave, but the other teachers in my department coached winter sports and stuck around, waiting for afternoon practices to begin.

My phone buzzed and I read the screen.

On your way?

I promised my dad after the busyness of the fall, tonight would be the start of a total veg week.

Yup.

I grabbed my coat and headed to the door when the loudspeaker crackled and a voice growled, "Katie Wilk, if you're in the building, report to Mr. Ganka's office. Immediately."

I should've left when I had the chance.

Walking the plank would've taken less time and been less painful. My plodding footfalls echoed in the empty corridors. By the time I reached the office my heart thudded in my chest. When I changed careers, I'd sent out dozens of resumes and accepted the only job offered in education, teaching math at Columbia High School. I loved what I'd been doing. Why would Mr. Ganka want to see me?

The administrative assistant Mrs. McEntee always gave me good advice and had helped make my first few months of teaching successful. I trusted her to give me a heads up regarding what Mr. Ganka wanted. Her desk, however, usually a hub of activity with phones ringing, computer keys clacking, and students circling with an urgent request to see the principal, sat empty.

I readjusted my jacket and knocked on Mr. Ganka's door.

"Come in."

I tensed at the unexpectedly terse response but turned the knob and pushed open the door. Mr. Ganka sat behind his desk. His fingers were tented in front of his face, one eyebrow raised high enough to meet his flat-top. His mouth cut a severe line between his jowls. Mrs. McEntee sat in the corner, fiddling with her laptop, and avoiding eye contact. The boys' basketball coach and fellow math teacher, Trevor Michaels, leaned against a short bookcase. He crossed his arms over his chest and glared. A man and woman sat in two of three chairs in front of Mr. Ganka's desk, rigid, eyes forward, not acknowledging my arrival.

"You wanted to see me?" Before I could close the door, another body bolted through the gap and scooted into the remaining chair.

Dillon Maxwell.

My stomach clenched.

He grinned. "Good afternoon, Ms. Wilk."

His syrupy voice sent pins and needles down my back. This couldn't be good. Dillon had done everything possible to upset my classroom this year. He'd often arrive late, flip the light switch in my windowless room, and throw the class into darkness. Then he'd turn the light back on and invariably hand me an excused tardy slip. He'd apologize, slump into his chair, and make a production of searching for a pencil or slapping a notebook onto the desk. Sometimes he threw paper wads toward the trash can from across the room, 'practicing' his shot. Other times he'd sharpened his pencil within a centimeter of its existence, inspecting its point, and when it didn't meet his weapons-grade standard, he'd grind again.

"Hello, Dillon," I said flatly.

Mr. Ganka laid his hands on the desktop and leaned forward in his creaky chair. "It seems we have a problem."

My eyes flew open as the words tumbled from my lips. "What problem?"

Coach Michaels unfolded his arms and stood erect, six and a half feet of solid muscle. Red crept up his neck.

"Dillon says you're biased against athletes. That you have favorites and are failing him to keep him from playing in our holiday tournament. It's the principle athletics fundraiser of the year and the Cougar Claw is on the line with our biggest rival. Not to mention the city council promised new uniforms if we win." The confusing words poured from his lips. "We need him. The point guard runs the offense. Dillon is our best dribbler and holds the conference record for most steals."

That didn't surprise me—stealing.

The bird-like woman turned her perfectly made-up face to me and said in a high-pitched voice, "And he could be named to the All-State Mr. Basketball Team. You are denying him that opportunity."

"Now, Mrs. Maxwell," Mr. Ganka said in a soothing voice. He nodded at the man seated next to her. "Mayor Maxwell."

Dillon's mother drew a tissue from her purse and daintily sniffed, before she patted her perfectly coifed hair.

The mayor glanced at his wrist and said in a deep, gravelly voice, "We're attending an event in St. Paul tonight. Ganka, I want this fixed."

"Ms. Wilk," said Mr. Ganka in a placating tone.

I'd known him to be a fair and reasonable man, but he needed the facts. I inhaled and raised my chin. "I'm sorry Mr. Ganka. He is failing and he wouldn't be if he'd done the minimum amount of work."

"Stop telling lies." If looks could've done damage, Mrs. Maxwell's laser-sharp glower would have crippled me. No doubt Dillon got his eyes from her.

"If he's failing your Applied Math class, you're teaching it wrong," Coach Michaels said.

"But he's the only one failing," I said. "Everyone can pass if they do the homework. That's the way the curriculum was designed." I crossed my arms over my chest. "If my students simply turn in the completed assignments, they are guaranteed to *pass* the class. Our department feels it's more important our students know how to balance a checkbook, fill out a tax return, and figure a sale price. They should be able to ask informed questions without fearing or hating numbers." I turned to Coach Michaels and raised my hands to emphasize my indignation. "You know that."

"Take a breath," said Coach Michaels.

Dillon's sickly-sweet tone sliced through the tension. "No one can meet your unrealistic expectations Ms.—"

He made me grind my teeth, and I cut in. "Excuse me." I took a calming breath. "The course was designed to encourage students struggling with math."

"Struggling with math?" Mayor Maxwell's gruff voice repeated my words.

I sensed his ire rising, and feared a dressing down, but forged ahead. "Dillon doesn't even have the courtesy to come to my class on time."

"How dare you talk to my son like that. It's obvious you can't teach." Mrs. Maxwell lifted her chin, a lioness protecting her cub.

Mayor Maxwell's voice questioned again, "Struggling with math?"

I blinked back tears. I loved teaching my Applied Math students. Some had difficulty with school. They didn't want to be here and wouldn't allow themselves the luxury of enjoying any class, so I used whatever means available to make using numbers a positive experience. We played games with dice and cards, used calculators, drew floor plans, and doubled or tripled favorite recipes in a Family Life lab. Completed assignments earned a chit and favorable test scores provided bonuses. We pretended to purchase stocks and watched the market. Every student had a bank account, and I had a stash of inexpensive gizmos, gadgets, and candies they could buy with their fake money.

But what if Mrs. Maxwell was correct?

My confidence dropped to my shoes and my shoulders slumped.

Mrs. McEntee cleared her throat, which caught everyone's attention, and read from her screen. "Dillon's been late to his Applied Math class eighteen times." She looked over the tops of her glasses, landing on Mrs. Maxwell. "And you, Mrs. Maxwell, have written an excuse eighteen times."

Mayor Maxwell's head swiveled at the speed of molasses. He leveled his gaze on his wife and turned back to Mr. Ganka. "Dillon's always been proficient at math. May we see his records?"

"Yes. I think that'll clear up any misunderstanding. It doesn't look like you brought your gradebook with you, Katie."

I shook my head and caught Dillon smirking.

"Why don't you run and get it?

I didn't want this to go on any longer than it needed to. "Mrs. McEntee, may I pull up my records on your laptop?"

Her lovely eyes twinkled, and she smiled. "Of course, Ms. Wilk."

The Maxwells and Mr. Ganka rustled in their seats. Coach Michaels grunted. Sparks flew from Dillon's dark eyes, but he didn't move.

Mrs. McEntee handed me her laptop. I entered my

credentials and pulled up a class spread sheet. I blackened all the students' names except for Dillon's and set the laptop in front of Mr. Ganka.

I'd entered the skill practiced in each assignment across the top. Numbers filled the page except for the row headed by the name Maxwell. There I'd recorded a total of five grades since the start of school—four assignments and one abysmal test score. Mr. Ganka rotated the screen for Dillon's parents. They sat forward in their chairs.

Coach Michaels leaned over their shoulders to look for himself. His jaw turned white. His eyes met Dillon's. "You came in for a refresher and we reviewed how to figure a tip with a calculator before school that day. All you had to do was turn in the assignment. Even if Ms. Wilk didn't do a great job …"

I bristled.

"And I'm not saying she didn't." Coach Michaels nodded. "You had it completed. And look at this test score." He shook his head.

"Her test wasn't anything like what we went over. She wrote a bad test." Dillon sounded convincing and looked relieved.

Coach Michaels' chin jutted out and he stood tall. "The department agreed we needed continuity of instruction. The first semester tests came from the course I taught last year." He towered over Dillon. "I wrote that test. You are failing."

Mayor Maxwell said, "Dillon, you need to fix this." He turned to Mr. Ganka. "What can you do?"

"Ms. Wilk, what would it take for him to pass."

I had a feeling Dillon understood math. I think he just hated me or liked making everyone kowtow to his audacious whims. The tournament started in five days. "I believe he's capable, but he needs to complete every assignment." I shook my head. I was sure he could pull it off, but I didn't know if he would.

"She can tutor him." Mayor Maxwell said, clearly a command. "Beginning tomorrow morning. He will do the assignments. Schedule the necessary meetings and he will be there. The city's donation of uniforms is dependent on winning the tournament."

"Tomorrow is Christmas Eve, and the holiday break begins." Mr. Ganka rubbed his chin when he caught the look Maxwell gave him. The scowl vaporized whatever Mr. Ganka had been about to say. He sighed. "But my office is open, and I'll be here. We can work on it."

Dad and I intended to spend our first Christmas in Columbia together. "I can be here in the morning." The words left my lips before I could think about the commitment. I wanted him to succeed, if for no other reason than to prove it wasn't due to my lack of skill. "I'll have to check my calendar, but I planned to stay around for most of the holiday." What else would I do? I had over two hundred hours of unstructured time to fill or be bored to tears.

Coach Michaels said, somewhat contrite, "I'll help when I can, but the wife and I are spending Christmas at her parents' home in Bemidji, and we're leaving at ten, immediately after practice tomorrow. Dillon can practice, can't he?"

Mr. Ganka nodded.

Coach Michaels tipped his head my way. Before slipping out, he added, "Dillon, I expect you to do whatever you're told."

Mrs. Maxwell said, "I'll make sure Dillon studies, and

he will pass," making it seem like it was my fault.

"Mom," Dillon whined. "It's vacation."

"Not anymore," the mayor said. He turned to Mr. Ganka. "If he completes his work, can he play in the tournament?"

"That'll do it," said Mr. Ganka.

Mrs. Maxwell rose and dragged Dillon out the door. Mayor Maxwell stood and shook Mr. Ganka's hand.

"Have a great holiday, Mayor," Mr. Ganka said.

"Same to you, Phil."

When we no longer heard their footsteps, Mr. Ganka cleared his throat. "I'm sorry it went this way, Katie. I should've known better. They are the most vocal parents I know and if Dillon would listen and toe the line, we'd all be much better off. Do you need anything for tomorrow?"

With a student like Dillon, I didn't want our time spent together to be awkward or for him to misconstrue any intentions. "Could we meet here, in the office?"

"You can work at my desk." Mrs. McEntee held up her hand to waylay any no-you-don't-have-to-do-thats. "I can work at the counter and any hint of impropriety will be nipped in the bud." She'd read my mind, again.

I tugged at my collar, letting the heat escape.

"It's settled. Have a good night, ladies."

Mrs. McEntee waited until Mr. Ganka left. "Good girl." She shook her head. "But watch yourself. You're the only teacher with enough gumption to call Dillon out on his ill-preparedness. And you don't seem to care about his parents' ambitions. See you tomorrow."

Maybe I should have cared.

CHAPTER TWO

I left the quiet of the office and entered a world of ref whistles, shouts, and pounding basketballs emanating from the gym and following me to the math department. I fished out my key and opened the door. Without the life and light of the students, the empty, bleak rooms amplified my aloneness. I grabbed my coat and briefcase from the closet and noticed a file open on my desk which wasn't there before. Maybe a late assignment or a message of sorts? What I found had me frowning.

One of my favorite folders lay open on my desk, listing famous female cryptographers—encoders, and cryptanalysts—puzzle solvers. I had wanted to follow in their footsteps and attended the Royal Holloway in London. I worked in cryptanalysis with my best friend, found true love, lost it, and went home, only to find it again.

And then someone killed him.

It all happened so fast. Dad, Charles, and I were biking on a trail near my hometown. Dad had yelled, "Gun!" He still suffered minor effects from his traumatic brain injury, taking a bullet meant for me. Charles knocked me off my bike, covered my body with his, and took two more bullets. He died from his injuries. And they never found the shooter.

Blinking back tears, I replaced the file and rolled my chair under the desk, back in its place, revealing gouges around the lock on my top desk drawer. My finger traced the sharp indentations.

I inserted the key and cautiously pulled the handle. With nothing jumping from the gap, I opened the drawer fully. My favorite pens, mechanical pencils, and white board markers rested in their individual depressions; the ruler, protractor, calculator, and compass filled a mesh tray. But my record book was missing.

The door to the commons area banged open. I clutched my chest as the drumming of feet rounded the corner into the office.

Three students marched to the side of my desk with sharp creases etched on their young faces.

"Ms. Wilk," said Lorelei Calder, "we want to help keep you from getting into trouble over the Christmas break."

I laughed. "Whatever do you mean?"

They looked at each other and shook their heads. "We heard you being called to the principal's office, and we waited for you. You've been known to find trouble when least expected."

And they would know. To secure my teaching job, I consented to supervise the mock trial and science club, and the girls were three of the inaugural members of both extracurricular activities. They'd weathered the new ups and downs with me.

My shoulders twitched. Palms sweaty, my retort stuck to my lips. *But what if trouble comes looking for me?* Since I'd moved to Columbia, my dog, Maverick, and I had been accepted as a probationary search-and-rescue team. We'd been practicing our new skills. We'd broken up a drug ring, located a lost boy and an injured law enforcement agent, and even found a few bodies since school began. Each of these girls had played a part.

I swallowed hard. I had to admit they might be onto something.

"You have to go with us," Lorelei said, frowning. She was an opinionated, sometimes too-smart-for-her-own-good junior, taking advanced courses in math, communications, and science.

"Where do you want to go?"

I wasn't trying to be funny but the intensity smoldering in her hazel eyes squelched even the thought of laughter. She pushed her glasses up on her nose, raised her chin, and squinted.

"Brock wants to take us fishing. Ice fishing. In the cold. On the ice. Tonight." She brushed back tendrils that had escaped from her long blond braid and blew out an exasperated sigh. Every bit of her five-foot three-inch frame, usually packed with grace and confidence, quivered.

Often trailed by an adoring pack of groupies, Brock was a six-foot four-inch senior athlete, captain of the baseball team, and homecoming royalty. He followed Lorelei around school with such tenderness in his eyes, doing everything he could think of to merit her approval. She pretended to ignore him, and they fit together like yin and yang.

But ice fishing?

"Why would he want me to go ice fishing with you?"

"His mom and dad work tonight and they want a crowd and a responsible adult to supervise, and she likes you." Carlee Parks-Bluestone's eyes lit up with mischief. "And we can keep you out of trouble."

"I don't think I'd be any good. I've never been fishing. And Carlee, are you going to fish wearing that cast?"

Carlee laughed. "You'd be surprised by what I can do. I'll just wear a big old wool sock over my toes."

"It'll be fun," said Kindra Halloran. In early December, her family had been blindsided by the unexpected reappearance of her estranged dad. It had been hard on Kindra, but our mock trial team had helped her pull through. The sparkle in her bright eyes had dimmed a bit, but she scrabbled to reestablish trust in people. "Lorelei has some ideas for an experiment using different types of fish food." Kindra giggled. "Imagine that."

If hauling fish through a little hole in the ice would help bring more light back into Kindra's eyes, I was all in.

"What do I need to do?"

"Brock has all the equipment, but you'll need a fishing license," said Lorelei. "We're going to buy ours now. Can you meet us at Fuller Park Landing at six-thirty? Brock said he'd set up where we could see him."

I nodded.

"Dress warm." Lorelei waved as they left the math department.

I looked back at my desk and noticed the scratches again. I searched the drawers and the shelf for my record book.

The only clue to its whereabouts lay in Dillon's smirk

when Mr. Ganka asked me to show the Maxwells his grades, and I was certain he wasn't about to share any information. With my compulsion to keep records safe, I'd inadvertently thwarted a plan to discredit me by making a digital copy.

Using the office machines, I printed another hard copy of my grade book and buried it among the cryptanalysts' biographies. I left the math offices with much less confidence in its safekeeping than before.

CHAPTER THREE

I pulled my hood tight against the howling December wind trying to sneak under my scarf. I picked my way over the ice, through the empty parking lot to my rental—a dented, rusty, white Ford Focus. Two months ago, my Jetta ran into a majestic buck and couldn't even limp away. The stand-in, an unpretentious 2002 van purchased from an impound lot, disappeared one night, and returned minus the radio, the front bumper, three wheels, four hubcaps, the rear seat, the gas cap, and the windshield wipers. The replacement value wouldn't cover the cost of a bicycle helmet. Dad didn't enjoy driving much anymore and wanted me to have his pride and joy, a cream-colored Crown Victoria. I declined ownership but had borrowed his solid auto and it slid into a creek during a snowstorm. I lucked out. The mechanic told me he could get Dad's beloved car back into its mint condition if I'd drive the old beater and he could take his time fine-tuning the dream car.

It took the entire drive to my apartment to heat the car and afforded me time to regret my offer to tutor Dillon. Mr. Ganka did a fine job of subtle arm-twisting. If I could only get Dillon to use some of his smarts turning in completed assignments instead of concocting devious ways to get out of doing the homework, he could probably ace the course. I mentally ran through what I might accomplish in an hour, conjured up countless stumbling blocks, shook my head, and groaned. I couldn't pass the course for him.

My thoughts had taken up so much room in my head, I barely noticed when I arrived home. I parked the car, grabbed my briefcase, and hauled myself up the steps. Usually, Dad yanked the door out of my grip, but not today, and with my hands full, I fumbled around in my bag, fished for my key, and opened the door. A black streak flashed into the yard. I smiled while waiting for Maverick to finish his yardwork. It would be a vacation week for him too.

"Dad?" I called.

A clunking sound came from around the corner in the kitchen, followed by a loud grunt, and the splash of water.

"Dad?" My briefcase thumped to the floor, and I hurried to find the source of the commotion.

Dad sat on the floor, both hands shoved in front of him, his face turned away from the torrent of water spraying from underneath the sink.

Between glugs, he said, "Turn it off. Turn it off."

The spewing water hid the valve from Dad's vantage point. I reached in, turned the knob, and the water stopped.

Water covered his trousers and shirt. Droplets dribbled

through his hair, down his cheek and chin, and off the end of his nose. I handed him several dish towels but held onto the last one until he answered my question. "What do you think you're doing?"

He hung his head and muttered, "I lost something down the drain."

I stared for a moment before I burst out laughing and handed him the other towel.

"What's so funny?" He tried to maintain a serious expression, but it melted, and he chuckled as well. "Our floor needed a good washing anyway."

I took a huge breath and plunked down next to him. "What did you lose?"

He sobered immediately. "My wedding ring went down the tubes."

I stopped laughing too. Dad and Elizabeth were on a temporary hiatus. Elizabeth had eighteen months of non-stop caregiving for Dad following his injury and she needed the break. I arranged for Dad to stay with me for the time being.

"I think plumbing might be just outside of your area of expertise. Let's call someone who knows what they're doing."

"I've got a number."

"Did you get a recommendation from Ida? Our landlady probably has her favorite tradesmen. You know how she gets."

"I met Steve at the Y in my spinning class and …"

A wailing alarm drowned out his words and Ida rushed in through the adjoining door, carrying a steaming pot. Our landlady lived in the front half of the Queen Anne style home, and we'd come to think of her as family. She set the pot on the stove, removed her oven gloves, and crossed her arms over her generous assets. Her face pinched, and she said, "I installed an alarm to monitor appliance failure and it has a sensor to detect excess water under the refrigerator and sink."

Her green eyes and her freshly dyed red hair seemed to spark, and before her anger blew up, Dad and I scrambled to dry up the rest of the floor. The alarm stopped braying,

"Harry," Ida said. "What's going on? What are you doing?"

"Sorry, Ida. I'll get a plumber over here as soon as possible." He climbed to his feet and left the room, looking for his phone.

Her reproachful look transformed to one of concern. "Is Harry all right?" The door between apartments seldom stayed closed for long. Ida watched over Dad and always had his best interests at heart.

"He's fine. He took apart the sink, looking for his wedding ring, and he's never been very handy."

"That's a relief. I thought the alarm would be useful when the apartment is empty. Water damage is the worst. And I guess it comes in handy with a do-it-yourselfer as well." She grabbed the edge of the counter and buried her nose under the sink, nodding approvingly. "It looks like you have it all under control."

"Where do I get a fishing license?"

Ida stood and crossed her arms again. "Walmart. Why? What have you planned for your break?"

"I'm going to chaperone some of my students ice fishing." I shivered thinking of sitting on the ice surrounded by the shrieking wind. "Do you have any advice?"

Her green eyes glowed with mischief. "Dress warm.

Any other exciting goings on?"

"Tomorrow, I begin tutoring one of my students. He hasn't done the work. But if he can get a passing grade in my class, he can play in the holiday basketball tournament, and Coach Michaels thinks they have a shot at winning."

"That's a big deal here."

"So I've been told, and I've been identified as the deciding factor in whether they win or lose."

"You do know, you can't be held responsible for lack of effort on the part of a student? Every student signs a high school league form stating they understand the rules they need to follow to participate in a co-curricular or extracurricular activity. There are consequences."

"It's the mayor's son."

The tiniest grunt escaped. "Good luck with that. It won't be pleasant. Maxwell believes he's entitled to free lunch, free service calls, and unlimited get-out-of-a-speeding-ticket cards. He's an all-around unpleasant person. He's hard on his son, and his wife puts up with an awful lot."

"She lets him slide. And maybe she lets Dillon slide too."

Ida nodded at the pot. "My vegetarian chili. We can talk about the rest of your vacation tomorrow. Enjoy supper and have fun fishing." She tipped her head and with a thoughtful expression said, "Do you need anything? I think I have Casimer's old fishing equipment downstairs. He loved to fish." She sighed, reminiscing about the love of her life. "He didn't catch them often, but he loved to tell stories as if they were all big ones."

"Brock should have everything we'll need, but thanks." I uncovered the pot on the stove and inhaled the aroma of peppers, tomatoes, onions, garlic, and spices I couldn't identify. "Are you joining us?"

"If you insist."

The only thing I made well in the kitchen was a mess. On the other hand, Ida made the best everything. Dad usually had to choke down anything labeled vegetarian, but her chili won awards at the county fair every year and he loved it. She cooked with ingredients she grew herself and topped every recipe off with her not-so-secret ingredient—love.

"I baked Italian loaves this afternoon. It'll go well with the chili. I'll run and get one."

I rummaged through our refrigerator and, after checking the expiration date, opened the bag of lettuce. I tossed the contents in a bowl with crumbled feta cheese, garlic croutons, and black olives to up my game.

Dad hummed a tune as he reentered the kitchen.

"Any luck, Dad?"

"My friend Steve will stop over at ten in the morning and help me dissect the pipe to look for my ring."

"I'll be long gone by that time, but good luck."

"What are you doing tomorrow? Doesn't your break start?"

I gave him the same story I'd given Ida. "I want my student to pass, but he's making it very difficult. I think he hates me."

"No one hates you."

Hate might be an extreme word, but Susie Kelton came to my mind. When I moved to Columbia, I met Dr. Pete Erickson in the ER, having my head examined and stitched. He was funny, handsome, charming, and had shown interest. Susie was his nurse. They had a dating history, and she'd done everything she could to win him back. I'd been reserved, afraid to commit. They'd recently taken advanced training in forensics together to help with Pete's coroner duties. I missed my chance. He and Susie were now engaged.

I was afraid to ask who came to mind when Dad rolled his eyes.

Ida returned for supper, carrying a laundry basket loaded with fishing doohickeys, poles and reels, and canvas clothing, topped with a loaf of bread. The aroma of butter and garlic complemented the herb-scented black bean chili.

No one made food better than my landlady and we were fortunate she always made enough to feed an army. We sat and Ida sang a table blessing. My spoon was on its way to the bowl when she asked, "When do we get to know what's in the envelope?"

"I'll open it on Christmas Day." Months ago, I'd been saddled with a dog I didn't think I could care for, and Ida had sent a message to the kennel to come and reclaim Maverick, but by the time the veterinarian arrived from England, I wouldn't think of giving him up. The vet gave me an envelope I hadn't yet had the heart to open.

My spoon closed in on the bowl again. I closed my eyes and inhaled. With such a delicious start to my vacation, what could possibly go wrong?

CHAPTER FOUR

The long lines of overflowing carts and cranky last-minute shoppers at the check-out lanes made me second guess my consent to go ice fishing, but a store manager waved me and my single item to the service desk, and I checked out too quickly to change my mind.

I drove the busy streets to Fuller Park Landing and parked as close as possible. Trussed up against the below-zero temperatures in thermal mittens, a leather hat with furry ear flaps, waterproof boots with cleats, and wrapped in a woolen scarf and old snowmobile suit from Ida's laundry basket of Casimer's fishing sundries, I half waddled, half skied behind Maverick to where I could see people, and beads of sweat rolled down my back.

Kindra and Carlee waved from the landing entrance.

"Ms. Wilk. You came," said Carlee. Maverick moved in for a good rub.

"You sound surprised. I picked up a license and everything."

"If you hadn't come, Lorelei's mom wouldn't have let her go out on the ice. She should be here in a minute." Kindra turned and pointed. "Look at all those ice houses. It's a mini village."

Vans, trucks, four-wheelers, and snowmobiles parked next to shelters in red, yellow, blue, black, and orange, built in all different shapes and sizes. Four outstanding editions sported oversized mascots in Minnesota Viking purple and gold, Wild green, red and gold, United silver and blue, and the Columbia Cougar royal-blue and gold. Puffs of steam billowed from the chimneys of the heated boxes. Sounds of laughter and music carried over the ice. Generators hummed. Life pulsed from the gathering of fisher people.

I wondered how the ice held so much weight.

"Brock told us his favorite fish house is the Columbia booster. It has two holes, a heater, fridge, stove, oven, microwave, big screen TV, and two Murphy beds," said Kindra.

"Sounds like a home away from home." I stomped my feet to keep warm.

A horn tooted, pulled next to us, and Lorelei leapt from the Calder car.

"She's here, Mom. I told you. I'll be careful, I promise. And I'll get a ride home from Kindra." She slammed the door and followed her friends to the edge of the lake, toting a bright pink tackle box.

The passenger window slid down. "Thanks for chaperoning, Katie," Marietta Calder said. "I'm sorry. I just can't seem to relax." Her pensive gaze looked inward. "We almost lost her."

"I know. We'll be careful." Marietta pulled away from the curb and I took a deep breath. At the start of school, with the best intentions and trying to protect her friends, Lorelei deciphered a coded invitation to a party where drugs were shared like candy and the consequences nearly killed her.

"Come on, Ms. Wilk," Lorelei said anxiously. I smiled. *To be young and in love.*

I eyed her warily. "Do you know what we're looking for?"

"Brock has a four-person blue and gold portable pop-up."

"What's a pop-up?"

"It's like a tent." Lorelei giggled. "You should see your faces. Don't worry. It's insulated. Brock has chairs and anything we'll need to catch fish plus snacks and hot beverages. He's done this a million times. He's a pro. It'll be just like summer fishing."

"What's in your box?" I asked.

"Oh this?" She shrugged. "I have corn kernels, a jar of trout dough fishing bait, bread crusts, rubber worms, and some flashy lures. I want to experiment."

"I've never been fishing—summer or winter," I said.

Lorelei hedged. "There's always a first time." She brightened. "Kindra, you've been fishing."

"No, I haven't. You've been fishing though, right, Carlee?"

"Well …" She hopped a bit, regaining her balance over her casted ankle.

The girls tittered nervously, realizing none of them had any idea what Brock had in store for us.

"Thanks for being here, Ms. Wilk. I didn't want him to fish alone, and my mom is still skittish letting me out of her sight, but Brock needs us." Her voice trailed off.

"What's up, Lorelei?"

"Brock got new contacts today and he's adjusting." She sighed. "And I just didn't want him to be out here on the ice at night by himself. I think it's crazy. He's already out there, setting everything up for us."

I cinched my coat collar closer to my neck. "Let's see if we can find him," I said before I weaseled out of the experience.

I took a tentative step onto the ice and heard a scratchy voice behind me yell, "Scaredy-cat. Ice measured nineteen inches this morning."

A scruffy man hobbled onto the ice next to us. He wore a long, stained coat with frayed cuffs and tears at the elbows, an unraveling knitted cap, ripped black trainers, and gloves with holes at the ends of several fingers. Flecks of something unidentifiable dotted his scraggly beard. Coarse, gray-streaked hair covered his shoulders, and below his chin rested a black bowtie.

"Who're ya lookin' for, girlie?" he asked, slurring his words. "I know 'em all." The gap where his front teeth should have been made his smile appear sinister. He raised a paper bag to his lips, took a long swig, wiped his mouth with the back of his hand, and waggled an eyebrow over one steel gray eye.

"Hi, Xavier," Lorelei said. "How are you doing today?"

He puffed up. "I'm Ta Great Xavier," he said, adding the sobriquet. He squinted. "Do I know you?" Maverick edged closer and nudged Xavier's hand. Xavier petted him absentmindedly, while staring at Lorelei.

"No, but my friend Brock said you know everybody, and I should ask you for directions."

It could have been my imagination, but the man seemed to stand a little taller as he said, "Brock. That Arnold's son?" He scratched behind Maverick's ear.

"Yes, he is."

"Boy can't fish worth beans." He spat on the ice. "Head toward the point." Lorelei's gaze followed his crooked finger to a wall of lights on a huge home across the ice jutting out into the lake. "Fire engine, take a right." He shook a gnarled finger at her. "But stay away from my spot. And don't follow me." Paranoia crept into his voice. He shuffled toward the parking lot, up the embankment.

Lorelei whispered a thank you and stepped onto the ice. The girls and I followed, hoping the directions brought us close. Engines roared behind us. I glanced back and caught a glimpse of three riders, jumping off neon-green and black snowmobiles. They skulked up to Xavier bent over a trash receptacle.

"Wait," I said. The girls stopped.

I started back and heard one of the riders say, "What are you digging for now, you old goat?"

Two of them dumped a paper bag of garbage over Xavier's head. The other slammed the trash lid. Xavier flinched, threw off the cover, and continued digging.

"Leave him alone," I said, marching sturdily over the slippery ice. Maverick barked and pulled.

The faces, hiding behind ski masks, glanced up and at one another. They turned and ran.

Xavier continued raiding the can as though nothing had happened. I stepped next to him. "Are you alright?"

He muttered and hummed the opening bars of the

William Tell Overture.

"Xavier?" Maverick nuzzled his side.

He scratched behind Maverick's ears again and said, "Ta Great Xavier. Do I know you?" His cloudy eyes didn't focus.

"No, but my friend Brock said you know everybody, and I should ask you for directions."

He repeated his conversation with Lorelei verbatim.

"Thanks, Ta Great Xavier. Have a good night." I joined the girls, shaking my head.

"Dillon is a bully," Kindra said. "He didn't have to do that."

"Dillon Maxwell? How do you know it was him?"

She looked at me. "Did you notice anything special about his cap?"

"It was knitted, blue-and-gold, very long, and had a visor," said Lorelei.

"His grandmother knitted that cap especially for him to keep her 'little Dillon warm'. He's a nasty piece of work."

I shook my head. Tomorrow's meeting was turning into an even more unwelcome chore. My heavy feet trudged down the row of icehouses. Every step carried us over deeper water, but the houses, vehicles, burly men, rowdy kids, and patient women hadn't broken through the ice yet, so why should we? We walked until we came abreast of the bright red vintage fire engine, refitted as a fish house, sitting flush on the ice.

A polyester fire hose was gathered accordion-style and hung next to a shiny silver fire extinguisher. Two hooks secured an ancient wooden extension ladder to the side above a fireman's axe. Twinkling lights blinked from the retractable wheels in a traveling circle. A snowmobile posed at the door, aimed for shore, awaiting the evening's finale. We turned right and found Brock forty feet away, jumping up and down and waving his arms. The blue tent door flapped in the wind. Lorelei waved in return, and we stepped up our pace.

Maverick stopped, raised his sniffer, and cocked his head to the right. He usually acknowledged a sound I would hear moments later, but this time I heard the ice crack too.

CHAPTER FIVE

"Kindra, hold her," I said, a moment before Lorelei understood what had happened and screamed.

Brock disappeared, swallowed by the freezing water beneath his feet. Maverick and I trained for water saves and ice rescues. I squelched the desire to run out on the ice, shove my hand into the maw, and tow him to safety, but Maverick's search-and-rescue teacher, CJ Bluestone drilled into us repeatedly, "Nothing good happens if you both drown." I quickly ran through the important steps I needed to remember. Maverick barked and pulled. "Maverick, wait. Carlee, call 911."

Brock broke the surface and gasped.

"Brock," I yelled. I wasn't going to lose him. "Look up. Keep looking up. Keep paddling. Kick hard." I needed a safe way to get him out of the water and off the ice without doubling the catastrophe.

Maverick barked and pulled me toward the fire engine. A few fisher-people, curious about the desperate cacophony of screaming voices and a yapping dog, stepped out from their shelters. Maverick stopped and sat in front of the fire engine, continuing to bark. Xavier came out of nowhere and ripped the ladder off the side, dragging it across the ice toward Brock.

"Grab the hose," he said.

I snagged the hose and followed him.

"I told you to stay away from my spot." Xavier slid the ladder toward Brock. "Kid, grab the end." Xavier's gruff voice didn't carry far.

"Brock, grab the end," I repeated.

Brock thrashed around the edge, breaking off chunks of ice, creating a larger hole. His arms looked heavy, and he acted like he hadn't heard us.

"Brock!" Lorelei screamed, trying to pull away, but Kindra held her, using all her strength and a calm, reassuring voice.

"You'll have to go get him. Crawl along the ladder and elongate yourself to distribute your weight more evenly. You'll be less likely to go through the ice," Xavier said with a clear-headedness I hadn't expected. "If you can't reach him, toss him the end of the hose. Hold tight and I'll pull you back."

I heaved the hose over my shoulder and crept over the slats toward Brock. Maverick bounded toward me, and I held up my hand. "Wait." I put as much force into that word as I could.

Maverick would add another sixty-five pounds to my

one hundred twenty-five and we could go through the ice and join Brock. Maverick sat and whimpered.

I scrabbled forward, blocking out the voices rising behind me. The end of the ladder hung over the hole, but my fingers were still inches shy of Brock's hand. His chin bobbed in and out of the water and his panicked eyes locked on mine. Then they took on a resigned look.

"Don't you dare." I splashed icy water into his face. "Brock. I'm going to throw you a hose." Brock shook his head. Icicles hung from the lock of dark hair dangling in front of his pleading eyes. "You're going to be okay, but you have to grab the nozzle." He nodded. I tossed the hose. He reached for it and missed, sinking deeper in the water. "Brock." My voice scared even me, and his eyes widened. "You have to catch the end or … or Lorelei is going to kill us both."

I retrieved the hose and lobbed it again, and this time, Brock reached with a surge of adrenaline. His hands clasped the end, and I pulled him toward me. I seized the fabric on the back of his jacket and hauled him onto the end of the ladder.

The ice cracked again. The ladder tipped forward and water splashed my face. My torso dipped into the water and Brock slid from my grasp. Maverick barked and all sounds ceased. I reached over Brock's back and gripped under his arm, yanking him forward and tightening my hold. I laced my other arm through the rungs.

"Pull." My voice reverberated across the frozen water. The ladder jerked and caught on a chunk of ice protruding from the surface.

I reared back like a bucking horse, upsetting the balance, and raising the front enough to chip off whatever held us in place. I wanted to call out, begging Xavier to pull faster, but I had no breath. I couldn't feel my fingers and I shuddered. All I could think of was to hang on to Brock. I closed my eyes and gritted my teeth to keep them from chattering.

Maverick licked my face.

Sound returned full force. We scraped through the ice and snow amid voices and sirens. Someone tore Brock from my arms. I saw him rolled onto his back and onto a stretcher, a shiny stethoscope snaking its way to his chest.

Maverick licked my face again. I reached out to pet him, to tell him I'd be fine, but he was shuttled out of the way. I wanted my dog, but someone hauled me upright, wrapped a thick blanket around my shoulders, and steered me to the rear of the ambulance. Energized, seeing Brock shoving the oxygen mask off his face, I piled in.

Kindra caught my eye and with the barest of nods, assured me she would take care of everything. She held a sobbing Lorelei. Maverick sat in front of her, head cocked in a question, and Carlee brushed the top of his head.

The metal doors clanged shut and cut off my view. The siren wailed and the engine roared, but I focused on Brock's welcome moaning and complaining.

"Leave me alone. Let me go," he said.

The ride seemed to take forever, and Brock argued with the emergency technician for the whole trip. It felt like everything would turn out well, but I couldn't track time. It all ran together until the siren stopped.

My fingers clenched tighter as someone tried to yank the blanket off my shoulders. I fought back. "I'm fine. Take care of Brock."

"Katie?" I looked up and took in Pete's kind face and

concerned eyes. "We've got Brock. We need to get you out of here. Come with me."

I quaked with such intensity I couldn't get my legs to move. He took my elbows, helped me stand, and guided me down the steps.

"What were you doing?" he asked.

"Ice fishing." My teeth rattled behind a forced grin.

He delivered me to a cubicle manned by Susie. She shooed Pete from the room, dragging the curtain closed. "Get out of those wet clothes." When I took too much time she added, "Would you like me to help you?"

I redoubled my efforts and she slipped out. The buttons and zippers came undone, and I changed into dry scrubs.

I curled under the heated blanket a nurse delivered and my jumbled thoughts thawed. What happened? How was Brock? Did Kindra get the girls and Maverick home?

As if on cue, Maverick barreled around the corner, wriggling through the narrow entryway and onto the examination table, lapping my face and licking my happy tears. The rings of the privacy curtain screeched across the rod and Kindra, Carlee, and Lorelei snuck in. They pulled the curtain closed behind them.

"Are you okay?" Kindra asked.

"Chilled, but I'll be fine." I shivered, but at least I could put together a sentence and force the words between my lips.

Lorelei's eyes were shiny with tears. "Do you know where Brock is?"

"No, but he was fighting the EMTs in the ambulance the entire ride here."

She hiccuped and a little laugh escaped.

"He'll be himself in no time at all." I really believed he

would be fine, but wished we knew more.

The curtain opened again. Susie led Ida to the triage room. "She's all yours, Ida." Then Susie disappeared.

Ida tossed a puffy brown coat, a knitted blue hat, and matching mittens onto the table next to me. She placed a new pair of suede fashion boots next to the door. She crushed me in a bear hug. Stepping back, she put her hands on her hips, and gave me an irritated look.

"Did Dr. Erickson release you yet?"

I shrugged and slipped into the coat.

"And where is Brock?"

When I shook my head, she spun out of the room. I pitied whoever she came across first. She would find out about Brock and her directness would most assuredly result in my speedy release as well.

Lorelei swiped her eyes and Kindra brushed her arm.

"He'll be okay," Kindra said. "He will. Between Ms. Wilk and Xavier, Brock spent very little time in those frigid waters."

Xavier.

"Did anyone see what happened to Xavier? He reacted and knew just what to do. I don't know if I would have come up with that solution as quickly as he did."

"He disappeared into the crowd as soon as the EMTs arrived, and I didn't see him again," said Lorelei.

"I'd sure like to thank him."

Ida returned, dragging Pete by the lapel of his white coat. He had an indulgent look on his face, so she probably caught him between patients.

"Can she go home now?" Ida asked. She released him and crossed her hands in front of her.

Pete smiled. "Everything checks out. I'll sign the forms

and release her into your capable hands."

Kindra cleared her throat. "How's Brock?"

"If you head to the waiting area, you'll see him in a few minutes. His dad is on his way."

The girls looked at me. "Go," I said, making shooing motions.

Pete watched them leave and shook his head. "Brock asked only two questions. Repeatedly. Where's Lorelei? And when can I get a new phone? Katie, how did you manage to find the only square yard on the entire lake with thin ice?"

"It wasn't me." I tried to laugh as I patted around me, my heart racing, searching for my own phone. If Ida was here, Dad had probably heard about my dousing, and I needed to call him to tell him I was fine.

Pete reached the stand behind me, sliding the plastic bag of wet clothes to the side. He said, with a mischievous glint in his eyes, "Is this what you're looking for? I'll take a finder's fee. One dozen snickerdoodles should do it."

At the sight of my phone, the ice at the forefront of my mind melted away, and a warm calm washed through me, making my toes tingle as the nerves came alive, prodded by teensy pins and needles.

Ida plucked the hefty wet sack off the stand and lugged it toward the door. Pete gave me a hand off the examination table. When my feet touched the floor, we heard a crash and excited voices. Pete vanished. Ida glanced at me and raised her chin. I tugged Maverick's leash and we trooped toward the noise.

"Who decorated that ugly tree?" Xavier brandished a gnawed chicken leg, pointing it at an elderly man who pivoted in his chair and turned his back. Xavier spun one hundred eighty degrees. "Was it you?" He pointed the bone at another unsuspecting patient in the waiting room. "Bah. Humbug." Xavier released a maniacal giggle and did a little soft shoe.

Two uniformed men pushed through the double doors. Xavier threw the bone and it hit its mark before clattering to the floor. One of the men wiped slime from his cheek. A silent message passed between them and before Xavier made his escape down the hall, they seized him. He flailed, swinging his arms, and yelling unintelligible words, but they held tight.

I stepped in front of Maverick to keep him from entering the fray.

Lorelei halted the security officers. The scowl on her face didn't bode well for a conversation. She spoke and listened. She looked stunned, stepped to one side, and officers dragged the scrawny man toward the exit.

Xavier thrashed and squawked. He wrestled with the security officers, writhing and bucking, and almost tore free. The lights made his sallow complexion, agitated eyes, wild hair, and dirty clothes even more noticeable, and he resembled the Incredible Hulk bursting out of his Dr. Banner persona.

"Don't give her more." He lurched toward a pale, young girl cowering in the corner of the waiting room. "Just don't!"

The girl began to wail, and fat tears trickled down her cheeks. The woman seated next to her tried to cuddle her, but the girl stiffened and pulled away, crying harder.

"I'm not stealing." Xavier wrenched an arm free and knocked one of the guards to the floor. He pointed at a maintenance man. "You watched. I didn't do it." He twisted and dropped to his knees. "You can't throw me out. This is city property."

Xavier's erratic behavior had us all befuddled. "William Tell. William Tell," he said. His eyes met mine and he relaxed enough for one of the guards and the maintenance man to resecure his arms. Xavier slumped, and they dragged his dead weight near the sliding glass door while he intoned the opening notes of the overture.

The crazy glow dimmed in his eyes.

Xavier caught movement from the triage suite as a statuesque physician stepped out, reading a chart. Her wide eyes met Xavier's and he tilted his head to get a better look. He sneered. "I see things. Remember, I know things." He squirmed again in the arms holding him. "Let me go."

Pete's calm voice halted their movement. "I'll take him."

"But, Doc, he's a …"

Pete nodded but walked up to Xavier. "I'll take responsibility for his being here tonight."

The officer shook his head but released him. Pete spoke quietly and escorted Xavier across the waiting room, tugging on Xavier's sleeve to keep his attention, and led him through the door to the examination rooms. Regular noises in the room resumed.

"That's it. Show is over, folks. Let's get back to the tasks at hand." The officious sounding woman holding the chart called from behind the check-in desk.

The haughty look in her eyes held some displeasure, perhaps annoyed by the spectacle in the waiting room. She had a stethoscope draped over the shoulders of the pristine white coat she tugged closed. The blood-red polish of her nails flashed as she cinched the buttons, one by one.

Her finger followed a line on a page in front of her and she announced, "I'll see Quinn Karlman now." She tucked a flyaway strand of straw-colored hair into her French roll. Those startling eyes took in everything and she read a question in the little girl's face. She tilted her head. "Quinn. Remember me? I'm Dr. Coltraine."

The little girl snuffled, and the woman next to her wiped her nose. Quinn hopped off the chair and took the woman's hand. "Momma?"

"You'll be okay, Quinn, honey."

"But I want Dr. Pete."

Her lips pursed and Dr. Coltraine looked down her nose at the little girl. The bustling room went silent as if it expected an eruption. "You're sick. You need to get well. Let's get this done." She spun on her heels and stomped through the door. Her mother dragged Quinn, following the rapid clacking with slow, plodding steps.

Brock startled me by clearing his throat. I clutched my chest in mock faint, or maybe not so mock. "You're okay."

"Thanks to you," he said.

"And Xavier." A tiny question and then understanding flashed in Brock's dark eyes. "He pulled us off the ice," I said, nodding.

Flanked by Kindra and Carlee, Lorelei locked her arm around his and he smiled warmly. He grabbed her hand and brought it to his chest. Kindra bent her head and examined her boots, shying away from the twosome when Lorelei grabbed her and pulled her in for a hug. Brock yanked Carlee in, whispered to the girls, and stepped my way.

"Ms. Wilk? I don't know what to say."

"You're good. There's nothing to say." Maverick wiggled between us.

Brock's brow furrowed and his fingers scratched Maverick's furry head. "Can we talk someplace a little more private?"

We exited the first set of sliding glass doors into the entryway, and he walked to one side.

"I want to thank you again." He looked down. "But what I really want to tell you is ..." He shuffled his feet. "I don't even know how to say it. I was so scared. When the ice cracked open and I went down, it felt like there were dozens of frozen fingers wrapping around my ankles and pulling me into the dark, but I looked up and knew I didn't want to let go of the light. And then you were there making me think. I'm sorry I didn't check out the depth of all the ice where I set up. I always do that. I can't believe we could be so close to the village, and it's still standing tall without any problems." He shook his head, dislodging his disbelief. "Anyway, I hope you'll forgive me. I promise it won't happen again."

I gently took his ice-cold hand. "We're good."

The door slid and Ida, Kindra, Carlee, and Lorelei strode out to meet us.

"Now what?" asked Kindra.

Brock's grin was contagious. "I think I'll pass on fishing any more tonight."

Mr. Isaacson, Brock's dad, caught the last few words as he joined us in the entryway. "I'd say that'd be a great idea. Maybe we can fish next week." He turned his brown eyes to me. "Thank you, Ms. Wilk."

Tongue-tied, I smiled. Tears threatened to leak from my eyes. It could have turned out so differently.

"Lorelei, I know you wanted to protect Xavier. What did the guard say to you?"

"They asked if I could take him someplace safe and warm for the night. To be honest, I hadn't thought about where he would go. But he'll be in the hospital with Dr. Pete tonight."

Ida said, "Let's get your wheels, Katie. You kids, go home and hug your parents and tell them all about tonight before they find out from an old busybody like me."

We waved goodbye and headed toward Ida's car.

"Katie," Ida began. "What happened?"

I wrapped my arm around her and told her what I remembered. I took a small breather and asked, "Was it my imagination, or did Pete look especially sad when he took Xavier out of the waiting room?"

"You didn't imagine it." We reached her car and the locks clicked.

I opened the door, slid inside, and waited. "That's all you're going to say?" She revved the engine of her purple Plymouth Barracuda. "Why was he sad?"

Ida checked for traffic more carefully than usual. She exhaled. "Pete has been instrumental in requesting funds, soliciting corporate sponsors, and petitioning grants in an effort to raise awareness, expand the reach of our local shelter houses, and build some tiny homes."

I waited.

"Until the remaining grants come through and the buildings are secured, some of Columbia's homeless seek a moment of respite or refuge against the elements in the emergency waiting room, or library, or the mall during regular business hours. Moms, dads, grandparents, kids. Pete's seen it all. And he has a personal history with many of them. The mayor gets a ton of complaints, but he's invested in the new buildings so it will be a win-win when they find places for all the dislocated and close the encampment."

"How tragic!"

"I don't have much sympathy for Xavier, though. He's a Scrooge and has had plenty of offers of assistance. I wouldn't have anything to do with him and I think he should be locked up." Ida's strident voice rose in rage. "He's selfish and a con artist. A menace to himself and others."

I bit my lip before I said, "His lucid moment tonight pointed me in the right direction, and we saved Brock. I think I will be indebted to him forever."

She blinked, a little surprised, and nodded. "Your dad's waiting. I'll meet you at home."

"Am I in for a lecture?"

She gave a small chuckle.

CHAPTER SIX

Maverick licked my ear, and I rolled over, out of his reach. He jumped on the bed, and I pulled the covers over my head. He pranced around, and I giggled, unable to catch my breath. I sat up, took one look at the clock, and leapt from the bed. I dove into sweats and pounded down the stairs, into the kitchen where Dad and Ida sat, drinking something chocolatey from a mug.

"It's nine forty-five." I glared. "You both know I have to tutor one of my students today at ten. I didn't even hear my alarm. Why didn't either of you get me up?" I inserted a recyclable beverage pod for hot chocolate in the coffee machine and pushed all the right buttons.

"I turned off your alarm early this morning, before it could wake you," said Dad.

"Why would you do that, Dad?"

"I told you she wouldn't be happy, Harry."

He ignored Ida and ticked his arguments off on his fingers. "Well, let's see. You saved a student's life last night. You almost froze to death." I started to argue, but he held up his forefinger and continued. "You went to the hospital. You got home very late. It's vacation." He made a fist. "And you nearly gave me a heart attack. I even called Mrs. McEntee. I did you a favor."

"I promised Mr. Ganka I'd be there." I huffed.

"When will you be back?"

My irritation poured out. "When I'm finished."

Dad looked penitent.

"I'm sorry. Please let Maverick out. I've got to go," I said. I grabbed my hot chocolate and raced out the door.

I put the ice-cold car in gear, backed out of the garage, and came face-to-face with a big, red truck, thundering up the drive and blocking my exit. I honked. Exiting my car, I motioned for the driver to roll down his window. "I have an appointment. Could you please let me out?"

His lips formed a wicked grin. "What'll you give me?"

Seriously!

"A lot of trouble if you don't." My ears felt hot, and I'd bet the red and yellow sparks from my eyes ensured his compliance. He revved his engine and roared out to the street.

I rumbled through the icy roads and arrived just as my car's heat vents spewed warm air, with two minutes to spare. The lot was almost empty, so I parked close to the main doors and dashed through the front entry. I slid to a stop in front of the office and took a breath before pushing open the door.

Dillon stood by Mrs. McEntee's desk, pulling on his

coat. "I thought you weren't going to make it, so I made plans."

One glance at the clock and I said, "Sit." I meant it. Mrs. McEntee saluted.

Dillon didn't remove his coat, but he sat. I dropped into a second chair. I extracted what I needed from my briefcase one item at a time. I opened the records file on my laptop.

"Do you need a chaperone, Ms. Wilk?" Dillon said quietly, his ice-blue eyes danced as he shot Mrs. McEntee a challenging look.

My face felt warm, and I gritted my teeth. "Assignment five," I said, and curled the first four completed pages over the top. "Do you need a refresher?"

"Nope. I'll let you know when I want your help." His slick honey-voice grated on my nerves. He picked up the pencil and arranged the eraser and calculator he'd need within reach and set to work. I pulled out a paperback and sat quietly, my eyes roving the pages of the book, reading the same words over and over. I loved the story of naval cryptanalyst Agnes Meyer Driscoll, but couldn't stop thinking about Brock going through the ice.

After an hour, Dillon said, "Can I be done for today?"

He'd landed on assignment twenty. I checked his answers, and, except for one error, he'd done well. "If you can do this twice more, you'll be caught up. Do you want to do the exams for the two units you've finished?"

"May as well. My mom will want an accounting. Would you please write her a note, so she'll let me out of the house?"

He aced the tests, and I wrote the note for his mom.

"Why didn't you do the homework the first time

around?" I asked.

"Because then I wouldn't get to spend all this special time with you, Ms. Wilk."

If he wanted me flustered, he knew which buttons to push. "When's your next practice? We can coordinate your tutoring session with your basketball schedule."

He sniggered and his eyebrows crawled across his forehead. "Monday morning at eight, but I can meet anytime anywhere."

I ignored him. "Mrs. McEntee, could we work here again on Monday at ten fifteen?"

She clicked a few computer keys and, without looking up, said, "Certainly."

Dillon packed up and glided out of the room. When we were alone, Mrs. McEntee said, "He's a real piece of work. My skin crawled from all the way over here."

"Could you hear him?

"Not all his words. But I could feel his smarmy personality floating across the room. I'll have to fumigate before school starts again." She shuffled pages on the desk in front of her. "I do have a favor to ask."

"Shoot."

"The Student Council collected toys for Rachel's toy drive. She's a nurse—"

"I know Rachel. She loves her kids, doesn't she? I saw her in her element on the pediatric ward at Columbia Hospital. She guards those kids with her life and would give anything to see them all smile and be well."

"Could you drop the school collection off today? There are some gifts for her patients and she and her crew are going to deliver the rest tonight to the children who need them. Our students were so proud of all the things they gathered."

"I'd be delighted." I followed her into the commons. "I can't thank you enough for letting us hang out in the office to work. I just don't understand Dillon."

"I noticed he never asked a question. He knows how to do all the assignments, doesn't he? He just didn't do it. He certainly didn't take the easy route." She stopped in front of a cardboard barrel heaped with toys of every size and shape. "Here it is." She shimmied a clear plastic bag over the open end so nothing would topple.

I spun the barrel on its edge and rolled it a few feet. "I've got this."

She handed me an envelope. "They also collected cash for the committee members to use as they see fit."

The loudspeaker boomed. "Katie Wilk, report to Mr. Ganka's office."

My respiration increased. Mrs. McEntee walked me back to the office and shook her forefinger at her boss. Mr. Ganka wore a red and white Santa hat and a red tie with a blinking green Christmas tree.

He ho-ho-hoed and said, "Mrs. Maxwell called and wished us a Merry Christmas. Katie, you won round one. Ho-ho-ho."

"Merry Christmas, Mr. Ganka. And you too, Mrs. McEntee."

"Merry Christmas, Katie," they said in unison.

I rolled the barrel out to the car and hoisted it into the back seat with a grin which almost hurt. Our students had come through with items they'd enjoyed receiving themselves: superhero figurines, noisy electronic playthings, dolls, green slime, plastic and wooden blocks, tiny cars, musical instruments, crayons, markers and coloring books, plastic trains, grisly dinosaurs, board games, card games, and stuffed animals.

I sang along with the holiday radio station all the way to the hospital. I nabbed a hand truck and carted the barrel to the pediatric wing, excited to see Rachel's face.

I plopped the barrel in front of her desk.

"Oh, wow," she said and clapped. "What a haul." Her smile dimmed and she bit her lip, eyeing the exit.

"What's bothering you, Rachel?"

"Sorry I'm distracted." She cleared her throat. "These are great. We need toys this year. It's going to be a tough one for a lot of kids."

"And …" I prompted.

"Someone has been stealing from our supply at the hospital. I'd already chosen specific gifts for some kids and several of those presents are gone. Vanished. Vamoose. I can't imagine anyone wanting to take toys away from the children, but it happens. Dr. Coltraine hints it's our maintenance crew, but I don't know. When I asked Jim about it, he said it's all the riffraff allowed to use the hospital waiting rooms as their own personal home away from home."

"What is Dr. Coltraine's position?"

"She's the doc in charge of the emergency room, Dr. Pete's immediate superior."

Rachel grinned as she unwrapped the top of the barrel. "This stockpile is really going to help. Thanks for bringing them by, Katie. Give me a second. I have a thank you."

We exchanged envelopes and I left with a spring in my step and questions bombarding my good mood. Would Dad like what I got him for Christmas? Would Ida appreciate my gift? Would I attend Christmas Mass? Why would anyone steal from the children? But the question of why Brock had gone through the ice while trucks, snowmobiles, and houses did not was foremost in my mind.

I dropped by my apartment and picked up Maverick. We headed out to Monongalia City Park to take a walk, but wanting answers, I changed my mind and made my way to Fuller Park Landing instead.

Daylight burned the luster off the ice fishing village. The sun vaporized the mystique of the fish houses sparkling by moonlight, and during the day the deserted sheds appeared old and well-used. The bulging trash receptacles could use emptying. Neon pink markers waved atop wires stuck into the snow at ten-foot intervals, indicating the depth of the ice.

Maverick and I followed the same path as last night, across the ice towards the huge home on the point, up to the fire truck. The hose had been returned to its neat accordion fold and the vintage ladder hung on the hooks. It seemed we'd walked a lot further to get to Brock's pop-up last night, but I stumbled into the yellow caution tape just beyond the fire truck.

A dark gray discoloration outlined the formation of new ice over the hole which had swallowed Brock. I shivered. Maverick sat.

Brock had no chance to see it last night, but by the light of day, I could see the perfectly square shape to the hole.

"Maverick, stay." I dropped the leash and skirted the tape. I wriggled closer to examine the edges. The overnight temperature had plummeted. It wouldn't take long for the water to freeze solid, and the ice would camouflage the evidence. There may even be other dangerous areas across the lake where the ice had a shallow profile. I wanted proof the ice had been compromised. Our capricious Mother Nature didn't orchestrate Brock's accident. It had been manmade.

I stepped carefully, my eyes glued to the surface, examining it for signs of another void or a booby trap, like watching for a trip wire. I stayed outside the tape, circling, feet from the edges and snapping photos. I checked the results on my photos. Even zooming in, the photos didn't have the clarity I needed.

Momentarily deafened by growling engines, I pocketed my phone and secured Maverick's leash. The snowmobiles coasted onto the ice, sliding directly toward me. I gripped the leash and murmured gentle words to calm Maverick.

I recognized the windblown-red uncovered faces and wasn't surprised to see Dillon and his long blue-and-gold stocking cap. I stood in place. He and his cronies dismounted their sleds and clomped across the remaining distance, wearing boots with metal cleats.

"Hey, Ms. Wilk, what are you doing out here?" Dillon said in his saccharine voice. He checked out the area as if he really hadn't been here last evening.

"Examining the ice," I said.

"You should be careful, Ms. Wilk. It's dangerous. Can we help you?"

"No, thank you."

One of the young men took a misstep and landed on his back. He rocked and rolled onto his knees and his leg went out from under him as he attempted to stand on the slippery surface. His friends howled with laughter. Filled with determination, he tried again and threw himself forward. This time he knocked my foot out from under me.

I fell backwards, grabbing at the flimsy yellow tape. My heart raced as I skidded, in slow motion, toward the hole in the ice. I attempted to brake my momentum by clawing the surface, but my fingers couldn't find purchase.

The leash jerked in my hand, slowing my glide. Maverick pulled and I hung on until my measured crawl stopped. I remained motionless, sprawled across the ice. I heard boots tromp toward me and a crack.

A panicked voice called, "Don't move." Seconds later I heard, "Back away, slowly."

As the boots crunched in reverse, the leash jerked in my hand. Maverick pulled me a centimeter at a time away from the opening.

"Wait." I cued and Maverick stopped. I listened. Nothing happened. With my weight distributed as evenly as it could be, I rolled onto my front and shimmied on my belly, a tiny bit closer to the edge. I pulled out my camera and snapped a few photos at arm's length. The photos caught the sharp edge I wanted to capture for … whom? Why? Was cutting a hole in the ice a crime? That's what all the fishermen did.

"You're crazy, lady." Dillon said. Someone pulled at my boots and dragged me past the caution tape. "You're welcome."

"Thanks." I should've already thanked them, but it *was* their fault I'd fallen. I closed my eyes and rose to my hands and knees.

"Now, you're on your own," he said. "We're out of here."

Their retreating footsteps hammered the ice, and the machines bellowed to life.

The last of the engine noise receded. I sat, and let

Maverick lick my face when I got within range of his tongue.

I could always talk over troubling questions with Jane and thought to punch in the number to call my best friend but remembered she and Drew were on their way to visit her dad for Christmas. Instead, I typed a text to my new friend, Police Chief Amanda West.

I checked my message for inaccurate auto corrections and enlarged the photo to make sure she could see the edges of the ice. My eyes were drawn to the water. I peered more closely and had to swallow a scream. Something else floated in the water.

CHAPTER SEVEN

Scrambling on ice was tricky. Maverick must've felt my unease. He woofed in displeasure and rushed to my aid. I hurriedly crab-walked toward shore and told myself it was a trick of the light, an apparition made in the shadows by the ice and overhead clouds, or my imagination making something appear where nothing existed. I pushed send and took a breath.

Seconds later, my phone buzzed.

"Katie, where are you?"

"Amanda, did you see the photo? I think there's a body at the ice fishing village on Lake Monongalia."

"Stay where you are." She disconnected the call.

I edged to the shoreline, sat, and peered onto the lake. Maverick did the same, but as he nestled into my side, he whined.

Three cars arrived with flashing lights, but no sirens. No need to rush. Nothing could be done for a corpse. Officer Ronnie Christianson exited his car first. I cringed. He trudged across the ice, hitched his pants, and rearranged his jacket over his paunch. He loomed over me and sneered, "You, again. What are you doing here?"

Before I responded, Chief of Police Amanda West climbed from the second car. Ronnie looked over his shoulder, then back at me with disdain. "You're in luck."

When the chief's position opened before Thanksgiving, Ronnie had expected to be given the job, and he hadn't forgiven the former chief of police for encouraging the search for a new chief. The city council received several applications from well-qualified individuals. Columbia and Chief West were conducting a mutual trial. So far, I liked her and, though our latest weather was brutal, I think she appreciated everything else Columbia had to offer. However, she'd lived here for less than a month and she'd already worked one homicide. I hoped another body wouldn't upset the delicate balance and cause her to look for a position elsewhere.

She slammed her car door and met Ronnie on the ice. They held a brief conversation. She strode in my direction. I wiggled my fingers.

As word spread, fisher people stirred from their tiny houses, and in my need to ease the tension, I let the words from the song Glinda sang on the Wizard of Oz irreverently fill my head, *Come out, come out, wherever you are.*

"Here?" Amanda asked, dragging me from my reverie. I nodded.

She gestured to her officers. They set up a wider perimeter and slid tubs and packs of tools and equipment within reach. Amanda secured a cable to her belt, ducked under the caution tape, and cautiously stepped on the ice nearer the hole next to a diver sheathed in a dark-gray wetsuit with a single silver tank. He checked the cable tethering him to the police vehicle. He pulled the mask over his face, inserted a mouthpiece, and dropped into the abyss.

I turned at the clang of another door slam.

Dr. Pete Erickson trailed a gurney, manned by two uniformed EMTs, to the shoreline. He searched the growing crowd and caught my eye. He shook his head and marched my way.

"What did you find now, Katie?" He thought he was being funny until he saw the look on my face and stopped teasing. Maverick rocked from paw to paw, and Pete scratched behind his ear. Gray encircled his tired eyes and the five o'clock shadow looked hours old. I wanted to reach up, straighten his mussed hair, and ask him where his cap was. Instead, I burrowed deeper into my coat.

"I'm not positive," I said. "I took a photo and sent it to Chief West. She responded with the other officers and … you. I think there might be a body in the water where Brock fell through last night. It looks like the ice was carved out with precision and hasn't totally refrozen."

He rubbed his hand over his chin and eyes. "Cut out? Brock parked near someone else's fishing hole?"

"This hole was huge."

We both looked onto the ice when water splashed and the diver bobbed to the surface, hauling something to the edge. Two officers pulled the bundle of fabric onto a blue, plastic tarp. I looked away and my damp eyelashes began to freeze together. It looked like a body.

"You and Maverick, go sit in my van. The heater's on and it's warm."

Chief West summoned both Pete and Ronnie. From my vantage point, Ronnie seemed reluctant to join them. Maybe he harbored a bit of resentment. Pete's dad was the former chief of police and Ronnie had not been chosen as his replacement.

Maverick and I walked through the mumbling onlookers, and I almost bypassed the coroner's van, but curiosity and the cold got the better of me and I climbed in. With a front row seat, I watched the proceedings through the windshield. Pete and Amanda circled whatever had been brought to the surface and bent down. Pete gestured to the EMTs, who headed over the ice, hoisted the load onto the gurney, and wheeled it off the frozen surface.

The EMTs headed toward me. My heart raced. I did not want to be in the van with a body so Maverick and I got out and walked toward the fire engine, keeping tabs on the intense activity on the ice. Ronnie and another policeman knelt on opposite sides of the hole, observing the opening. I gasped when the diver bobbed to the surface once more and shoved forward another unwieldy bundle, sloshing the cold gray water. Ronnie and his partner dragged the heap onto thicker ice as the diver heaved himself from the lake and slithered away from the opening. He tore the mask from his face and slid the tank from his back. Amanda draped a long, black covering over his shoulders. He shook his head and she put a hand on his arm.

The EMTs deposited the first body in the back of the coroner's van. Relieved I'd escaped being caught with the corpse, I blew out a puff of air. They snaked their way through the crowd to pick up the second form. Pete accompanied them on the return; his hand rested on the rail surrounding the gurney. He clenched his jaw so tightly, it looked like his jawbone was trying to break free.

The EMTs slid the second gurney into the back of the ambulance and Pete clambered into the driver's seat of the coroner's van. He stared at the expanse of lake in front of him. He hesitated, then the engine revved. He threw his arm over the seat and turned to monitor his reversal. The wheels spun. He let up until the tires caught some traction. The vehicle jerked, and he bolted in the direction of the hospital, following the ambulance.

The wind picked up and began to whistle through the channels between the fish houses. The officers dispersed the crowd. Some fishermen chased items skittering across the ice. Pieces of trash spiraled from the top of the garbage cans, lightly touching down like tiny dancers before spinning out of sight.

Amanda tramped over the ice, testing each step. When she stood in front of me, she said, "Looks like he went in at the same place and, as you believed, it had been manmade, cut with precision. The victim—"

"One victim? But your diver came up twice."

"Yes. The first heap is just a bale of old paraphernalia held together with bungee cords, but Officer Rodgers brought up a body too. That was probably the face you caught on your camera. The victim belonged to one of the groups of homeless, sheltering under the bridge on the north side of the lake. Dr. Erickson, Pete, recognized him."

"Did he tell you who it was?"

"Xavier Notrecali."

I felt like I'd been socked in the gut and grunted.

"Katie," she said with concern. "Did you know him?"

I nodded. I inhaled and coughed as the cold air took my breath away. I blew out as much of the frigid numbing agent as I could. "Xavier helped direct the rescue last night."

She scrunched her forehead. "The crazy one?"

I almost smiled. "Not too crazy to nab the ladder off the fire truck and yank Brock and me to safety. He seemed quite aware of how to maneuver on ice. He sounded as lucid as you or me when he told me what to do. He showed up at the ER later, and I got the feeling he was checking on us. I …" He'd saved Brock's life. Of that, I was certain. Maverick leaned against my leg.

"So Xavier knew where the hole was. Maybe he thought he could get rid of some stuff in the open water and fell in. Pete's pretty shaken and I didn't know what to say."

"Do you want me to call Lance? Warn him?" If Amanda's trial as chief of police was successful, she'd be replacing Lance Erickson. He'd had heart issues and had to give up the career he loved. When I came to Columbia, he'd been first on the scene when I needed help, and he was on my speed dial.

"Yes. Please. Someone should know."

I punched in his number and had to leave a voicemail, sharing what Amanda had said. I waited until she finished talking to her officers. She escorted Maverick and me to my car.

"I won't need you for anything today, but could you stop in and make a statement on Monday? And could you keep it under your hat? We have next of kin to notify."

I nodded.

"I'm sorry, Katie."

"Me too." On Christmas Eve, Amanda would have to notify next of kin, if there were any she could find, forever changing the meaning of this holiday for them.

I opened my car door and white splattered against my windshield. We turned and saw a person wrapped in rags, winding up, preparing to hurl another snowball in our direction. I ducked or the second one would have smacked me in the face.

"They killed him," the toothless mouth screamed.

CHAPTER EIGHT

Amanda put her head down, pulled her collar up, and plodded through the snow. "Ma'am," she called, but the pitcher fled before the chief could confront her.

"I wonder what that was about," said Amanda once she returned. Her phone buzzed. "Give me a sec." She spoke briefly, pocketed her phone, and said, sadly, "Merry Christmas, Katie."

"Same to you." Maverick jumped in, and I slid in after him, but before I pulled the door closed, I said, "Amanda, do you have somewhere to be this evening? If not, come join us."

"I might just do that." She waved. I backed out and headed home.

I meandered the streets, taking the long way, admiring

the decorations, grieving a bit for Xavier, and remembering Charles, regretting never having celebrated our first married Christmas together.

Maverick licked my face, bringing me to the present, happy for my dad, my landlady, a good job, great students, and a dog I loved. I tuned my radio to the holiday station and headed to 3141 North Maple Street—home.

Ida had warned me. Christmas was her favorite December holiday. She buffed and shined, making everything gleam. She cooked, baked, boiled, roasted, and broiled all her favorite foods. Her decorations rivaled the city's lights, blinking from every tree in her yard, around the scrollwork of her iron fence and gate, within the wreaths and animated statuary, and from every window on the front of her house, welcoming and merry.

A cheery grin inched its way over my face but stopped when I saw the big red truck clogging the end of the driveway. I parked on the street and tried to recharge my good mood.

Maverick and I traipsed to the rear apartment through the mounds of snow. I stamped my boots, dislodging the fluffy white covering, before opening the door to loud music, accompanied by two out-of-tune baritones in the kitchen, crooning one of my favorite carols, *White Christmas*.

I yelled, "Hello."

"We're in here darlin'."

I peered around the corner and tiptoed into the kitchen, expecting water to be spewing over the floor again. Dad sat on a high stool, flashing the finger displaying his wedding ring. "I'm the overseer. Steve's working his magic on the pipes." He took a swig of something frothy in a mug; a white mustache hung over his upper lip.

"Not vocal pipes, mind you," croaked a rough voice.

I inhaled and stopped breathing. Stale smoke wafted from the overalls covering Dad's plumber-friend, and I backed away.

Metal clanged and the voice called for the exchange of one of his tools. Dad delivered, securing a monkey wrench in the outstretched hand, like a nurse supplying a scalpel to a surgeon. The voice called for a coupling nut and a trap. The pieces disappeared with a jangle and a few thunks. "Valve grease," the voice said. Dad placed a tube in the outstretched fingers.

I heard a solid tap, and Dad's fellow-Y-spinner elbowed his way out of the cupboard and sat, wiping his fingers on a dirty rag.

"Steve White." A live cigarette dangled from his lips.

I took a quick breath, stepped forward, and shook the hand offered. "Katie Wilk."

Steve slid back under the sink. "Har, run it."

I grabbed a towel and wiped the grease and grime off my hands as Dad turned the handle on the faucet.

"Looks sealed to me." Steve slid out again, and continued, "But call me if you see any water. My peepers aren't as good as they used to be. Maybe you, with your young eyes, should take a look, Katie." He hacked, coughing, and his eyes watered before he caught his breath.

Dad extended his hand. Steve rocked a bit, and after a few grunts from the two of them, he stood, waiting expectantly for me to check his work.

With one hand planted on the sink, I stuck my head underneath, not knowing what I should look for. I found shiny pipes, no dripping, and a clean cupboard.

"Looks good to me. How long have you been in the

business?"

"It's just something I picked up. I retired and moved to town and was working part-time maintenance work at the hospital. But it's not fun anymore so I steer clear. Them ER docs think they know it all."

They certainly do. I hoped I didn't say the words out loud. I asked, "What did you do before?"

Dad said at the same time, "Are you joining us, Steve? You know you'd love it. Think of all the new people you'll meet."

I scrunched my forehead. *Join us?*

"You heard me squawk. I ain't got a voice." He stubbed out the cigarette, and not finding an ashtray, he wrapped it and put it in his pocket.

"It doesn't matter. Everyone loves carolers. Ida's got a bunch of Katie's students coming and she'll be there too." Dad's eyebrows danced and a knowing smile inched its way across Steve's grizzled face. Dad turned to me. "Are you caroling with us, darlin'?"

"Who did Ida get to sing?"

"Ida called Lorelei and she pulled a group together."

Lorelei would gather quite a crew. "Where are you caroling?"

"We're going to sing for the senior residents at Sterling Manor followed by a performance at the children's ward at the hospital. Rachel asked Ida to provide a little entertainment. There'll be cookies and cider." His voice lilted, hinting the treats should be enticement enough.

"That sounds like a lot of fun. I'm in." I checked the time. "Meanwhile, what did you do for lunch?"

The adjoining door banged opened, and Ida waltzed in, beautifully attired in red and green spangles and sequins, carrying a Dutch oven filled with something that smelled like clam chowder.

"Make room, Katie. Lunch is served."

I cleared space and she set the pot on a trivet. "Get out some bowls, small plates, and silverware. I need a hand, Harry. We'll get the salad and baguette."

Dad followed Ida, mimicking her fancy strut behind her back.

Steve stripped the overalls from his broad shoulders and wriggled his legs out, kicking the offending outfit into the farthest corner of the room on top of a pair of worn work boots. I could smell the minty gum he popped into his mouth. Using the back of his hand, he slicked his hair down. He tugged on his shirt and adjusted the top button. He rubbed his hands over his stubbly chin. Sitting down, he leaned back, and feigned nonchalance while I arranged our table for four.

Ida hugged a bowl of greens, dotted with deep red cherry tomatoes and chunks of yellow and white cheese, and a foil-wrapped loaf of bread. Dad jostled a tray of beautifully decorated cookies and candies onto the counter between the piles of tools.

"Sit," Ida ordered.

"I invited Amanda for the evening. I suppose I should text her with our itinerary."

Ida answered, "Caroling at Sterling Manor at four thirty, before their dinner. Caroling in front of the hospital until we meet in the children's ward at six, after their dinner. Our supper at eight followed by midnight Mass."

"You're coming, aren't you, darlin'?" Dad asked.

My fingers danced over my phone. "Sure." It pinged in response. "Amanda's hoping to join us at the hospital and stay for supper."

We bowed our heads, and Ida gave a blessing before we dug in. I didn't fully appreciate their humor but enjoyed hearing hearty laughs from Dad, Ida, and Steve. I just couldn't get the square shape carved in the ice out of my head.

CHAPTER NINE

At Sterling Manor, the residents joined us singing and many used most of the correct words. What words someone didn't know, they invented with gusto. More than one senior, with sparkling impish eyes, used the *jingle bells, Batman smells* lyrics, and received a tap of reprimand from a well-intentioned friend. Our farewells took forever.

We carpooled to the next destination, and when we arrived, Dad held tightly to my hand. He knew I'd rather cut and run. Visits to hospitals brought memories of his gunshot and surgery and Charles' death, but, over time, the intensity of those emotions decreased, and my aversion had lessened. We stood outside the hospital and gazed at the sky, studded with glinting luminaries.

Biding our time outside until after the supper hour,

we ran through four of our songs before my allergies kicked in. At least that's what I told Steve when I teared up after warbling another beloved holiday special, "Oh Holy Night."

"Ri-ight." His head went up and down, but his eyes twinkled. I never actually heard his gruff voice singing, but his presence was a welcome addition.

Kindra's sister, Patricia, was deaf, and she taught us to sign *Jingle Bells*. The repeating words made it easier to learn.

The church bell pealed six times, and our choir strolled through the atrium, serenading the lonely registrar. She beamed. Jim leaned against a broom handle and applauded our small troupe. We made our way to the elevators and crowded inside.

The bells jingled in Patricia's hand as she signed, and Kindra interpreted. "There aren't many people here. That's good, isn't it?"

"I think they try to get as many patients home as are fit to go," said Ida. "But there are a few who won't make it home tonight."

Kindra signed Ida's answer to her sister.

The doors whooshed, and Nurse Rachel stood in front of us. The baffled look on her face clearly indicated she'd been anticipating someone else. She grabbed my dad and they stepped to the side. Behind her we watched a curvy elf delivering candy canes to young and old. Susie Kelton glanced our way, first with eagerness, then a frown. We weren't who she expected. Of course, I hadn't expected her either.

During the month of December, Rachel had the atrium piano wheeled to the pediatric ward where some of her patients or their caregivers would share music of the season and it guaranteed a visit from carolers. Ida rushed to the piano, threw open the cover, and ran her thumb over the ivories from one end of the keyboard to the other in a cheery glissando. She sat. We circled her and launched into our first chorus. When we began our fifth carol, the elevator bell dinged, drawing all eyes like a heavy-duty magnet. Ida stopped mid chord.

Before the black-booted figure could fully emerge, Ida pounded an introduction, leading us in an enthusiastic rendition of *Here Comes Santa Claus*. Mouths dropped and eyes opened wide as a skinnier-than-usual, red-suited Santa hitched up his pants, cinched his belt over a soft middle, and hefted a bag of colorfully wrapped gifts over his shoulder. He ho-ho-hoed across the room and dropped into an upholstered wingback chair.

Susie sashayed to Santa's side and whispered in his ear. He whispered back. "Santa doesn't have a lot of time. He has places to go and people to see tonight. But he has gifts for each of you. Let me hand them all out before you unwrap yours. Then we can do it at the same time, okay?" she said to the kids.

Santa removed the packages from his pack, smiled knowingly, and read the names. Hands rose timidly, the children not believing their good fortune. Susie scurried around the room, distributing presents, receiving hugs in return.

Soft piano notes danced quietly in the air, and Ida swayed as she continued to accompany the activity.

Rachel put her arm around my shoulder. "Thank your dad for me. He does Santa well in a pinch."

"What happened to your real fake-Santa?"

She shook her head and shrugged.

"Were you expecting Dr. Erickson?" The first time Pete played Santa when we caroled earlier in December, the kids loved him.

"ER docs are so unreliable," she said, chuckling. "Can't seem to keep a schedule. Thank you and your students for coming too. It's good to see Miss Parks looking so well." Carlee had broken her ankle in several places and had spent almost a week on the children's ward, recovering from surgery, but she maneuvered fine in her walking cast. "We have five patients tonight. Most will make it home this weekend. There's only one patient who is questionable."

I followed the tilt of her head and almost didn't recognize the little girl from the ER last night with her pale face and twitchy demeanor. She sat in a wheelchair, twirling a strand of stringy hair around the finger of one hand, and chewing a nail on the other. Standing behind the wheelchair, her mother rested her head on the stiff shoulder of a big man. His arms were crossed over his barrel chest, and he glowered at Rachel.

Goosebumps traveled up my arms and I shivered.

"What's wrong with her?" I braced myself for a devastating diagnosis. The little girl didn't even light up when Susie placed a gift in her lap.

"They can't pinpoint what's wrong, but they're doing tests and she'll be here for a little while."

I searched Rachel's inscrutable face.

The elevator doors dinged again, and a nurse's aide arrived, pushing a cart with hot cider and cookies, bringing Amanda with it.

The bright lights reflected off her shiny shoes and gold shield. The creases in her uniform could slice cake. A thick braid threaded with gold ribbon hung down her back, and her subtle makeup enhanced her natural beauty.

"Am I too late?" The words came in a rush.

"Nah. We're taking a break. What do you have there?"

"I have a few copies of a Christmas story I thought the kids might enjoy. I hoped to be here earlier, but I didn't think bagging them would take such a long time."

I took half the toppling pile and set them on a nearby table. I picked up a wrapped book and turned it over in my hand. "These are fancy. Did you attach a pinecone and chocolate Santa to each one?"

Amanda blushed. "Is it too much? One of my goals is to make police more accessible to kids and I thought if I brought books tonight and sang, more of them would decide we're not the bad guys."

"Of course not." I gave her a quick hug. I'd only known her a month, but I like her and hoped she'd stay in Columbia. "Let's hand these out."

Amanda smiled lopsidedly as we topped off each gift pile. Each child received the wrapped book with starstruck eyes, awed to be treated by both Santa and the chief of police.

Finally, Santa stood and held up a sagging pack. "Merry Christmas everyone. I'd best be on my way. I've got the world ahead of me tonight. Be good. And remember." He winked. "I'm watching."

The voices joined together and said, "Merry Christmas, Santa." The kids dove into the packages, and Santa and his elf disappeared.

Torn and wrinkled paper littered the floor, and oohs and aahs filled the room. Ida continued to play softly until that first yawn. Knowing how contagious they could be, she waved us together at the piano and the roomful sang

We Wish You a Merry Christmas, before we headed out.

I assumed exhaustion explained the silence of the carolers, but on our elevator ride, Brock cleared his throat and worked up his courage to make a request.

CHAPTER TEN

The sponsors of the holiday ice fishing contest are requiring a team of up to eight anglers for the tournament, needing an average age of twenty-four. I know you had a rude introduction, but Ms. Wilk, would you care to join my team?"

My jaw dropped and my palms itched. I barely heard the grinding gears of the descending elevator over the pounding of my heart. The door dinged but no one made a move. A hand shot out and pressed the button to keep the door open.

Lorelei broke the silence. "Please?"

"Send me the info," I squeaked. "I can't make any promises." I remembered the icy water rushing over my hands trying to claim Brock, and pictures of Xavier filled

my head. But if Brock could make it back on the ice, so
could I.

Maybe.

Ida snorted and released the elevator button. Everyone
exhaled at the same time and poured out of the confining
box. I stumbled behind them. Before falling on my face, I
felt powerful fingers wrapped around my upper arm.

"I've got you."

"Thanks, I …" I looked up into laughing chocolate eyes
and watched a glorious dimple form as the face flashed a
smile. I retrieved my arm. "I appreciate your help. Merry
Christmas, Dr. Erickson."

Dad stood behind Pete and rolled his eyes. I didn't
know what he expected. Pete was taken. I forced a smile.
"And Happy New Year."

I thought I detected Pete's smile fading a bit. What I
wouldn't give to be the one to make him really smile.

"Your dad was kind enough to take my place this
evening, and I'm most grateful. I have a patient I'm very
concerned about, and time got away from me. Merry
Christmas, Katie." He looked over his shoulder. "And
Happy New Year, Harry."

Pete stepped into the elevator and the doors closed
him away.

"Darlin'," Dad said with a disapproving voice. "You're
still friends, aren't you?"

Ida snorted again and trotted after Steve.

I sagged. "You're right. I wasn't thinking. Brock asked
if I'd fish on his tournament team." Dad's left eyebrow
rose. "I haven't decided yet, but I promise I won't be so
curt next time I see Pete." I inhaled.

"As long as the ice depth is checked, fishing sounds like

fun," said a very chipper Amanda.

I pulled my cap on my head and we headed out the door toward our vehicles. "I don't know how to fish," I confessed.

"The sponsors are all about safety protocols. They mandated a minimum average age for each participating team, although whyever they chose twenty-four as the age of a responsible adult, I'll never know." Amanda snorted. "I do know Brock's grandfather founded the club putting on the contest and the powers that be didn't want to disqualify Brock outright just because he went through the ice. Instead, the board passed a rule last night, intending to keep him and other youth safer. Brock needs a team with dependable and conscientious adults, not necessarily fishermen or women, to prove he's capable of fishing safely after his recent polar plunge."

"That wasn't his fault," I said and secretly applauded the call to safety.

Amanda looked thoughtful and nodded. "If he needs more years to balance his team, I'll help. I'll up the average enough."

I didn't know how old she was, but certainly no one would question the chief. "You fish?" I eyed her suspiciously.

"Walleye, perch, sunnies, men, women …" She gazed at the night sky. "It would give me an opportunity to mingle with members of the fishing village and become part of the community without drawing attention to myself as law enforcement. I'd like to talk to that snowball thrower if I can find her." We stopped and she climbed into her patrol car. "I'm going to stop at home and change, and I'll be along shortly."

"Bring an appetite," said Dad.

She pulled from the curb.

Dad said, "I would bring the average age way up."

"I don't remember you fishing."

"Darlin', there are many things you've never seen me do."

Ida gave a hearty laugh. "I would hope so, Harry," she said, walking toward our car arm-in-arm with Steve. "Look who else is joining us for supper."

* * *

I drove down our street and stopped in front of Ida's flashing, but tasteful, decorations. What a welcome! I couldn't wait to huddle in front of a crackling fire and listen to more glorious piano playing. Before caroling, we'd set Ida's dinner table with her china, crystal, and polished silver cutlery. She'd planned the meal in advance, and it had bubbled in her slow cooker for hours while we sang our songs. She promised tender ribs unlike any we'd had before, accompanied by Dad's twice baked potatoes. I'd made a strawberry Jell-O and pretzel salad with cream cheese and whipped topping from a recipe Lorelei had given me, promising I couldn't ruin it.

We propped the adjoining door open, better to ease the way between apartments, and barely had time to hang up our coats when Ida's doorbell rang.

I opened the door and smiled broadly. Amanda lugged inside a canvas bag of clanking bottles. I helped her unpack them and read the label on the first of three.

"Sorry. I didn't ask what we were eating and didn't know what wine to bring so I brought a variety." Ida's Christmas caftan floated behind her as she glided forward with her arms held wide. "Amanda, welcome. Dinner is ready." The nose on her Rudolf apron blinked red and Steve snickered.

Dad scrutinized the wine labels, selected a red, and headed for the far end of the sideboard. Steve removed the cork, poured a short glass, and handed it back to Dad who swirled the liquid, inhaled its aroma, and sipped, playing the part of a sommelier. Deemed worthy, Steve refilled Dad's glass, poured four more, and handed them around.

"Did you figure out what happened to Xavier?" Ida asked Amanda as she herded us into the dining room.

"Bet he was drunk," Steve said. "Xavier's always guzzling a bottle of something."

Dad gave Amanda an apologetic look, lifting his glass. We appeared to be doing the same with our holiday libation.

"Did you know Xavier?" Amanda asked.

"It's just idle chatter I heard," Steve said.

We sat around the table and Ida led grace, but before Amanda could even taste her wine, her phone dinged. She read the screen and her forehead scrunched. "Excuse me." She stepped out of the dining room.

Ida's eyes shifted to the door and back, waiting for Amanda. After a minute or two, she said, "A police chief's time is never her own." Ida started passing the dishes around the table. We took healthy portions of the delicious smelling foods. Maverick drooled, watching for any dropped savory.

When Amanda returned, she was zipping her coat. "Thank you for the invitation, but something's come up."

Ida's green eyes blazed. "Don't leave yet. Give us a minute while Katie fixes a plate to take with you, and I'll box some treats. You're going to work, I presume, so you'll need to make amends with those stuck working with you on Christmas Eve."

"You don't have to do that …" The look Ida gave would have stopped a train. "But thanks," Amanda said.

I followed Ida into the kitchen. She harrumphed and whacked two plastic serving containers on the counter. I let her get as much out of her system as she could and said, "Don't hold back. I know you're angry, but can you tell me why?"

"Somebody is intent on screwing up Christmas. It's not fair." She looked at my container. "Give her more potatoes. And lots of the red salad you made. She'll need all the energy she can get. I don't think the dispatcher would've called Amanda if they didn't need her for something serious."

We snapped the lids on the containers and put them in Amanda's canvas bag. Ida put on a big smile and strolled back into the dining room.

"Enjoy, my dear," she said, handing over the bag. "Do let us know if we can do anything for you. Join us, if you can, for midnight Mass. We'll save you a seat until eleven fifty-five when the squeezing together begins."

Amanda nodded, and I walked her to the front door. "Are you going to be okay?"

Amanda shook her head. "I have a full plate now, that's for sure." She struggled to laugh, hiking the canvas strap over her shoulder.

"Is there anything I can do?"

She replied with an enigmatic, "You've done enough already. Merry Christmas, Katie."

CHAPTER ELEVEN

We stuffed ourselves, laughed, and told outrageous tales. Still chuckling, Dad rose from the table and followed Ida into the kitchen. He returned, delivering a *Bûche de Noël* which looked too real to eat. Awed by the textured log covered by a thick, luscious frosting in multiple shades of brown and surrounded by cocoa-dusted meringue mushrooms, Steve moaned and patted his stomach. "I don't think I can enjoy dessert yet and that looks too good to pass up."

"Harry," Ida said. "Katie and I are going to clean up. You and Steve make a fire. We'll be in shortly."

I'd never known men to be excused and women relegated to clean up in Ida's home. She'd always challenged Dad to do his share, but the way she smiled, with a starstruck face, told me a different story.

Dad and Steve refilled their glasses and retired to the living room. Ida and I cleared the table and stored the food in stackable containers in the fridge. She washed the dishes and I dried, trying to think of a way to casually ask what she thought about Steve but my phone rang. Because my hands were full, I hastily grabbed the phone and answered before I checked caller ID. "Merry Christmas."

"Katie, this is Chief West." My hand clenched the phone, and I straightened my back, listening intently to the official sounding call. "Could you make it to the station tonight? We have some questions for you."

"May I ask what about?"

"Xavier Notrecali."

"I'll be right there, Aman—Chief."

I disconnected the call and Ida looked up at me with worried eyes. "What is it?"

"I'm needed at the station." Ida balled up the dishcloth and reached for the apron ties behind her neck, but I stopped her. "You stay. I won't be long. I don't know all that much. Serve that lovely dessert and I'll be back before our gentlemen even know I've been gone."

I relished the quiet drive through the multi-colored lighted streets and viewed driveways overfilled with cars, imagining families visiting for the holiday. Dad and I had observed Christmas quietly until he married Elizabeth. Then we'd enjoyed a host of new traditions. I remembered the splendid Christmases with Elizabeth and my step-sibs, Austin and Sandra, and wondered where they'd be celebrating this year. This would be Dad's first Christmas away from his wife, and, although Elizabeth and Dad had an amicable separation—just time away, she'd said—I hadn't heard from any of them. I didn't know if a proper protocol existed, but I promised myself we'd give them a call tomorrow.

The harsh lights at the station glinted off the hood of my car and the visions of Xavier's body replaced memories of my past Christmases. I wondered why Amanda needed me so soon. I pulled my cap down and got out of the car. I shoved my hands in my pockets and trudged to the entry, puffing clouds of steam into the cold air like a kid trying to avoid another trip to the principal's office.

The officer at the desk checked me in and Amanda stuck her head out the door before I could take a seat. "We can see you now."

We?

She marched into a conference room, and I followed. She sat at the head of the table and pointed to the seat opposite her between Officer Ronnie Christianson and Officer Daniel Rodgers. I bristled at Ronnie's disapproving look. He'd been an adequate temporary chief of police for three months after Pete's dad suffered several small heart attacks, until the search team found Amanda.

"Hi, Katie," Officer Rodgers said with a smile.

"We need to know everything you know about the victim." Ronnie slapped his notebook on the table and flashed a pen, then opened the notebook with great fanfare, pretending to latch onto my every word.

"I didn't know him. Not really. I met him on Lake Monongalia Thursday night." When no one asked a question, I filled the empty space with more words. "I'd been invited to go ice fishing with some of my students. I'd never been ice fishing but one of the parents thought I'd make a good chaperone. We were told to ask Xavier for directions. He knew where everyone was on the ice and gave us perfect instructions."

"Had he been drinking?"

"I don't know. Maybe. He held a bottle wrapped in a paper bag, so I couldn't see what was inside."

They waited and I continued with my narration, wondering what startling revelation I could give them.

"After he was accosted by those snowmobilers—"

"What snowmobilers?" Officer Rodgers asked.

Amanda sat forward in her chair

"Xavier was combing through the trash and three snowmobiles stopped. The riders jumped off, dumped a bag of garbage over him, and slammed the lid on his head. We chased them away—"

"Do you know who they were?"

"There were three males—maybe males. They wore facemasks so I didn't see their faces."

"When it's below zero, everyone wears a facemask." Ronnie amplified his disbelief with a snort.

I should probably have told them Kindra recognized Dillon, but that was hearsay, wasn't it? She never saw his face. They could check out the lead. Somebody might have known who they were.

"And then?" Amanda gave me an encouraging smile.

"My students—"

"Names?" said Ronnie.

"Lorelei Calder, Carlee Parks-Bluestone, and Kindra Halloran."

"Go on."

"It seemed as soon as we made contact with Brock Isaacson, the ice cracked, and he went under." My heart rate picked up and I felt the terror of seeing him disappear into the icy water. I took two deep breaths. "And Xavier did everything he could to help me get Brock out."

"He knew where everything was, you're saying?" said Ronnie.

"Not only where everything was, he was very levelheaded. He reminded me to distribute my weight across the rungs of the ladder we'd sent out on the ice toward Brock. He told me to throw the nozzle of the hose if I needed more length to reach him and when we were ready, I screamed 'pull.' The ladder scraped through snow and ice. I didn't see who pulled us in, but Xavier set the successful rescue in motion."

"And at the hospital?" Officer Rodgers urged me to continue.

"I only saw him for a few minutes. He was agitated and caused a little disturbance in the ER, acting a bit crazy, but when he saw us, he settled down. It felt like he'd come to check on us, and when he saw we'd made it to the emergency room, he seemed relieved."

"Did he say that?" Ronnie asked, squinting, making me want to squirm.

"I guess not, but ask Dr. Erickson. He took Xavier into the triage rooms after the ruckus. Pete, I mean, Dr. Erickson told the security officers he'd take responsibility."

Amanda looked at Officer Rodgers.

Ronnie shoved away from the table. "Told ya."

"Officer Christianson." Heat curled around my ears. "I know we don't always see eye to eye, but whatever does that mean?"

"We're trying to discover Xavier's whereabouts after the confrontation in the ER waiting room and we received the same information from multiple sources. Dr. Erickson was the last one to have been seen with Xavier."

I relaxed and sat back in the chair. "There," I said. "Pete will be able to give you all the information you need."

Amanda looked down. Officer Rodgers aligned the three pages on which he had taken notes, and Ronnie smirked.

"What did I say?" I asked.

CHAPTER TWELVE

When I asked if they knew what happened to Xavier, they clammed up and Officer Rodgers escorted me from the building, wishing me a Merry Christmas." I ranted between mouthfuls of rich, gooey, chocolate goodness topped with vanilla ice cream. "A Merry Christmas." I released an exasperated sigh.

"Why did they need you tonight?" asked Dad.

I shrugged. "Ronnie was there. He asked who was with me when I met Xavier. They knew about Brock, of course, and I told them about the girls. I wish I hadn't. Amanda wouldn't bother the kids on Christmas Eve, would she?" I scarfed down two more huge bites. My hand holding the spoon dropped to my lap, and Maverick's tongue licked it clean faster than a lightning bolt. I shook the spoon at my dog and chuckled, looking into his innocent brown eyes.

The spoon clattered in the empty bowl. "I have to talk to Amanda." I stood, determined to discover why she asked about Xavier's death, and why law enforcement had so many questions.

"Not now," said Dad.

"It's time to head to church," said Ida at the same time.

"But it's ten thirty-five." I sounded like a whiney kid. I shook my head.

"We'll leave at eleven to make sure we get a seat. With the added benefit of a forty-five-minute prelude of Christmas music, church will be filled."

I dragged myself up the stairs, a continuous list of questions scrolling in my head. With the temperature falling as well as the snow, I chose a pair of forest green corduroy pants and a red-and-green sweater. I caught most of my shoulder-length hair in a clip on the top of my head and curled the tendrils around my face. I applied a tan eyeshadow and a dark brown mascara to my eye lashes, highlighting my blue eyes. A shiny lip gloss finished off my look. I delayed as long as I could.

Ida sat on a kitchen chair in her faux fur coat, tapping her foot and drumming her fingertips. She held a large white cardboard box on her lap.

"We're going to be late," she huffed. "Every year for …" She lifted her chin and her left eyebrow raised. "… more years than you've been alive, I've dropped off some of my Christmas delicacies at the ER right before I went to Midnight Mass." She made a production of glancing at the smart watch on her wrist and tapping the timepiece. "There isn't time now. I guess you'll have to do the honors after the service."

I wanted to attend the service. I had no doubt the music would be lovely, and the ritual liturgy of the Mass would calm my nerves, but I wasn't sure I was truly vested in my religion anymore. I knew God couldn't answer all our prayers, but it was difficult to accept God's decision to allow Charles to die. Ida and Dad wanted me to attend with them, but would God miss me much?

We stepped out into a crisp starless night. The car started but icy air blew from the vents. We arrived at ten minutes after eleven, and the lot overflowed. I dropped Ida and Dad at the door and parked the car on the street a block away. Once inside the church, I located them in the second to last row, already enjoying a lilting children's choir, singing, *What Child Is This*. Families crushed together in the crowded pews. Ushers set up extra chairs in the vestibule and I thought wide thoughts to disguise saving a small space for Amanda, if she decided to join us.

The musicians varied in age from middle-elementary piano and vocal students, tugging and scratching at their necks, wearing brand new clothes with just-out-of-the-package rectangular creases, to senior citizen members of the full choir, outfitted in brilliant golden robes. An ensemble of accomplished instrumentalists and vocalists concluded the concert with a not-to-be-missed performance of the *Hallelujah Chorus* from Handel's *Messiah*. The transcendent music carried me to a peaceful place.

Amanda didn't show, and I was so caught up in the lovely spectacle, I didn't see Pete and Susie join the throng until the processional started. Pete saluted over the head of Ida's three-year-old neighbor, Emma, one of the few little ones still awake, dressed as an angel, leading the Holy Family and a group of short shepherds down the aisle to the altar. I pasted on a smile and mouthed, "Merry Christmas." He nodded.

Ida nudged me and I slid closer to Dad to make room for some latecomers. I threaded my hand through his arm and rested my head on his shoulder. Ida nudged again and I looked up into the twinkling eyes of CJ Bluestone as he and his daughter, Carlee, squeezed next to Ida. While he was deployed to far off lands, his wife disappeared, and he never knew he had a daughter. Fate brought them together and their presence together tonight was a miracle. I decided I could give thanks that *some* stories had a happy ending.

I settled into my seat and listened to the readings, responding appropriately, and counting my blessings, when a loud beep sounded. I followed the annoyed looks to a red-faced Pete, who shut down the noise, read the screen, and quickly exited the church. Susie kept her emotionless face forward, pretending they hadn't come together.

The rest of the Mass dragged. I tried to pay attention. I really did. But I couldn't concentrate. Was Amanda still at the police station? What happened to Xavier? Why had Pete been paged? How was Dad going to fare without Elizabeth this Christmas? Would Ida like my gift?

The service ended, and Father Anderson waited to personally greet his congregation at the back of church. Distracted, I knocked over a big display of bright red poinsettias. I heard a snigger and turned to find Susie Kelton's eyes on me. The heat curled around my ears, and I hurriedly stood the flowers upright. I greeted Father, and raced to the car, ostensibly to warm it up, but I wanted to get away from the crowd.

Sitting in the icy car, waiting in the long line to pick up Ida and Dad, I solidified my evening plan. I'd drop Dad and Ida home then deliver the treats to the ER and maybe get one question answered by Pete or I knew I'd never sleep.

A jolly Ida slid into the backseat. With a sprightly voice, she said, "Have you been a good girl, Katie? What do you expect from Santa this year?"

I smiled. "I hope I've been good enough. It's been a big year. Moving here. Meeting you. Dad moving in. Loving my job." Even if not everyone loved *me* in the job. Dillon's attitude pummeled my confidence. I hadn't always done what was expected: Chief Erickson repeatedly asked me to stay out of his way; I found a child but nearly lost Maverick to a furious river; I made flawed choices with serious consequences; I jumped into situations without considering the consequences of my actions, like volunteering to tutor Dillon. I shook my head, jarring loose the morass of memories siphoning the cheer from my heart, and concentrated on the positives.

We drove through the empty streets. The city lights ignited the twirling snowflakes shaken from the blanket of heavy clouds hiding the stars and the moon, a tranquil vignette.

"How about you?"

"Doubtful." She giggled, then yawned. Dad and I followed suit.

Ida perked up as we drove down Maple Street. "Let me get the box of goodies. I think anyone who has to work on Christmas Eve deserves a treat." She hopped from the car before I set the brake and returned with the treats.

Dad and Ida waved as I drove to the hospital.

Carrying the box holding the chocolate, vanilla, and pumpkin treasures gave me easy access to the deserted ER. A security officer allowed me to enter after she snagged two frosted cutouts. Three nurses, passing through, nabbed a half-dozen Scottish shortbread cookies to 'share.'

Jim, the maintenance man, sidled nearer the offering and timidly plucked an Angel Kiss out of the box. The registrar grabbed a napkin and two pieces of fudge. She took her first bite, closed her eyes, and sighed.

After buttering her up with the candy, I asked, "Is anyone else here?"

She mumbled a response and tilted her head behind the desk. Before I could thank her, her phone rang.

Jim stood in front of me. The pockets in the red sweater vest he wore over his wrinkled scrubs sagged with a scrub brush and a can of cleaner. It looked like he'd had a long day. His short salt-and-pepper hair stood out in all directions. Gray circled his hazel eyes, and the bristles on his five o'clock shadow looked like sandpaper, but he smiled. I offered him another treat and at first he declined, but eventually everyone succumbed to Ida's tempting treats. He nabbed another meringue delicacy, opened a supply closet, grabbed a cart, and pushed it down the hall. I froze in place for a second, deciding which way to go, then followed him.

He popped the remains of the sweet confection into his mouth, saluted, and disappeared around a corner.

Soft voices drew me past rooms cordoned off by gray privacy curtains, toward an office area alive with beeping monitors screens, stacks of supplies, computers, printers, and desks and I almost ran into Pete and Susie.

"Promise me you'll help watch out for her. There's something terrible going on," Pete said. "She needs someone."

I swallowed hard. Not wanting to intrude, I guiltily backed away, and took refuge in the last cubicle, waiting for the opportune moment to retreat.

Susie dusted snow from the sleeves of her coat, tore

off black earmuffs, and tossed her chestnut waves. "You promised you'd turn off your beeper, and you embarrassed me." Pete reached for her shoulders, and she pulled away. She stood next to him, her hands flying out of control. "She always comes first. That's just it. And if it's not her, it's someone else. I can't live this way. And look at you. You only wear black. Who does that?"

"Susie, you know how important my patients are. Our patients. We talked about it."

"I need you."

"At this moment, she needs me more. You understand. You see it every day."

She squinted and her face turned red. Seething waves of anger rolled off her. She looked ready to explode. She twirled a glistening ring, yanked it from her finger, and dropped it into Pete's hand. "I can't marry you. I'd always be second," Susie whined.

"Susie, we'll get through this," Pete said.

I couldn't imagine why she would give up such a wonderful guy with a big heart. He'd helped lessen the pain of losing Charles and brightened the prospect of beginning life in a new place. He'd rescued me. I wasn't sure what the end of their relationship would mean.

The door behind me clicked, and heavy footsteps pounded in the short hall. I ducked deeper into the dark space as Chief West, and Officers Rodgers and Christianson trooped past. I peeked. Pete and Susie stared at Amanda.

I couldn't hear what she said but watched Susie's eyes widen and she left the office.

"Murder?" At least that's what I thought I heard Pete say. He shook his head. "Chief, Xavier's death had to be an accident."

I craned my neck to peer around the corner and hear

better. Amanda hesitated and said, "Xavier Notrecali did not drown. Our preliminary investigation determined he was dead before he went into the water. We believe it was murder. At the very least, a coverup."

Pete's forehead crinkled.

"You cited the cause of death as accidental drowning." Amanda watched his face.

"You were right there. I assumed Xavier died by drowning, but no autopsy had been ordered and there was no reason to suspect anything other than accidental drowning. I've been working a very unusual case that's been all consuming. I must have missed it. How could I have been so wrong? May I see the body again?"

Ronnie stepped forward. He sneered. I didn't think he'd ever forgive Pete's dad for supporting the search for a new chief of police and took his displeasure out on Pete whenever he could.

"We ran a tox screen. Xavier died from an overdose of tetrahydrozoline. You were the last person to be seen with the victim. Pete Erickson, you are under arrest for the murder of Xavier Notrecali. You have the right to remain silent. Anything you say can and will be used against you in a court of law. You have the right to speak to an attorney and to have an attorney present during any questioning."

My mind screamed over his grating voice, *You have the wrong man. He couldn't have killed Xavier.* Pete had been Xavier's' guardian angel. He let him stay in the ER rather than brave the elements. Pete was a doctor and a good man.

My nose tickled. I wanted to sneeze.

CHAPTER THIRTEEN

I cupped my hand over my nose and mouth, to muffle the blast should it happen. I squeezed my eyes and curled up. *Don't sneeze,* I repeated to myself. *Don't sneeze.*

"It's a mistake." Pete shook his head. "You've got it all wrong."

I knew he couldn't be guilty of murder. My blood coursed through my neck and pulsed so loudly I couldn't hear what else was said. I held back the sneeze.

Pete wouldn't kill anyone, but Ronnie tightened the handcuffs and propelled Pete into the hallway. I shrank back even further as Ronnie perp-walked Pete past my hideaway. He gave Pete an unnecessary shove out the door. Officer Rodgers followed closely.

I peeked around the corner again. Amanda caved in on herself.

I couldn't stifle my sneeze any longer. It erupted and I slinked out from behind the curtain. Amanda looked up.

"You know he couldn't kill anyone," I said. It was the only thing of which I was certain.

"Evidence says otherwise. Were you eavesdropping? Did you hear enough?" Her clipped words cut like a blade.

"I'm sorry. I hadn't intended to listen in, but …" I held out the flimsy box.

"But what, Katie? With your eloquent corroboration and by Dr. Erickson's own admission, he was the last person to see Xavier alive. Several staff members witnessed Dr. Erickson accompany Xavier out of the waiting room. Xavier did not drown. And given their history, it's safe to say there was ample motive."

"What history?"

I noted the scorching look in Amanda's eyes. "Officer Christianson keeps warning me. I didn't realize how often you've inserted yourself into investigations in the past. You may mean well but stay out of it." My jaw dropped. She stomped ahead of me, out of the room.

I set the box on the counter next to the registrar. Gone was the welcoming smile; the corners of her mouth turned down and her eyes were big and round and sad.

The doctor in charge of emergency services, Dr. Coltraine, sashayed through the double doors, shaking her hair free from her cap.

"What's going on? Where are they taking Dr. Erickson?" She peeled off a pair of leather gloves and rapped her knuckles on the counter. "Hello-oo. Why didn't anyone call me? I need to know what's going on. If I hadn't attended the Christmas service, I never would have driven by and seen him get hauled away." Her angry voice drew the registrar out of her shock.

Her tirade trailed off as I crept out of the ER and took a slow circuitous route to my car, thinking.

The wind picked up and the snowflakes soared in a corkscrew around my face. I pulled my hood tight and traipsed to the car. I'd try to do exactly what Amanda wanted. No involvement. No trouble. She'd figure out soon enough for herself; Pete couldn't have done anything to Xavier.

The wipers tick-tocked a familiar rhythm, swiping back and forth. I drove to Ida's, assuring myself if anyone knew the history between Pete and Xavier, it would be Ida. I'd satisfy my curiosity in the morning, staying safely away from Amanda's enquiry. I yawned as I drove onto Maple Street and blinked back surprise. All the lights in Ida's lovely Queen Anne style home gleamed. I hoped late night Christmas lights was a Columbia tradition and not an indicator of Ida or Dad waiting up for me. It was after three. My well-intentioned visit had flopped, and exhaustion sapped my energy.

I opened the door, tiptoed into the living room and Ida turned up in front of me, arms crossed over her abundant chest. She certainly was not playing an elf getting ready for Christmas.

She said, "How could you?"

"How could I what?"

"Rachel called to tell me Amanda arrested Pete on suspicion of murder. Weren't you there?" The Columbia gossip train worked well even in the early hours. "What do you know about it? How could you let that happen?" She'd known Pete his entire life. They had a special bond.

I gathered her in a hug and emotions poured over me—

anger, sadness, disbelief, disappointment. I gave her the short version, omitting Susie's return of her engagement ring.

"Ida." I struggled to get the words out. "What would make Amanda believe Pete had a reason to kill Xavier? Who was he?"

She sniffed. "Xavier is a successful soloist and recitalist, a world-renowned violinist and prolific composer, or rather *was*. He won the Alicia Carter Award and performed his works on the stages in four continents. He blamed his unbridled, decadent lifestyle on his creativity. 'I'm right-brained,' he'd say as an excuse for his excesses in food and drink, his uninhibited life on the edge." She began to rant. "He threw money at his problems, buying gifts to placate anyone he'd made unhappy, throwing extravagant parties. People indulged him and maybe took advantage too." She threw up her hands.

"He traveled the world with a raucous crowd, alcohol, drugs, carousing. After one extremely successful tour, celebrating too much, rumor has it Xavier's wife caught him with his manager's girlfriend. They'd been drinking and he and his wife had a huge fight, but they reconciled. The Notrecalis decided to make their way home anyway. Evidence pointed to Xavier's wife driving." Ida gritted her teeth and hissed. "She caused a fatal accident. Xavier lost his wife in a head-on collision."

She took my hand and pulled me to the sofa. She patted the seat beside her. I could barely hear her voice. "And Pete lost his mom. She was driving the other car."

The blocks tumbled together, and I moaned. "They killed his mother. But Pete was so good to Xavier."

"Pete always tried. I think he overcompensated because

he didn't want any bit of hate and anger to consume him. It could have once, but he lives his oath—do no harm. Pete's family and the community suffered a great loss. His kind mother was one of my best friends. I watched Lance struggle for a long time and, even as a child, Pete helped his dad through his grief.

"But Xavier never got his life back on track. He said he didn't remember the accident, and he couldn't explain his crushed thumb and broken leg. The royalties from earlier in his career petered out—some kind of legal circumlocution—and he could no longer support himself. Child services removed his son and his stepdaughter disowned him. A few years later, after much prodding by his frustrated manager, he started to write music again. Xavier hoped for the next great sonata or partita or rhapsody, something with which to rebuild his career but the critics rejected his attempts. He tried to perform, but his friends ignored him, and his audience had moved on. He could have done something with his life, taught or found another career, but he gave up and fell too far down that manic rabbit hole. He disappeared for a while but, since he's come back, he's been homeless."

Her intense honesty caught me off guard.

"Susie gave Pete his ring back," I blurted.

I couldn't say anymore. Overcome by the events of the evening, my shoulders convulsed. Ida put her arm around me, and Maverick jumped on the sofa, next to me. He laid his head on my knee and his big brown eyes blinked a message of support.

Bright sunlight streamed through the living room window. I burrowed under a soft blanket, trying to return to dreamland, but my hip sank between the cushions on the couch. I flopped onto my back and rubbed my eyes. I stretched and wriggled out kinks in places I didn't know I had. The clock on the wall read six thirty-five. With my three short hours of sleep, my joints creaked in protest as I sat upright.

A fire crackled in the fireplace. Somebody had been busy.

Maverick followed me up the stairs.

I splashed water on my face, cleared the mascara circles from under my eyes, brushed my teeth, and changed into comfortable bright green sweatpants and a matching sweatshirt with sequins. My hair was a mess, but Ida and Dad had seen me worse.

The smell of coffee, sausage, eggs, and something sugary drew me to the kitchen. Maverick followed so closely, I almost tripped through the door. I was surprised my stomach growled. It seemed I'd been eating non-stop for the entire month of December.

Dad sat at the kitchen table on one of the mismatched chairs. Ida flipped pancakes at the stove. She'd made mounds of meats and piles of eggs.

"Merry Christmas," I said without much cheer.

"Morning, darlin'. Ida told me about your night. I'm sorry. You should have gotten me up." Dad stood and I walked into his open arms.

"Have you heard anything new this morning?" I searched Ida's face for any sign the Columbia gossip tree had caught wind of Pete's arrest.

She shook her head. Her tired eyes had lost their bright green shine.

"Today will be a better day. Today they'll figure out Pete had nothing to do with Xavier's murder. Have you thought of anything, Ida? What can we do?"

Dad pulled a chair away from the table and the legs screeched. "Sit."

Ida put on the finishing touches and Dad plopped a plate heaped with Christmas breakfast food in front of me—a red and green flecked frittata, a steaming pastry dripping with caramel, an apple, cranberry, and pear compote with cream, two blueberry pancakes, and sausage links. "Eat." He put two more plates on the table, and they joined me. Maverick stood at attention next to my chair, drooling.

The savory food went down too easily. Ida replaced the empty dish in front of me with a notebook and a pen and paced. "Xavier did not drown." Dad turned to look at her, then tilted his head, listening to the rest of her recitation. "Xavier died from some drug. Unfortunately, we saw Pete lead Xavier out of the ER into the back offices and Xavier wasn't seen alive again."

"No one *reported* seeing him again," Dad said. "That could make all the difference." He stored the leftovers in plastic containers and stacked them in the fridge. "And if Pete is not the murderer, then some other person would have been the last to see Xavier, correct?" Ida nodded but looked perplexed.

"It's a misunderstanding. They have to investigate. I know he'd never hurt anyone," Ida said.

"You told me Xavier had children. Do you know where to find them?" I asked.

I trembled at the thought of someone bringing news of my dad's death to me on this treasured holiday. I hoped they had a strong support group. "How old are they? Do they still live in Columbia?"

Ida shook her head slowly. "Xavier's son was a surprise child, and a toddler at the time of the accident. His father's manic behavior caused social services to remove the boy from his family and place him in the foster care system. Xavier's stepdaughter was on break, home from college. After the incident, she went away, and I don't think anyone ever heard from her again."

A stepdaughter and son. Two children would have this joyful holiday forever tarnished by Xavier's death.

"Is there anyone else who would have had feelings one way or another regarding Xavier?" I scribbled a note. "Do you know where his manager is?"

"As a matter of fact, I do." Ida shifted uneasily in her chair. She rose, went to the sink, and ran water to wash the dishes. "And so do you."

CHAPTER FOURTEEN

M e? Who? Where?" My phone buzzed, and I was tempted to ignore it, but picked it up and said tersely, "What?"

"Katie?" The voice sounded far away.

My questions were replaced by real cheer, and I sang into the receiver. "Merry Christmas, Jane. How's your dad?" When I heard no reply, I checked the screen face to make sure we were still connected. "Jane?"

"We didn't make it to Atlanta. The plane had issues and departure time was delayed and then it started to snow, and they postponed the flight indefinitely. Drew decided to drive back here and get a flight later in the week." Her voice rose and the words spewed out more quickly. "It snowed the whole way back. We exchanged some unkind words about his driving ability, and I'm a total wreck."

I peeked through the window over the sink. New snow sparkled like gems in the sunshine. Featherlight flakes drifted from the tree branches through the air, dusting the cars, the ground, all the surfaces, like a painter touching up the world of white. "Where are you?"

"We're at my apartment. My refrigerator is empty. The grocery stores are closed. Drew is crabby." She inhaled. "And I don't expect Santa to find me this year."

"Come on over," I said. Ida cocked her head. I mouthed, "Jane and Drew."

Ida nodded vigorously.

"Breakfast is ready and waiting."

Ida dried her hands, unpacked the food Dad just put in the fridge, and placed two sets of dishes on the table. The bell sounded minutes later.

I pulled open the door. Jane dropped her brown eyes, looking sheepish, and a large canvas bag slid off her shoulder. Drew removed his boots, rushed past her, and wrapped Ida in a tight embrace. "You've saved our lives," he said in an overly dramatic voice. "Really!" He wore a thick cream-colored cardigan sweater with indigo blue jeans, and without a hair out of place, he looked like he stepped out of the pages of a fancy men's catalog. Jane wore a Christmas-red knee-length sweater jacket over red pants. She removed two pairs of fuzzy slippers from her bag, slapped them on the floor, and slipped into the ones that read 'nice.' Maverick drooled on the pair that read 'naughty.' Drew grabbed a paper towel and wiped them, then slid his big feet inside.

Jane rolled her eyes when she took in my attire, but before she could reprimand me, I grabbed my best friend in a hug, and she raised her head. "Merry Christmas." She looked over my shoulder and her eyes grew to the size of basketballs, admiring the breakfast feast laid out for them. "Oh, Ida."

I put my hands on my hips, pouted, and said, "You don't think I can make breakfast."

"No," came the resounding response from four full-throated voices as Jane and Drew sat in front of the smorgasbord. Maverick barked.

I giggled and said, "Not you too?" I scratched behind his ears.

"What's new?" Drew said between bites of eggs and sausage.

For a moment I stared, mesmerized by Drew's out-landish tie. A flat bulb the size of a quarter blinked red and white patterns where the nose on a cartoon Rudolph should be. Ida coughed and I continued. "A homeless man died on Lake Monongalia—"

"Oh, no! Did he fall through the ice?" When Jane didn't get an answer, she put down her fork and shook her long blond curls. "Katie, not again." I didn't laugh. "What happened?"

"The death has been ruled a homicide."

Drew tried to read my face. He shook his knife at me and said, in a concerned voice, "And?"

"They arrested Pete."

After a moment of frightening silence, a belly laugh erupted from Drew. He grabbed his non-existent stomach and pretended to ho-ho-ho. Ida, Dad, and I couldn't join him, and the laughter faded as he realized I hadn't been joking. He shoveled the last morsel into his mouth and gathered his place setting. The dishes clattered when he set them in the sink. He reached for Jane's unfinished breakfast plate, and she mimed stabbing him with her fork. He poured two cups of coffee, one for Jane and one for himself, and sat down at the table.

"Explain."

We answered the questions as best we could, and ended up where we were when Jane called. "We have to do something. He didn't kill anyone," I said.

"I agree, but we also can't step on Amanda's toes. She's in charge and the evidence she has points to Pete, at least in her eyes," said Drew.

"I don't think Ronnie will go out of his way to prove Pete isn't guilty." I'd seen his sneer and said, "His attitude regarding Pete and Lance is jaded. But maybe we can talk to Officer Rodgers."

"And Susie?" said Jane.

Ida said carefully, "I'm not sure that's a good idea. They broke up last night."

Drew let out a huff. "Geez. That's horrible timing. Pete's fiancée returning her ring right around the time of his arrest, looks like she doesn't trust him or believe him. Is there any way we could get her to take him back?" He looked at Ida then me and after a moment he groaned, "Ow. What was that for?" He rubbed his shin where Jane might have kicked him under the table.

"Ida," I said. "Xavier's manager might be a suspect. It's a long shot but maybe he's held a grudge for all this time and an opportunity finally presented itself. Who was it?"

Ida's fingers drummed the tabletop. Dad put his hand over hers. She looked at him and wriggled herself a little taller in the chair. "Xavier's manager was Mayor Maxwell."

"Our mayor?" My heart thudded against my chest and

my palms sweated. "He's been a promoter his entire life?"

"In various capacities, I suppose he has." Ida took a deep breath. "But Xavier still made him money, so I don't see him committing murder."

Drew sat back in his chair. "If Maxwell was making money, how could he leave his client penniless and homeless?"

"Xavier couldn't handle finances and wasn't a very good father. In the very beginning he was quite successful, and he was wise enough to want to protect his investment for his family. He had an attorney draw up a document to secure money he put away that he absolutely could never touch—a spendthrift trust. Until Xavier died, Maxwell took care of the investment and received a stipend, a small percentage of the investment, which would be rescinded if Maxwell dipped into the assets to assist Xavier. It was meant to protect his children from his debauchery and his hedonistic ways. He also added a morals clause to preclude their slipping into the same wanton behaviors."

"Do as I say, not as I do." Drew's comment didn't go unnoticed.

"Unless he died, Xavier wanted his children's inheritance to remain untouched until each reached the age of thirty, then mete a portion out over time until his death just in case they carried his self-indulgent gene. Even in his present state, he wouldn't let Maxwell draw from the principal. Occasionally, Xavier would take a small offering from Maxwell, but now the money will be dispersed, and Maxwell won't have that source of income."

"How do you know all this?" Drew asked.

Ida glanced out the window. She turned back and looked at Drew. "My husband was an excellent attorney.

When I helped the firm clean out Casimer's office and safe after he died, I came across Xavier's paperwork. It's all legally recorded if you know where to look."

An uncharitable thought popped up in my head. "Xavier was a real piece of work but that doesn't mean Maxwell didn't have an alternate motive to kill Xavier. What about that girlfriend of Maxwell's?"

"His wife now."

I gawked. It was a small world.

"How do we start?" Ida said, oblivious to my surprise.

We looked to each other for a solution. Finally, Dad said, "Xavier was a local celebrity in his day, I take it. There should be a record of his successes and failures. We can research online today, but because of the twenty-year gap in time we may find additional information in the archives at the library or at the newspaper office Monday. Ida, are there any musicians who performed with Xavier still in Columbia? Personal stories have much more impact than reading the printed page and you never know what someone might let slip when they recount the history firsthand."

"Most of the musicians stayed only a short time and then used their connection with a famous violinist to launch their careers. The cellist who played in Xavier's string quartet stayed the longest. She idolized him, but she took her admiration too far. She quit the group after the accident and rebuffed any attempt to have her play without Xavier until she received the same snubbing he did and no longer performed anywhere. But I don't know where she is now."

Maverick barked.

Dad answered the knock at our door.

A tan blur bolted through the opening and playfully

attacked Maverick. Maverick mirrored Renegade's bounding back and forth, jumping from paw to paw, challenging best friends to a free-for-all until CJ whistled and both rear ends hit the ground. *I have to learn how to do that.* Carlee stood on the top step next to her dad. "Merry Christmas." Her teeth chattered.

"We brought a gift," said CJ. "Merry Christmas." He held out a tube wrapped in butcher paper and tied with a green lace ribbon.

"Dad," Carlee said, shaking her finger. "Tell the truth. You said it would be fine." She was too antsy to wait and blurted, "It's too cold at our house. Can we stay here?"

CJ cleared his throat. "Our furnace went out and the earliest the emergency crew will be able to check it is this evening." Carlee inherited the old house across the street from our neighbor, who thought Carlee and her dad needed a place to call home, and they'd just moved in. So far, they'd needed a new clothes dryer, a grill, a microwave, and maybe a new furnace.

"Join the crowd." Ida reached for the package. A grin spread across her face when she read the label. "Tenderloin. Santa's being very good to me."

I hoped she was right.

CHAPTER FIFTEEN

CJ removed his felt hat and hung up both their coats. My friend shook his glistening black hair and turned. His brilliant smile lit the room. When circumstances threw us together, I'd almost had a crush on him, but he'd busied himself, learning the ropes of being a good father to a daughter he never knew he had. We'd become good friends. He'd taught Maverick some tricks of the search-and-rescue trade and had been instrumental in our acceptance as a probationary team.

"Have something to eat," Ida said with a huge smile, serving up two more helpings. "We have plenty."

After clearing her plate, Carlee patted her flat tummy and said, "I'm going to warm up by the fire."

Dad said, "I'm with you. How about a rousing game

of cribbage?"

"I've never played."

"Then welcome to my parlor." Dad pretended to twist the ends of a handlebar mustache and his eyebrows did the rumba. Then he rubbed his hands together and let loose a dastardly, "Heh, heh, heh."

Carlee halted in the doorway to the living room, cocked her head, and said, "Mr. Wilk, you haven't even opened your gifts yet."

"Later," Dad said. He set up a card table next to the Christmas tree.

After they'd settled into their game, CJ's penetrating eyes looked us over, one by one. He said, "You do not look very merry. What's happened?"

Ida, Jane, and I stared at Drew. He took a deep breath and retold the story. It was just as horrible this time round.

"What are we going to do?" I asked.

CJ paced and Renegade and Maverick pranced next to him, their nails clicking on the floor. He stopped and asked, "Should we include Susie in on our team?"

Jane, Drew, Ida, and I all said at the same time, "No."

Drew continued, "We don't know why, but Susie returned his ring. We don't want to give her a heads up if she isn't on his side and we don't want to make this worse for Pete."

"I kind of know why she returned his ring," I said. "I might have heard her tell him that she wasn't happy playing second fiddle to what sounded like his care of a patient."

Jane nodded. She commiserated but understood the importance of Drew's job and had to figure out how she fit into his life. Drew knew how difficult life could be for her—worrying whether he'd be safe. Standing behind her, he wrapped his arms around her shoulders and dropped his chin onto the top of her head. She closed her eyes, leaned back into him, and caressed his arm. Drew served as a field agent for the Minnesota Bureau of Criminal Affairs, and she could lose him at any time.

"Susie's in the health care field. She works side by side with him and surely, she knows, in his profession, he makes life and death decisions all the time," Jane said, and her voice squawked with impatience.

We all thought for a moment and then Drew said, "Harry's idea of research is a good one. We can do that from here right now."

Jane dug her laptop out of her bag and began tapping. Her hand cupped her mouth, stifling a moan. "How dreadful! Who'd have thought such a prolific and expressive artist would plunge to such depths of depression and ultimate homelessness."

Drew glanced over her shoulder and bent at the waist to get a closer look. She grabbed the notebook from the end of the table and jotted some notes. "My goodness, but he led an extraordinary life."

She frowned and turned the screen for us to see. The larger-than-life personality sat in a high-backed chair, leaning forward with his chin braced in his hand. The subjects, a tall, blond woman jostling a toddler with a mop of messy dark hair on her hip and an owlish, shy teenager hiding behind thick black frames, gazed at the handsome man adoringly.

"I realize Lance might not want to discuss Pete, but I'm going to call him. He might have some insight for us." Ida stepped into her apartment and closed the adjoining door.

"Listen to this," Jane said. "Musician extraordinaire

Xavier Notrecali and his wife, Erica, were involved in a fatal accident early Saturday morning. Erica Notrecali was pronounced dead at the scene and was presumed to be driving when they collided with the car driven by Christa Erickson." Jane spun the screen for us to see. "Wasn't she beautiful?"

"Pete looks like his mom," I said.

Next to the photo of Pete's mom was a photo of the scene, two cars mashed together, windshields shattered, doors open, a pair of bent, round tortoise shell glasses tying humanity to the tragedy, dark stains on the driver's seat, and traffic cones cordoning off the site.

No one breathed as we considered the implications.

Jane inhaled, steeled herself, and continued reading. "Xavier was thrown from his car and suffered non-life-threatening injuries. Christa Erickson was airlifted to St. Cloud in serious condition. Alcohol is presumed to be a factor. Charges are pending."

Jane's hand dropped into her lap. "Do you think it's possible Xavier was actually driving the car, and because his wife died, he let her take the blame?" She backtracked, reading the incredulity on our faces. "Never mind. I'm letting my imagination take over."

Drew shook his head. "Jane, that's an avenue we have to explore. Maybe someone found out—"

"But wouldn't that look worse for Pete?" Jane questioned.

"We know Pete did not kill Xavier. The truth can only help," CJ said. "We need to unearth someone else who might have wanted Xavier dead. He may not be missed by many, but no one deserves to be murdered."

Jane tore another sheet from the notebook, wrote

Xavier's name at the center, and drew lines connecting it to the words cellist, Maxwell, Pete, Lance, stepdaughter, and son. "Isn't this how you begin, Katie?" Then she drew three extra lines. "You never know."

Under stepdaughter and son, she wrote 'inheritance.' Under Pete and Lance, she wrote 'revenge.' I steamed a little and Jane reminded me if we wrote the names down, and we discovered they couldn't be guilty, it would strengthen the motives of the others and removing their names would feel even better. She hoped. Under Maxwell she wrote 'grudge' and 'wife' and under cellist she wrote 'love interest.'

Ida's apartment door opened. "I invited Lance Erickson over for Christmas dinner."

"Did you tell him why?"

"Of course not. I thought better of it. He might not come." Her bottom lip stuck out. She expected praise for her quick thinking, but it didn't materialize.

We exchanged looks, wondering what trouble we'd be in when the former chief of police and the father of the main suspect heard we were investigating. I collected the loose pages and filed them in a folder.

A pleasant sound erupted from the living room. Carlee's laughter pealed like church bells.

"You're just good at cheating somehow." Dad feigned anger. "Let's play again." He kept her busy while we pulled up general information about the Notrecalis and Maxwells.

Curious about Dillon's dad, I found decades-old information about Maxwell and Xavier. High school classmates, neither attended college, but Maxwell began his career as a music manager with one prodigious client — Xavier. Usually with a glass of something in his hand, Xavier's phony smile plastered on his unctuous face showed up in photos taken at social gatherings with celebrities all over the world. Some photos captured the skylines of Los Angeles, Minneapolis, Chicago, Dallas, and New York. Years of program covers highlighted the concerts Xavier headlined. He figured prominently as a soloist at the front of an orchestra or boldly leading various ensembles. Scores of photos featured members of a quintet, bowing, or Xavier singled out, haughtily accepting adulation.

Grasping at straws I thought, *Could jealousy be a motive?*

One article cited the number of musicians' careers jumpstarted by performing with Xavier. I wondered what happened to those careers after the accident.

I took a second look at a much younger Maxwell. He showed up in the background of many of the photos and my neck crawled, noting Dillon's similarity to his father. Maxwell had promoted Xavier's compositions through catalog sales and recordings. That dropped off when Xavier no longer took the spotlight.

Loss of revenue? Follow the money?

Among my uncharitable thoughts crept the notion Maxwell did little to forward Xavier's career, but rather rode the coattails of his talented client. And I wondered who took the photos.

Coverage dwindled significantly after the car crash. Maxwell continued managing for a short time, and although the photo was twenty years old, Mrs. Maxwell had been his final client. She looked like Marilyn Monroe, but her vocal career faltered about the time Dillon was born and I couldn't find any more information about Mogul Maxwell Management Studios.

I added my notes to the growing mass of information and wondered if any of it would be useful. Looking at my friends' faces, it appeared we'd stalled.

CHAPTER SIXTEEN

Dad braced himself against the doorjamb. "She's one heckuva card shark. Who's going to get cleaned out by the ringer next?"

Carlee scooted past him, beaming. "I just got lucky." She whispered to her dad, "And Mr. Wilk let me win."

"I did not," Dad protested. "Maybe, a little at the beginning, but I played my A game and still got whipped."

Carlee grabbed a tangerine from the wooden bowl on the counter and peeled it. "Let's do a geocache. I've looked one up and it's designed for a winter break. This is the first in the Twelve Hides of Christmas series called, 'A Pair of Cartridges.'" She popped a segment of the juicy fruit into her mouth. "It's at the county park. Ms. Wilk, can you drive?"

"You kids go on without me. I need to start dinner," said Ida.

Dinner was six hours away.

"I'm staying to help Ida," said Dad. Then he mumbled, "Or maybe take a tiny nap."

"Count me in," said Jane, shoving her arm through the sleeve of her puffy, white coat. "I need fresh air."

"It's cold out there." Drew buzzed his lips but grabbed his jacket and wrapped a scarf around his neck. "Lead on, lovely ladies."

The snow glinted in the sunlight, as if someone had sprinkled a pearlescent glitter. We drove through a winter wonderland and parked in the lot. Carlee led the way, hopping on her crutches, periodically glancing at the app on her phone. Drew and CJ walked right behind her, asking questions, and discussing the possible outcomes of the day's football games.

The refreshing walk led us around Lake Monongalia to the boat landing and the short bridge connecting the walking path to the community park near the end of the point. Across the ice, we could view the entire fishing village. Snowmobiles, trucks, cars, and four wheelers zoomed among the tiny bodies moving about on the surface and no one appeared to fear falling through.

I worried.

"Girlfriend, you're awfully quiet." Jane hunched her shoulders against the cold air.

"Thinking, I guess. I'm scared for Pete. I know he didn't kill anybody. And they always say so many innocent people are sitting in jail for something they didn't do."

"We're all afraid for Pete. But I can tell it's something else. You aren't tracking with your usual fastidiousness, and you have me concerned."

I pressed my palms against my eyes.

"I am so mixed up. At any other time, I would've been happy Susie had broken up with Pete, but now I feel guilty. Foremost, I don't want anything bad to happen to him."

Jane's arm entwined with mine and we continued walking. "He's a great guy."

I nodded, my heart aching, remembering our kiss in September, standing in the rain. Circumstances beyond our control got in the way.

Carlee squealed and yanked me out of my reverie. "I found it." Drew and CJ lowered her from three feet off the ground, standing in the stirrups made by their clasping hands. The infectious joy written on her face dispelled Jane's misgivings. "Look."

Carlee held a strange, plastic container in her palm. The closer we got, the stranger the homemade contraption looked. She slipped a hook and the cache opened, revealing two hollowed out ink cartridges hinged together. She plucked a tiny roll of paper wrapped in clear plastic from the interior and unfurled it. "Do we have something to write with?"

"I have a pen," said Jane.

Carlee signed the log, nestled the tube inside, and secured the lid on the homemade container. "Up," she said.

Drew and CJ lifted her. She replaced her find and as they lowered her to the ground, a puff of white exploded at the back of Drew's head. He deliberately shook the flakes free from his collar, bent down, and gathered snow in a ball. Before he could retaliate, another struck. CJ doubled over in laughter, and Jane and I took cover, trying to locate the source. Drew turned around and ducked when he figured out Jane hadn't been the offender.

"Oh, goodie," Carlee screeched. "A snowball fight." She stooped, made her own sphere, and hurled it at her dad.

A projectile plastered my face. It had to be a friend of Carlee.

"Hey, you," Drew said. He stood and took another splat. "What do you think you're doing?" He brushed the snow from his face.

Jane and I turned. A bundle of rags launched another blob of snow from behind the bridge braces. Drew threw a bunch of snowballs in succession, drawing attention away from CJ who crept behind the culprit. When he stopped to re-arm himself, another snowball hit his chest.

The person stood up to get a better angle on Drew when CJ grabbed a shoulder. The person spun around and pounded both fists against his chest, screaming, "Rape!"

CJ released her, tripped, and fell back.

She screamed, "They killed him! Won't nobody listen!"

Before any of us could register what happened, she scurried behind the bridge and disappeared.

"What was that?" Drew asked as he tromped up the hill. He grabbed CJ's hand and hauled him into a standing position. "Anyone know who that crazy woman is?"

"I've seen her before and she said the same words then, 'They killed him.' Amanda wanted to speak to her, but she's quick."

"Who do you think she's talking about?" asked Jane.

"I think she's talking about Xavier."

"Do you think she knows who killed him?" asked Drew.

"Killed who?" Carlee waddled close and had quietly

joined us. Her dark, worried eyes looked like a pair of eight balls.

CJ wrapped her in a hug. "Sorry, honey. A homeless man died."

"You mean the man who fell through the hole Brock dropped into. I thought it was an accident. I hadn't heard he'd been killed."

CJ looked to me to address her misunderstanding.

"You remember Xavier, the man who told us how to find Brock and then helped get Brock out of the water? He died later that night. They found him in the lake, but he didn't drown. He was deliberately put there."

"Brock is going to be devastated. He liked Xavier. He told us all about him when we gave him a ride back to his car after the accident. Whenever Brock and his dad had a fish fry, which wasn't often enough for Brock, they'd invite Xavier and a few of his friends. Brock said he's been around since last Christmas. He even gave Brock an old violin." She scooped up a handful of snow. "What's this?"

She dusted the snow from her hand and held out her palm. A tiny gold charm nestled in the center. We jostled around her to get the best vantage point to view the tiny piece. CJ lifted it and dangled it from a bent jump ring.

A cello.

On our walk back, Carlee said, "Ms. Wilk, you've been trying to keep it from me, but I know Dr. Erickson has been arrested. It's all over the waves." She walked and talked as if it was a most natural conversation. "I want to help. Was he arrested in connection to the death of Xavier?"

Her dad grabbed her shoulders and kissed the top of her head. "Maybe."

I don't know what we'd been thinking. My students

always knew more about what went on in Columbia than any of us. And Carlee was a bright girl, but as much as she wanted to help, we had to keep Christmas a happy holiday for her—her first ever with her dad.

We agreed to wait until after dinner to discuss the charm. Maybe Ida would know who it belonged to. Maybe Lance would be able to shed some light on Pete's arrest. But we'd have to be gentle. Lance might have some of the same feelings about Xavier that Pete could have. But maybe we'd figure out a reason for someone else to have killed Xavier because we knew Pete was innocent.

CHAPTER SEVENTEEN

We returned to find Ida's dining room prepared for guests. Festive red and white dinnerware sparkled on the extended table. Tall white tapers set in silver candle holders, six-piece gold flatware, and crystal goblets added a celebratory flare. Each place setting boasted a linen napkin folded into the shape of a lotus flower with a chocolate center.

Miraculously, the gifts under the tree had multiplied and Carlee noticed immediately. "Dad, there's a gift here for you and me. And Ms. Mackey and Mr. Kidd."

CJ winked, and a knowing smile lifted one corner of his mouth. "Santa must have come while we were away. You see, he can find you anywhere."

"Da-ad. I'm seventeen. I know you're new at this

father thing, but you do realize I've known all about Santa for more than half my life." Her hands landed on her hips, and she looked like a young general. "Can we add our gifts now?" He nodded.

She bolted to the coat rack and rummaged around in CJ's pockets, retrieving small, gift-wrapped boxes which she arranged under the tree.

Carlee winced, startled when she heard a loud snort from behind Dad's door. He'd taken the napping route, so I went looking for Ida and located her bustling in her kitchen. I volunteered my gastronomic service, and she laughed. "You'll help best by getting out of my kitchen!"

CJ and Carlee couldn't return to their house until their emergency tech team restored the heat, and although Jane and Drew had heat, they didn't have much else to make their Christmas jolly, so Ida had set the table accordingly.

I pulled out an assortment of games and tuned into a holiday music station.

Jane looked at the *Sequence* box skeptically. "Do you expect us to learn at the same time we're trying to have fun?" She chose a deck of playing cards, riffling them like a pro. "Who's up for a game of bridge?"

Drew pursed his lips and scratched his chin. "How about a cribbage tournament?"

Carlee perked up. "We each put in two dollars, and winner takes all."

CJ smiled at his daughter. "I would like to learn the game." He'd do anything for her. Of course, so would I. This was the life she was meant to live.

"Another newbie. Just my cup of tea." Drew shuffled a second deck.

"Is it anything like poker?" CJ plucked the cards from

Drew's grasp, split the deck in one hand, pivoted the top half, wove the ends together, and created one deck. He turned over the top card, buried that ace of spades, cut the cards again, flicked them, arched the cards, and slid them together. He turned over the top card, which just happened to be the same ace.

Drew's jaw dropped. Fascinated, he said, "Ringers run in the family it seems. I'd forgotten you served as a Navy SEAL. I suppose you're quite good at cards."

CJ shrugged.

Carlee squealed. "Ms. Wilk, you can assign the pairings. Can I borrow two dollars, Dad?"

The player with the bye each round replenished a platter with light snacks of cheese and crackers or veggies and provided refills on beverages; we didn't want to spoil our appetites for Ida's Christmas dinner. At the end of the hour, CJ claimed the crown and the ten dollars and chose the next game, as far removed from poker as Go Fish could take us.

Jane bowed out and thumbed through the television specials listed on her phone. When she found *It's a Wonderful Life,* the games went back into the closet. Drew fed the fire, and I passed around mugs of warmed cider. Ida had scheduled dinner for four o'clock, so we snuggled into the comfy chairs. Maverick jumped up next to me and nuzzled under my arm.

Next thing I knew, the door between apartments banged against the stopper and Ida and Lance Erickson hustled through to my kitchen, rousing all five dozers. I jumped to attention, pretending to be awake, stifling a yawn, and followed Ida.

"You can't fool me, Sleeping Beauty," she said. "Trivets

please. Pull the cornbread from your oven in thirty seconds and remove the pail of batter from the freezer."

I stared at the baking contraption. I hadn't even known there was cornbread in my oven. She must have set it to bake while I slept. My embarrassed face warmed. Our landlady made the entire holiday feast, without help, and I'd slept through it. I rubbed my cheeks and wiped my eyes. "Sorry. I don't know what came over me."

Her gentle smile told me *she* knew what had come over me.

I carried the cornbread to the table and went back to search the freezer for a plastic pail. I removed the only one I could find and accompanied Dad to the dining room. He carried a tray with a thermal pitcher, three spice bottles, and a half dozen festive mugs. After lining them up on the buffet, Dad plucked the pail from my fingers and nestled it in a bucket of ice. He slipped the top to one side and scooped a large dollop of a frothy concoction, dropping it into one of the mugs. He added a shot of something to the mug, then filled it with hot milk from the pitcher and gave it a stir. He sprinkled cinnamon, nutmeg, and cloves on top and handed it to me. Ida and Dad waited for me to take a sip. My eyes closed, inhaling the ambrosial scent. *Oh, my!* "This is perfect, so soothing, and warm. Thank you."

"Carlee, dear, would you like a hot buttered no-rum to warm you up?" Dad asked, mixing up another warm, creamy beverage. She nodded and reached for the red and green mug.

Ida rubbed her hands together. "You deliver the drinks, Harry, and then there are gifts to open."

We moved back and forth between apartments, and once we all gathered in her living room, Ida said, "Drew, be a dear, and play Santa."

Ida loved giving gifts and wanted us to experience Christmas the Columbia way. In the weeks prior to the holiday, she and Dad made small gifts to be given to their nearest and dearest.

Each of us opened a shiny green bag with three truffles inside, homemade by Lance. Ida, Carlee, and Jane had made gifts for each of us and, if they were to be believed, the gifts also came from Dad, CJ, and Drew. Ida made personalized bookmarks using a holiday fabric and an appropriate charm for each of us. Dad took credit for closing the clamp from which the vintage charm dangled. My trinket resembled a tiny calculator. Jane fashioned a forest-green and navy-blue plaid velvet and pearl ornament for me to hang from our tree and Drew claimed he'd secured the hooks. Dad fastened his red and gold bauble next to mine and as we had so few, the welcome additions stood out. CJ and Carlee had collected teas and my bergamot Earl Gray smelled divine. My December time was at a premium, so I'd taken a shortcut and purchased homemade lavender and cedarwood soaps from Lorelei, and encased each bar in a folded origami box.

We finished sharing the gifts, collected the fanciful paper, and headed for the dining room.

"Katie and Jane, bring out the soup tureen and the salad bowl from my kitchen. Drew, be a dear and grab those extra chairs. Place them around the dining table. Dr. Bluestone can help."

"What can I do?" said Carlee.

The doorbell rang. "Answer the door," said Ida.

Carlee hobbled to the door and opened it. "You'd better come in."

Steve White had cleaned up well, after his gig as a plumber. He handed Carlee a glass tiered tray with mounds of beautifully browned Scandinavian rosettes, lightly dusted with powdered sugar. "Merry Christmas," he said. "I hope I'm not too late."

Ida appeared and casually pulled in another chair, rearranging them around the table. "Glad you could make it, Steve. You're just in time. Take your coat off." She blushed a bright pink.

Steve hung his fleece lined parka on the rack in the entryway. He tugged at the collar of his button-down red-plaid flannel shirt and finger-combed his hair before he retrieved his tray from Carlee and made room for it among the other goodies on the buffet.

Ida clapped. "Take a seat everyone."

After making introductions, Ida passed around permanent fabric markers. "You need to sign my tablecloth. Write a greeting if you'd like, but I absolutely must have a signature and date from everyone with whom I interact on Christmas. It's tradition." She sang the last two words as a stout and stalwart Tevye from *Fiddler on the Roof.* "I've had this tablecloth with me for every Christmas dinner since my wedding and I reminisce when I launder and iron it before packing it away." She pointed to a name written in big forest-green letters. "Casimer signed his name in large letters to fill the empty space." She tapped on another name scrawled in bright red and smiled wistfully. "And so did my dad." Names and warm messages written in all sizes and in a rainbow of colors covered the entire cloth, leaving very little area to fill.

When she'd collected the markers, having approved each addition, she sang our table blessing, and sent the first round of serving dishes around the table and they just kept coming. We had soup, bread, vegetable salad, a fluffy mint pineapple lime marshmallow mix, corn bread, a cheesy potato dish, and tenderloin cooked to perfection. Every one of the offerings could have graced the cover of a culinary magazine. With Pete's dad seated at the table, we kept the conversation on more lighthearted topics ... until dessert.

Carlee and I cleared the dinner plates. Dad refilled the cups with coffee or hot chocolate. Ida declined Steve's offer to help bring out the rest of the tasty desserts, so he topped off the water goblets. Cookies filled two more trays, but my mouth watered, ogling Ida's cream cheese frosted red velvet cake. Jane and Drew quietly discussed their plan to visit Mr. Mackey in Georgia. CJ and Lance chatted about the benefits and expectations of search-and-rescue canines and how well Renegade and Maverick might adapt to the roles.

We sat, savoring our warm drinks, and enjoying the sweet nibbles, until Steve said, "The scuttlebutt at the hospital is that an ER doc killed that old geezer, and for good reason I understand. He was a force to contend with."

The only sound came from the fire crackling in the other room. No one moved. I couldn't take my eyes from my bite of cake.

The legs on Lance's chair screeched and he rose from the table. "Thanks for the great dinner, Ida."

Ida stood too. "He didn't mean anything, Lance."

"Wait. I done it now, haven't I." Steve's confused attempt to backpedal ended up in his stammering. "That your boy? Sorry, Lance. I didn't know. I didn't think."

Ida put a hand on Lance's forearm. "Don't go. We all

know he couldn't have killed Xavier, for any reason. We've talked it over and we can help."

Lance gritted his teeth. He looked very much like his son when the white of his jawbone rose to the surface as he contemplated what he would do.

He inhaled deeply and said, "I thought it would be me that would get rid of Xavier, but Pete's always had his mother's heart and sense of justice. Even as a boy, he helped me get through losing her. There's no way he would have killed that old drunk."

"Tell us what to do."

His head dropped forward while he composed himself. When he looked up, his eyes were shiny. "I know you all mean well, but I put my heart and soul into Columbia for almost forty years because I trust the legal system. It works. Let Chief West do her job and she will exonerate Pete. He's in for the night because there's no judge to release him on Christmas—and certainly not with the charge of murder—but he will be alright. If you investigate, you will only get in the way and make everything worse." His eyes searched each of our faces for understanding. He looked at me for a very long time before he went on. "You have to let it go. Stay away from the investigation."

CHAPTER EIGHTEEN

Lance took the steam out of our forward movement with his impassioned plea to leave the investigation to the professionals. None of us wanted to hamper their efforts and put Pete's future in peril. Lance made each of us promise to leave the investigation alone before he bundled up and made his way out into the evening, huddled against the wind.

Seconds after Lance exited, CJ received a text from the furnace company. They were next on the list of emergency calls for Christmas day, and he and Carlee bade us goodnight. Jane and I cleaned up the kitchen. Ida dragged Dad, Drew, and Steve into her living room to listen to her play her favorite carols. Fortunately for Jane and me, the door remained open, and we could enjoy her lovely piano performance.

"What are you going to do, Katie?" Jane asked.

"What do you mean?" I said innocently, but I understood.

I wasn't eager to let it go. Pete was guiltless and I didn't want to leave his future to anyone who wouldn't do everything to clear him. I'd have to be careful not to get in the way. I trusted Amanda and Lance and I really wanted them to trust me, but I didn't trust anybody else.

"I know you. You're going to try to figure out who could've killed Xavier, but don't. I think Lance is right. We'll only get in the way."

"But Jane, if you would've heard Christianson, you'd be worried too. He's not going to do anything to help Pete." The panic in my voice filled my ears.

"You're overthinking what you heard. It was late. You were tired. He's just doing his job. And more importantly, so will Amanda."

"But—"

"No buts. You heard Lance. Stay away from the investigation."

Outwardly, I acceded, but in my heart, I promised myself I would not miss any opportunity to listen and maybe hear something that might help Pete. Because it really felt like he needed help.

By the time we finished, the kitchen sparkled. After a tender rendition of *Silent Night*, Jane and Drew wrapped up in their winter togs, wished us a Merry Christmas, and slipped out into the gusty evening in time to call their families.

I punched in Elizabeth's number and waited for her to pick up, but it went to voicemail. I thought she might be with Austin, but he didn't answer either.

My stepsister's phone rang once, and she picked up.

"Hi, you old thing." She laughed. She never missed an opportunity to remind me she was two years younger. "Merry Christmas, Katie. You caught me just in time. I'm on my way out the door, flying to Paris tonight. Is your dad there?"

I chuckled. "Never a dull moment with you. Merry Christmas. Here's Dad."

He took the phone, and I watched his gentle smile, happily catching up on her latest and greatest escapade. He loved all of us and I know he missed the rest of his family, especially on this holiday. Sandra was always doing something, going somewhere, on the move. Austin continually surprised me with his quiet intelligence when he'd expound on his next innovation. I even missed Elizabeth. She'd taken me in as one of her own and had been married to Dad for seventeen years. After the last year she'd spent overseeing Dad's recuperation, I knew she needed a break. She'd taken her dream job with Dad's blessing, but I hated to see him hurt.

Steve sat on the piano bench with Ida, watching her fingers fly across the keys, swaying to her beautiful music. He looked relaxed as well. I tried to put on a calm front; I sat and smiled and nodded my head in time to the music, but my insides churned and the mental gymnastics in my head made me dizzy.

Who killed Xavier? Certainly not Pete. And if Lance had killed Xavier, he would never have allowed his son to take the blame and spend one second within the confines of a jail cell. I wondered how much money Xavier had in his trust and whether the inheritance could be a motive to kill him. Maxwell would no longer benefit as trustee, but he could have payback for whatever happened between his wife and Xavier. Some of the folks at the hospital found Xavier repellent. Could he have been stealing toys, or maybe something else and letting someone else take the blame? He said he saw things in the ER. Which brought me to the ill little girl with her mother. Was she the patient Pete worried about?

A tap on my shoulder brought my thoughts back to the living room. "She wants to talk to you." Dad handed me the phone.

"Sandra?" I said, smiling. "What's up?"

"Thanks for the call, Katie. This is hard on all of us, but Harry sounds like he's doing well and so is mom. Keep in touch, okay?"

"Sure. Happy holidays, Sandra."

I stared at the phone in my hand. I missed her, but my reminiscences were interrupted by Ida.

"Katie, the day has flown by and there are a still a few gifts to open. Shall we?"

I hopped from the chair and dashed into our apartment, retrieving the gift-wrapped packages and cards from beneath our tree. I took one more approving look at our decorations and raced back to complete the Christmas day ritual.

I placed a short stack of gifts in front of Dad and Ida and an even shorter stack in front of Steve. He had a gift from Ida and a card from Dad, but nothing from me as I hadn't thought I'd ever see him again after yesterday. I shrugged, but he said, his eyes widening, "I didn't bring anything."

Ida gave a self-satisfied snort. Her supply of yarn and fabric art gifts of mittens, quilts, scarves, caps, and dishcloths were ready at a moment's notice. However, Steve's bulky gift had been beautifully wrapped with masculine paper and bore a gift tag with his name on it, so she'd had this one ready for him. He pulled out an afghan, arm-knitted with super chunky gray Merino felted wool. She'd explained the process to satisfy my curiosity earlier, but I didn't know the piece would come together so quickly.

Steve smirked when he waved the check Dad had given him. "You didn't have to, you know. I'll always help a friend." He glanced at Ida and smiled.

"You deserve it, and it's probably not nearly what I'd have had to pay a real plumber," Dad said and chuckled.

Ida's eyebrows flew to the ceiling, and she caught my eye. We'd have to keep watch under the sink and make certain Steve's plumbing skills were sufficient.

Dad gave Ida a copy of Connie Shelton's *Tricky Sweet* and a bottle of her favorite Chardonnay in exchange for a bulky cable-knit sweater. I'd ordered an apron for Ida from a company specializing in blowing up a photo and attaching it to a heavy-duty cotton canvas. The tongue hanging out on this enlarged Maverick was three times the size of the original, looking ten times as lethal. One of Ida's ancestors had been a passenger on the *Titanic,* so Dad and I gave her a three-dimensional jigsaw puzzle of the grand ship. Dad chuckled at my practical gift of jeans that didn't hang down on his nonexistent backside—he'd never fully regained all the weight he'd lost while recovering.

Dad fidgeted, watching me open his gift. I held the delicate chain on the fine gold pendant. "Oh, Dad, it's lovely." He jumped up, held out his hand, and hung it around my neck in return for a huge hug.

Ida cleared her throat and held out her present. I

opened a forest-green, hand-knitted cashmere scarf and wrapped it around my neck before bundling up and finally taking Maverick out for a much-needed walk through the neighborhood.

The lights on Maple Street glistened against the crisp flakes, sparkling like tiny gems. The ice and snow crunched beneath my footfalls. Muffled music and the hum of voices filtered through the air. I caught the stinging scent of burning wood. The low click of metal, like a car door closed without slamming, cut through the sounds. Maverick pranced a few feet and marked a spot, pranced again, and tugged the leash, his heart and eyes following a brown squirrel scampering over the top of the snow and up a tall evergreen tree. Maverick tensed. Footsteps clumped down the road behind us. I glanced over my shoulder and saw a hooded figure hurrying up the sidewalk. With the frigid temperatures, hurrying was the only speed of choice. We picked up our pace and as we alighted on Ida's front steps, Maverick turned and barked.

CHAPTER NINETEEN

D illon?"

"And a Merry Christmas to you too, Ms. Wilk."
Dillon Maxwell stomped the snow from his heavy, black-and-brown boots. "Like them? Santa brought my dad and I the best winter boots available. They're Kamik Nations."

Maverick sat and looked back and forth between us. "How did you know where I lived?" I crossed my arms in front of me.

For the first time since I'd met him, Dillon seemed to lose a bit of his bravado, but I reminded myself he was a consummate actor when he wanted something.

"Mrs. Clemashevski's address is listed in the phone directory."

I let down my guard a teensy bit. "What brings you here?"

"Would you be willing to do some of the lessons with me tonight so I can complete everything ahead of schedule?"

"They haven't moved up the holiday tournament, have they?" He shook his head. "Then whyever would you willingly submit to doing math ... on Christmas?"

He looked down at his feet and mumbled something I couldn't understand.

"What did you say?"

He raised his head and his blue Maxwell eyes glared at me. "My dad invited me to fish on his tournament team and he's never asked me before. He's probably hoping I won't finish my work or have time with basketball, but I'd like to ..." He looked back down at his feet. "... if I could."

Before I could laugh, or protest, or say no, Ida yanked open her front door.

"What are you doing out here? Come in and bring your friend." She peered into the yard. "Mr. Maxwell."

I forced myself to walk inside with Dillon in tow.

"Dillon has some make up work to complete. Do we have any plans that would get in the way of doing a lesson or two?" I sincerely hoped Ida could read my mind screaming, 'yes.'

Instead, Ida bustled in front of me, giving orders. "Mr. Maxwell, put your boots on the mat and hand me your coat. Harry, go warm up some cocoa. Steve, can you make up a plate of refreshments? We'll get these two settled at the kitchen table."

I didn't trust Dillon any farther than the front door, but I needn't have worried. The hour passed quickly. Dillon was on a mission to complete as many of the assignments as possible. And we were never alone. Dad delivered cocoa and Steve stepped through the door with a platter of his crispy, sweet rosettes and some frosted sugar cookies. Dad exchanged places with Ida who brought her newest knitting project to the table. She acted uninterested as she rhythmically clacked her needles, producing several inches of multicolored pastel rows. Steve checked under the sink and returned to Ida's living room—a constant marching in and out through an invisible revolving door.

At seven thirty Dillon handed over his completed pages and slurped the last of his cocoa. Dad took the dishes to the sink and Ida disappeared.

The assignment was perfect. "Dillon, you should probably have taken the advanced math class."

His blond hair fell over one eye and he smirked. I wasn't sure if it was to infer he couldn't do the work or didn't want to. Before I could ask, Ida returned with her tablecloth. "Sign, please."

Dillon hesitated.

"Everyone who visits my home on Christmas signs my tablecloth. You can't break tradition."

Dillon appeared to be at a loss. He picked up the fabric marker and scribbled his name, placing a five-pointed star next to it.

"Thank you," said Ida. "You don't know what this means to me." She clasped the linen to her chest and her eyes teared up.

I led Dillon to the door. He stuffed his arms into his coat. "Well," he stammered. "Do you have time to do any more tomorrow?" Dillon looked like this was the last place he'd like to be tomorrow, but the faster we finished the sooner my holiday time would be my own.

"Dad? Ida? Do we have anything going on? Would

Dillon and I have time for another short meeting tomorrow?"

Ida marched into the entry. She crossed her left arm over her tummy, set the elbow of her right arm on top of her left hand, and tapped her chin, pondering. She stopped tapping, and said, "Yes, but Mr. Maxwell." Her hands went to her hips, and she stretched to almost five feet tall, staring intently. She shook her forefinger at him, flapping the colorful sleeve of her Christmas dress. "You need to be here precisely at noon and finish by one. We have places to go and people to see."

"Yes, ma'am, Mrs. Clemashevski."

I think he beamed a real smile, but I wouldn't have bet on it. She turned and marched back inside.

He ripped open the door and ran headlong into Lorelei Calder. She backed up so suddenly, she would have tripped backwards off the stoop had he not reached out, grabbed her hand, and hauled her to safety. He held her for a moment too long, and a strange look covered his face. She shook free from his hold and flipped the furry hood off her head.

"Thanks," she said. Dillon took a deep bow, stood erect, and skipped down the steps.

Brock, following at her heels, was not amused. "What's he doing here?"

"Such a nice boy," Ida said,

Lorelei said, "We need your help."

"Merry Christmas," Steve said.

And I said, "What do you have there?" all at the same time.

"Hang up your coats, kids. I'll put on more cocoa. Steve—cookies. Ida—tablecloth. Katie, you sort this out," said Dad.

Brock very gently set a battered wooden case on the carpet, hung up their coats, and I led them to the living room.

"Dillon wants to play in the holiday basketball tournament and has makeup work to do." I felt it was important Brock and Lorelei understood Dillon's visit wasn't a social call. We sat around Ida's coffee table. The treat tray and cocoa magically appeared within reach, and they sipped and nibbled while Ida explained her tradition. They signed her tablecloth.

"What's going on? You two don't look like Santa has arrived yet," I said.

"Have you decided if you can be on my fishing team? After the other night, I figure you might have some reservations." Brock looked at his hands. "I guess we all do. But …" When he looked up again, he leaned forward and searched my face. "My grandfather started the contest and I'd be letting him down if I didn't participate. He taught me everything I know, and if I hadn't been so …" He faltered again and a hank of dark hair fell over his eyes.

He looked so dejected the words popped out before I had time to think things through. It was getting to be a habit of mine. "Of course, I'll raise your age average. I even have more years to volunteer if necessary." I glared at Dad.

Brock looked confused, then beamed. "I have a team of three committed fisher people and the average would be about …" He stopped and his eyes grew round. "How old are you?"

"Not old enough to raise your average to twenty-four but Chief West said she'd fish and so did my dad. How many anglers do you have on your team?"

"With Lorelei, you, and me, that makes three."

I couldn't fault his optimism and either Amanda or Dad would be happy to help. "Have you asked anyone else? Do you have enough equipment for everyone?"

"I have plenty. I even have two pop-ups." He rubbed his hands together in anticipation.

"What do you have there?" I tilted my head toward the case on the floor and Brock's smile faded.

"Go on. Show her." Lorelei hid behind the mug, sipping, her glasses fogging up from the warmth of the cocoa.

Brock lifted the weathered trapezoidal case and gently set it on the table. He slid hooks out of place and undid the latch. The rusty hinges screeched as he opened the lid and reverently lifted a polished, honey-hued violin with a lush red-brown grain. He held the instrument by the scroll at the top and the tailpiece at the bottom with the strings facing me.

"May I?" Dad said from behind me. He reached out and held his hand to receive the instrument.

Brock nodded ever so slightly as if any hasty movement might cause the violin to shatter and set it in Dad's hands. Dad inspected the workmanship, tilting it to get the light just right, catching the sparkle of the rich warm wood. He lightly touched the strings. Ida depressed a single tone on her keyboard and Dad tuned the pegs. He thrummed all four strings. Satisfied with its intonation, he handed the instrument to Ida. Her eyes glowed. The bow snapped free from the clamps in the case and Dad ran his hand along the stick. He yanked several long, dangling hairs from the bow, tightened the screw, and slid something wrapped in felt up and down. He waved the bow like a baton. Ida set the violin in his outstretched hand. Hugging it beneath his chin, he laid his head tenderly to the side. His eyes closed as he set the bow across a string.

I expected a sweet and lyrical melody but what we got was a bawdy rendition of *Grandma Got Run Over by a Reindeer*. Ida pounded the piano keys, adding a percussive dimension to the piece.

We clapped, laughed, and applauded, and with smiles all around, Dad segued into something lovely. After a few bars, Ida joined him. His fingers moved elegantly over the strings, sweetly caressing each vibrato, pulsating with intensity. She swayed and followed his lead, a little ritardando here, a bit of accelerando there. When they concluded, no one moved for a moment until Steve gave a wolf whistle. Dad's grin was stunning. My hands flew to my face to cover my astonishment, but he never noticed. After all he'd been through, he remembered one of my favorite pieces, Massenet's masterpiece, *Meditation*. I choked back a sob.

"What timbre and power! What brilliance! Where did you find this gem?" Dad held the instrument as if it were a mirror and he was admiring a most handsome reflection.

Brock frowned. "From Xavier."

CHAPTER TWENTY

Our smiles faded.

Dad carried the treasure to the sink where he could find the brightest light and read the interior label. His mouth formed an 'O'. He turned his head slowly and stepped to the table where he nestled the violin back in its case.

"It's very special, Brock. You should have someone who knows what they're doing look at it. If it is certifiable, it may be incredibly valuable."

Brock reached into the case and with the zip of Velcro, pulled a tab. He extracted a scribbled note and a yellowed sheet of paper, encased in plastic with corners folded to fit the shape of the inside space. He shoved it into Dad's hand. A smiled spread across Dad's face.

"A certificate of authenticity for a Mathias Albani, circa 1670. Do you play?"

Brock shook his head. He held the illegible note. "Xavier said he wanted me to take it before the circling vultures could get their hands on it. He was always talking about scavengers stealing his magnum opus. But now that he's gone, I don't know what to do. I don't know if he meant for me to keep it, or guard it until he needed it, which won't happen anymore. I don't even know if this is the magnum opus, but I'll sure miss him." Brock stared at his empty hands until Lorelei tightly grabbed one and shook it. He looked up with a rueful smile.

You may be one of the few, I thought.

Steve repeated two words. "Magnum opus? Great work. Xavier wrote music too, didn't he? Do you think he has a new composition out there?"

Ida cleared her throat.

"Out with it," Dad said.

"There was talk of his writing again. He never confirmed or denied the speculation. He was trying to pull himself out of the vodka-filled gutter. Since he came back, he's made himself more of a nuisance, showing up outside church or downtown in front of the arts center or near the fishing village or ..."

"At the hospital?" I finished.

"Yes." Ida fidgeted. "I don't suppose we'll ever know."

"His crazy girlfriend might know."

All heads swiveled toward Brock, and we waited.

"I don't know if she's crazy or his girlfriend, but she hung out on the ice. She always showed up with him, standing about ten yards away, like a shadow."

"Do you know who she is?" I asked. "Or where she stays?"

His eyes looked up to the right, envisioning a possibility. "I might. He called her Popovich. I know where Xavier hung his hat and she'd never be too far away. I could take you there. But what do I do with this?" He lightly ran his finger along the edge of the case.

"You can leave it here for the time being," Ida said, closing the case and setting it under the tree. "Brock, shouldn't you and Lorelei be getting home?"

Brock shook his head and his shaggy hair fell over one eye. "My mom and dad are out for the evening with friends. Lorelei has a midnight curfew, so if it's okay …" He checked with his girlfriend. "We'll go with you."

Ida glanced at the clock. "It's not too late, I suppose. Shall we go now?"

Lorelei's face lit up.

Brock and Ida rode in Steve's truck. Lorelei, Dad, and I followed in the Focus. We drove down Main Street, covering the same ground we'd covered looking for the geocache — was it only this morning? We followed the service road around the lake, through one of the Monongalia County parks, under the bridge, to a haphazard collection of tarps and tents, lean-tos and pallets, blankets and appliance boxes. My heart sank. The community extended beyond the beam from our headlights. We parked next to Steve and exited our vehicles.

"I'd expected a few, but this encampment looks more permanent than I imagined," I said. "They've settled in."

"The city council knows many of these people need a place to go and our local shelter simply can't house them all. Sometimes families would have been separated. Some of these folks can't maintain the sobriety requirement and some have pets they won't give up. The area is sanctioned. The restrooms and laundry facilities at the park are maintained. There is clean running water, and the heat is on in the big, insulated shelter. The school bus stops at the top of the hill." Ida pulled boxes from the back of the truck and stacked them in my arms. She closed the tailgate. "There is a cooperative church venture and every Sunday a hot meal is provided, and counseling services are made available.

"They even have a loosely organized association. It's a temporary solution for many and I wish they all had homes, but if they are going to remain living outside, it's the one policy on which Mayor Maxwell and I agree. At least until the work is completed on the more temporary accommodations, which I hope will be soon."

I looked more closely. Although a hodge-podge of shelters, if they could be considered that, I noticed the tidy appearance of the minute swaths of yard: straight paths trampled in the snow, a communal woodpile stacked in neat rows, rocks set in a ring around small fires, even sparse decorations adorned some of the entries.

Ida brought boxes of her delectable treats and carried them to a table under a sheet metal roof supported by four metal poles, and, by the line forming and warm greetings hailed, it appeared she'd been here before. Eager children jostled their way to the front, and she called some by name. I noticed many of them clutched a new toy in one hand. I smiled. Nurse Rachel and her elves had been here too.

Brock and Lorelei forged a path to the lakeshore, overlooking the lights of the fishing village. The location could have been considered prime real estate, but we stood in front of a sagging three-sectioned tent wrapped in the tatters of yellow caution tape and wondered if we dared enter.

"This is it." It would have been a novelty for the teen to

visit the eccentric artist in his abode. Facing reality, Brock's shoulders sagged.

A raspy voice called from the shadows, "Ain't nuttin' left. They took it all." A stooped bundle of rags tossed a snowball up and down in her hand. "And they killed him."

When she turned, Brock called, "Miss Popovich, remember me? You and I've met before."

She turned slowly, squinting at the speaker. "You Arnold's boy?"

"Yes, Miss Popovich. Do you think we could have a look inside Xavier's home?"

Hovel was more like it.

She shrugged. "Can't hurt him none. Nuttin' left."

Steve and Dad tied back the flaps and the three of us stepped inside. We took raspy breaths through the fabric of the sleeves at the crooks of our arms. The shanty was abandoned except for the putrid smell of decay. A pile of crumbled pottery pieces took up one corner. Stacks of damp, musty periodicals, newspapers, and booklets lined the north side, creating a short barrier to defend against the wind. Tiny tatters of paper skimmed across the tarp floor, as if dusted by an invisible hand. On my way out, I stooped and picked up a scrap with part of a treble clef drawn on a staff. I also picked up a piece of shiny red crockery in the shape of a tiny heart and pocketed them both.

"Told you," the woman said. "What ya lookin' for anyway?'

Dad said gently, "Anything that will help us understand your friend."

"He wasn't my friend," she shouted, though sounded like she wanted to cry. Her fists punched the air at her sides, and I strained to hear her next words. "He was my mentor." She dropped her head and the tears fell in earnest.

Where was Ida when we needed her? She always knew just what to do to make someone feel better.

We stood at an impasse until Lorelei said, ever so gently, taking slow, small steps toward her, "What did he teach you, Miss Popovich?" Close enough, Lorelei touched Popovich's shoulder, and the woman trembled.

"Everything," she said. "And I'm not Miss Popovich." She crumpled to the cold ground. "I'm Meghann."

Steve rushed to her side and knelt in the snow. "How can we help you? What do you need?"

She composed herself, swiped the end of her nose with the back of a hand wrapped in rags, and leaned on his arm to stand. She straightened the cloths around her middle, raised her chin, and, channeling a fine lady, said, "I'm perfectly capable of taking care of myself, kind sir. In fact, I may finally have found a way out of this rat trap." She examined his face and her eyes blinked rapidly. "Do I know you?"

CHAPTER TWENTY-ONE

Steve asked, "Do you?"

Meghann shrugged.

Ida had finished distributing her goodies and marched up the beaten path. She showed no sign of surprise seeing Meghann, but greeted her warmly, if curiously.

"Why don't you come home with us? We have a warm fire and …" Her eyes twinkled. "I have a piano. It's Christmas and we could sing carols."

Meghann yanked free of Steve's arm and scampered like a frightened rabbit behind the dried brush along the path. Steve held up his hands in a 'what did I do' gesture. He started back to the parking lot, and had only walked a few feet when a snowball smacked him in the back of the head. Steve swiped away the heavy white mess to keep it from melting down his back.

"Wait," she said. She bent down and we all instinctively dipped our heads, but rather than form another projectile to fling in our direction, she hefted an ungainly array of pages, edging every which way out of her grasp. She stomped to the head of our group. "Ready."

As if wary, Meghann stopped ten feet from the rear of Steve's truck. Brock and Lorelei jumped into the cab, but Meghann, more circumspect, stayed just out of reach.

Ida beckoned, waving her hand. "Join us."

Meghann's eyes shifted, looking side to side for an excuse to escape. Ida put out her hand. Meghann hugged the disorderly pile of papers to her chest and took tentative steps toward my vehicle. She crawled into the back seat and snuffled.

Light banter between Dad and Ida eliminated an uncomfortable silence and we rocketed onto Maple Street in no time. Steve parked his huge red truck in front of Ida's house, and with the myriad colored lights and fantastic decorations on the street, the truck was barely noticeable. Tonight might be the last night for some of my neighbors to go all out, sharing the spectacle to behold, and when I checked in the rearview mirror, I watched Meghann's eyes grow to the size of the moon.

I took in the view of our neighborhood. Next door, Pam and Adam Farley cuddled on their front stoop behind a Santa, sleigh, and four reindeer and waved. Precocious three-year-old Emma would have had a late Christmas Eve and a big Christmas day and was probably asleep, although she'd been known to surprise all unsuspecting adults in the neighborhood. Renegade circled CJ and Carlee as they put finishing touches on a snow sculpture resembling the Columbia High School mascot, a royal-blue and gold cougar. The big cat sparred with three vertical spheres of snow, complete with coal eyes, a top hat, a button nose, and an enormous smile made from little black dots which looked an awful lot like raisins.

The stingy amount of light illuminating our garage in the rear would appear gloomy compared to the front yard, so I parked behind Steve's truck on Maple Street so we could continue to enjoy the neighbors' glorious revelry.

Meghann stayed rooted where she was until Ida coaxed her with the promise of a plate of homemade cookies and candy and Dad's famous hot cocoa. Ida reached out her hand, and Meghann turned her back, curling up in the back seat, shielding the stack of papers she carried.

"Whatever you brought with you is safe. We don't want anything from you," Ida said. "Harry has the cocoa heating up and if you don't want to stay after that, we can take you back to your abode tonight, okay?"

Meghann crawled from the back seat but remained skittish, crouched over her valuable armload, guarding whatever it was she clutched in front of her. Dad held the door, the lure of warm yellow light drawing us all into the house.

Once inside, Meghann stood, ogling Ida's Christmas tree. She jumped when Steve shut the door and cowered when Maverick padded in from the kitchen.

"It's okay. You're a good boy, right Maverick," Ida said. Maverick brushed against Ida's leg, sat, and waited for her to pet him. "We've got a jigsaw puzzle to put together or we can play a game. Let's go sit at the table and, while we wait for Harry, you can tell us about your day."

Instead, Meghann took slow steps toward the piano. Two fingers twinkled the topmost keys in a tremolo reminiscent of birdsong in a Disney cartoon and the other arm gripped the pages tighter.

"Do you play?" Ida asked.

Meghann tentatively shook her head.

"May I?" Ida settled on the piano bench and began an arpeggio leading into *Silent Night*. Meghann closed her eyes and smiled. Her head slowly rolled on her shoulders as if she'd been transported to another world. When Ida finished, Meghann lost the dreamy look, but plopped herself on the corner of the seat next to Ida, and with her free hand, fanned the sheet music on the stand until she carefully teased out and opened one. "*The Wexford Carol*," Ida said, nodding in appreciation. She played the opening bars and sang the first few words of the haunting Irish melody. Meghann rose and quickly reseated herself on Ida's other side, plucking mid-range keys to accompany Ida's lilting voice. "You know the accompaniment line."

When the last tone drifted away, Dad applauded and said, "Cocoa is served."

We gathered around the dining table and Dad pulled out Ida's chair, then mine. Brock followed suit with a cockeyed grin on his face and held Lorelei's chair. Meghann slid hesitantly onto the seat Steve held.

She continued to grip the papers crammed on her lap beneath the dining table, but sat up straighter and daintily sipped the steaming beverage from Ida's delicate Wedgewood teacup, replacing it precisely on the saucer. A messy Russian teacake left traces of powdered sugar, and she dabbed at her lips before taking another precise swallow of hot chocolate. She cleared her throat and said, "Thank you for your kindness. This memory will last me a lifetime. I'm sorry for the way I've acted, but life has been challenging."

Without the edginess and fear, she had a smooth,

cultured voice and I could listen to her read a grocery list and smile.

"Can we see what you have there?" Ida edged closed.

Meghann examined the pages, then relinquished the stack to Ida with the tiniest hint of hope in her eyes. Ida ran her hand reverently over the top of the sheafs of paper. Her voice was full of wonder.

"It's music." As if planned, Ida added, "Brock, can you get out your gift?"

He pulled the case from under the tree. He set it in the middle of the table and opened the lid. Meghann gasped.

The doorbell rang.

Steve answered the bell to an unabashedly cocky Dillon Maxwell and his two pals who craned their necks to gape inside. Dillon held a helmet under his arm and, with the door open, I heard the thrum of the snowmobile engines.

"Good evening, all. Sorry to interrupt your party but I forgot my cap. May I?" He pointed toward Ida's coat rack and, sure enough, puddled on the floor was the blue-and-gold tail.

Steve gestured grandly toward the rack. "Help yourself."

Brock closed the case lid and slid the instrument under the table.

Meghann hunched her shoulders and clamped her lips together. The legs on her chair squawked as she backed away from the table. She rose hurriedly, and plastered herself against the wall, trembling.

Maverick barked; Meghann's eyes darted around the room.

Ida reached out her hand, but Meghann pressed herself into the corner. "Why's he here? What does he want?" she whispered, drawing her vest over her face. "He can't see me."

I stood next to her. "What's wrong Meghann? Is there anything I can do? Do you know Dillon?" She looked into my face and her eyes filled with confusion.

"Thanks. Gran would've disowned me." I heard his voice and peeked around the wall. Dillon swept in and out. He waved the cap over his head as he hopped down the steps. The motors roared to life, and I cringed at the whine as they sped away from the house.

As Steve closed the door, CJ dashed up the stoop with Carlee right behind him. "There's a big fire across the lake."

Even with the huge hulk standing in her way, Meghann shoved past him. The gentle man stepped aside but was taken by surprise and almost trapped her again when Meghann reached out and snagged the charm on the chain from around Carlee's neck.

"Mine," she screeched, running full tilt to the street and out into the night.

CHAPTER TWENTY-TWO

CJ lifted Carlee's chin and assessed the damage. He gave words of profound parental wisdom. "The pendant belonged to her in the first place, I would say."

Carlee nodded, almost in tears. "I didn't mean to take it to keep but I couldn't very well leave it where I found it, could I? I'm glad she has it back."

CJ nodded, turned to us, and said, "Drew called. They need drivers and vehicles to take some of the homeless at the park who require transportation to another temporary shelter. Steve, can you help? You might have room in your truck for a few of their belongings."

Steve moved toward the door when he heard 'they need.' I grabbed my keys. "My Focus will hold five."

"What's burning?" said Dad.

"We don't know yet. May Carlee stay here with you, Ida?"

Ida nodded, and Carlee took a seat next to her on the piano bench, wrapping her arms around the little lady. Their dog Renegade wriggled inside and plopped himself next to Maverick. Both tilted their heads expectantly.

"I'll help," said Brock, punching off his phone. "I got an okay from my mom."

CJ looked like he wanted to protest, but he thought again and jerked his head. Brock gave Lorelei's hand a firm squeeze and followed.

We headed out again, toward the county park. There were some gawkers mingling among the line of cars waiting to assist those who wanted to move to a new shelter up and away from the blaze. Occasionally, a thin flame scratched the night sky, stretching through the unnatural, eerie orange halo around the bridge by the park. Anxious, and with an insatiable need to know, Steve left his truck, and brought back the news. "It's awfully dry and there is a breeze but it's not as bad as it could be. The fire's contained. Only a few shelters and some of the trees on the point are destroyed. Some members of the community won't budge no matter how much smoke fills the night sky. They won't relinquish their little patch of the world for fear it might be taken. So far, no fatalities, but several families with young children and older folks want to spend a night away from the suffocating smoke."

When we finally neared the parking lot, the gray pall covered everything and made it difficult to see very far into the surrounding area. A handful of groups waited, still intent on new accommodations: two families with young children and three seniors in their twilight years.

One group piled into Steve's truck. Brock assisted the

elders crowding into CJ's truck, and a family of four got into my vehicle. Their clothes were clean but worn and threadbare. Each child clutched a small backpack and a toy.

"Anything else?" I asked.

"This is it." Their meager belongings fit in the single duffle bag toted by their mother. The dad sat as still as he could in the passenger seat, squeezing the life out of the folder on his lap and clutching the handle of a large clunking toolbox. While we waited for the church to which they were assigned to open its doors, he remained quiet.

His family poured out of my Focus.

He turned to me and said, "Thank you. I don't know what we'll do, but my kids will be safe tonight." He turned a ruddy face to me and twisted a sort of wry smile onto his face. "Know anyone who can use a good plumber?" He yanked a page from his folder and handed me his impressive resume. "Twenty-four-hour service," he said before he popped open the door and raced to join his family.

I folded the resumé and stuck it in my pocket.

We checked back at the encampment. The fire chief told us we were no longer needed, but to please accept heartiest appreciation from the entire crew, and Steve, CJ, Brock, and I caravanned home to Ida's.

Carlee and Ida still sat rooted to the piano bench, carefully paging through, sorting, and aligning the tattered and torn papers Meghann had left behind. Lorelei sifted through the straightened pages, seeming to reorder them. Neat stacks lined the edge of the piano, the coffee table, and end tables.

"What's to report?" asked Ida, not glancing up from the captivating task in front of her.

"The flames came from the direction of Xavier's dwelling, so I don't imagine there's much left. They'd called out three firetrucks," Steve said.

The wheels turned behind Dad's eyes. "There was no one there to light a fire and nothing there to combust spontaneously. What could've happened?" Dad planted a charcuterie board full of cold meat, cheese, olives, pickles, and nuts on the dining table between a tray of cookies and a basket of Ida's homemade potato buns next to bottles of mayo and mustard. "Do they think it was arson?"

Steve scratched behind his ear. "Why would anyone want to burn down an empty tent? It wasn't in terrible shape and could have been cleaned up and used by someone else. It wasn't in anyone's way. Everything is recycled out there."

"Did you catch sight of or hear from Meghann?" Ida asked.

"No, and I'm afraid her tent may also have met its fate. Theirs were the only two shelters on the point." Steve slapped together a sandwich, licking the dripping sauce off his fingers.

Life just became more difficult and challenging for Meghann.

Lorelei handed me a few pages. "I've been sorting by the date written on the bottom." She fanned the scorched upper right-hand corner. "It looks like someone tried to burn the papers but either they were too damp or too compact and that kept them from going up in smoke."

"Have you figured out what it is?"

Ida's eyes filled with wonder as she thumbed through the papers. "This seems to be a musical score, complete with multiple movements, but the pages are out of order and may not even all be here. If we can get it together, I'd like to see what some of it sounds like. Meghann is certainly taken by music. Maybe she was a composition student of Xavier's. She met him in the industry somehow. This is quite a body of work. The notation and instrumentation for each piece are very particular." She held up two sheets. She waved one. "This was written for a string quartet." Then the other. "This is for a chamber orchestra." She picked a third sheet up by its corner. "And this is written for piano and voice."

"Maybe another down and out musician?" Steve said.

Brock said around a mouthful of cookie, "She followed Xavier all over, like a groupie."

Wow, could that boy put away Ida's food!

"Meghann kept repeating that Xavier was killed." Ida's hands hovered over the musical treasure. "The way she said it, I thought it was just a feeling she had. But maybe she knows more than she's letting on, or maybe there's something she's not even aware of."

"We promised Lance we wouldn't investigate." The slight reprimand in Dad's voice didn't go unnoticed.

"Who's investigating?" Ida snapped. "If a clue just drops in my lap, what am I supposed to do with it? Disregard it as if it doesn't exist? Not happening on my watch." When her rant subsided, she added, "I just won't go out of my way to look for anything."

Dad rubbed his stubbly chin. "So we've just been doing our civic duty."

"That's right." Ida softened and the shiny tears in her eyes threatened to overflow.

CJ put a supportive hand on her shoulder. My stomach gave a little flutter. His kindness went out to everyone.

"It's Christmas and Pete's still locked up," she said. I

got an empty feeling in the pit of my stomach.

Carlee cleared her throat. She flipped what appeared to be a blank page back and forth, and her eyes opened wide.

"Mrs. C, look at this." She handed Ida a wrinkled sheet with quarter folds, shredded, scorched corners, and a rainbow of colored ink scrawled across the paper. Ida looked perplexed and held it up. The cover sheet displayed the composer's name, a date, and the title of the work.

"*Das Geheimnis der Meditation* by Xavier Notrecali." Her long exhale came out like a whoosh.

CHAPTER TWENTY-THREE

Dad reached out. "Hand it over," he said with a gleam in his eye. He set a pair of cheaters on his nose and tilted the glasses to get the right angle, deciphering the handwriting for himself. His forehead bunched up. "It does say Xavier. Do you think Meghann stole it?" Dad scratched behind his ear. "Maybe they wrote it together, but then her name should be on the title page, shouldn't it? Do you think Xavier gave it to her for safekeeping, just like he gave you the violin, Brock?"

Brock shrugged, stuffing a huge bite of leftover tenderloin into his mouth.

"But what a strange title. Looks like German to me," said Dad.

Lorelei performed a two-finger tap dance on her phone.

She inhaled deeply, and, trying to mask her surprise, said, "The secrets in meditation."

Carlee nonchalantly tossed out a comment that stopped the ruminating. "Or maybe she did away with him and just took the music." She didn't notice all movement ceasing until Maverick whined. "What?" she said.

CJ punched numbers on his phone. "Chief West. I am sorry to bother you, but would you be able to stop by Ida's? We have come across what might be considered evidence." We strained to hear her reply. "Thank you."

CJ slid his phone into his pocket. "She is not thrilled with our request, but she is on her way, and she is coming alone because she believes her officers need time with their families. She'd like us to remain until she can speak to us."

Brock stopped chewing and swallowed hard. Lorelei and Carlee looked at each other. Dad said, "I'll put on more cocoa."

Ida rattled a gift. She unboxed her one-thousand-piece monochromatic jigsaw puzzle, and she and the girls began the tedious task of separating the edge pieces and fitting them together. They organized the components by color shade and repetitive shape, connecting those they found and steadily built a vignette.

Renegade and Maverick pranced by the door, so CJ and I took them for an evening stroll. Some of the neighbors had turned off their decorations; the homes were dark. The frenetic day, with its festivities and its foibles, was coming to a close.

"How's fatherhood?" I asked.

CJ's tender smile glowed under the streetlight. "Couldn't have asked for a better gift. It has its challenges, but the only thing I can think of that would have made it better is if her mother had been here to see the wonderful young lady she's become." His smile faded a teensy bit. "However, I do not know if I can appreciate her male friends without hesitancy."

"Galen is an okay guy. I trust him."

CJ slowed. Renegade sat. Maverick pulled, then thought the better of it and sat next to Renegade.

"But can I trust my daughter?" He glowered for a second. His face lit up, and he said, "She is truly a handful." We silently traversed another block and he said, "Do you know how much Pete admires you?"

Where did that come from? With so much going on, I'd focused on ways to help get Pete off the murder suspect list but at that moment, thoughts of his liberation from Susie crept to the forefront. "He's a good friend who has a lot going on right now."

The wind picked up, and we quickened our pace. By the time we returned, Ida and the girls had completed more of the puzzle than I thought they could.

CJ's phone buzzed. "Yes," he said. "I understand. Thank you. I will tell Ida."

CJ pulled his coat from the hook. "We are all free to leave. Chief West has an emergency she has to take care of, but she will connect with you, Ida. I believe our possible evidence is currently low on her list of priorities."

"Did something else happen?"

"I don't know, Katie. I do know she is having a very long week and is deserving a break." He glanced at the clock. "It's time to bid your friends goodnight, Carlee." He held her coat out to her.

She yawned and stuffed her arms into her quilted jacket. Renegade stretched her paws in front of her and followed her family across the street to a now warm and cozy home.

Brock and Lorelei grabbed their coats. "It's been interesting. Ms. Wilk, can I count on you and your dad for the ice fishing tournament? It starts tomorrow at two."

I nodded, albeit reluctantly, and turned to Dad who radiated enthusiasm.

"Thanks for letting us hang out. Mrs. Clemashevski, what should I do with the violin? Do you think Miss Popovich recognized it?"

Ida caught my eye, and she shook her head almost imperceptibly. "I'm not sure. She might have, Brock. Maybe we'll check with her again. You can leave it here or take it with you."

He gave my dad a serious look. "Mr. Wilk, you play real well. Would you give me a few lessons sometime?"

"I'd be honored."

"Then, I'll leave it here for the time being, at least until I learn how to hold it." Brock mocked himself, writhing wildly, pantomiming drawing an imaginary bow over invisible strings.

Steve yawned. "I guess I'd better call it a day too. It would have been a long one, but it was filled to the brim and flew by. I'll sleep like a log tonight. If I may take my leave, your chefness." He bowed and kissed the back of Ida's hand. She blushed.

Dad and I stowed the leftovers while Ida sorted through the last few pages of the music. Dad put another log on the fire. I poured all three of us a glass of Cabernet. Dad and I relaxed on the couch and waited. The colorful dancing sparks and light crackling from our fire mesmerized me and set me to wonder what might have caused the fire at the homeless encampment.

Ida completed her task, hauled herself off the bench, and stretched. She picked up a slim pile of pages, peered closely at each, and reordered them between sips from the goblet. Satisfied, she sat again, and took another sip before straightening the pages on the music rack of the piano. She flexed her fingers, and played—tentatively, slowly, carefully. She stopped and scrutinized the notes and began the piece again. Her lips puckered and she frowned.

"This sounds dreadful." She closed the cover on her piano, grabbed the small sample of music off the stand, and stuffed it under the lid of the piano bench. "I must be too tired to be doing right by the composer." She rose and joined us by the fire. "Katie, don't you have one more package to open?"

I cocked my head and tried to figure out what she was hinting at. We'd unwrapped everything under her tree. I sat forward and craned my neck to see into the darker recesses behind the evergreen but saw nothing new.

Dad snorted. "She's obviously forgotten. I'll get it." He jumped up, looking spry for so late in the day, and paraded into our apartment, swinging his arms so much like a tin soldier, I could almost hear Tchaikovsky's march song. It dawned on me what he was after. My heartrate sped up just like notes in the piece and my breath came in shallow spurts.

The envelope from England.

"Katie?" Dad's muffled voice wafted through the door between our apartments. "Where is it?"

Ida and I looked at each other. Inwardly, I smiled. I could put off opening an envelope that was sure to conjure up both happy and sad thoughts about Charles. I'd adopted my lifesaving dog and, although I wanted to know what was written on the pages delivered by the veterinarian who had brought me the best handful of fur ever, a little delay would be okay by me.

Ida and I joined Dad in the search.

"I'm sure it was here, on the right side of the tree, on top of my gifts. But I don't see it now."

Dad side-eyed me, his disbelief radiating displeasure.

"Really, Dad. I don't know what happened to it. Maybe someone accidentally picked it up."

"Or maybe someone took it."

Ida glanced around the room. She plopped on the couch and pouted. "Meghann didn't sign my tablecloth."

CHAPTER TWENTY-FOUR

I hadn't set an alarm but, much to my regret, I woke long before dawn, looking into Maverick's wide brown eyes. He peered at me, blinked, and rocked on his paws, his leash dangling from his drooling mouth.

"Okay, I see you." I threw back the comforter. The cool room prompted quick dressing before plunging down the stairs, donning warm reflective gear, and trekking out into the new morning.

Maverick barked and yanked the leash. I shushed him. With our unstructured days, our erratic walk times messed with his schedule, but I didn't want to rile the sleeping neighbors. I hiked behind him, watching the streetlights blink off as the bright pink and violet colors blossomed over the trees and illuminated the Columbia skyline until remembering an old saying, "Red at night, sailors delight. Red in the morning, sailors take warning."

I mentally catalogued yesterday's events, astounded by how much Dad and I packed into our first Christmas in Columbia. We'd breakfasted with Ida, Drew, Jane, CJ, and Carlee. We'd found a geocache and played cards. We watched some of *It's a Wonderful Life*. Lance and Steve joined us for dinner. Brock and Lorelei visited and brought an antique violin possibly worth more than they'd expected. Dad played violin again. My lips curled up at the memory. We'd met Meghann and discovered a manuscript which may or may not be of any importance to anyone. We'd helped some of the homeless families get away from a fire which consumed several of the shelters. I frowned. That fire had taken away even more of what little some of those families still had, if not in possessions than in security and safety. We'd done a bit of research but hadn't helped Pete, and we promised Lance we wouldn't investigate or get in the way. To top it all off, Dillon came by last night and I regretted my promise to meet him again today. Not to mention Pete had been arrested very early the same day.

I urged Maverick to hurry and our last few steps took us around the rear of the police cruiser parked in our driveway. Ida's front door opened and Chief West waved us in. I glanced at my watch.

"What brings you here at seven fourteen?" I asked, hoping to elicit a smile from Amanda for my effort.

Daggers pulsed from her bloodshot eyes, and she didn't laugh. "Ida heard noises this morning and she thought it was you or your dad, but it looks like someone broke in and took your so-called evidence."

"Broke in *here?*" Maverick and I darted past Amanda into Ida's living room. Dad and Ida sat in two stiff-backed chairs next to the dining table. As always, Dad was dressed for the day in jeans and a bulky sweater, and he sipped from a cup. Ida dragged her faux fur dressing gown together in front of her. She brushed at her puffy eyes with a tissue.

"What was taken?"

"They swiped the manuscript," Dad said.

I couldn't believe of all the beautiful things in Ida's home, someone would choose to take tattered, dirty pages of music she thought sounded terrible anyway. The violin! But it was still beneath the tree. "How?"

"It appears someone just walked in and took it. The windows are intact. No one tampered with the locks." Amanda cocked her head. "I'll file a report. But it won't be high on our list of priorities. I just don't have the manpower to investigate a break-in right now. Are you sure the manuscript was stolen?"

"We think …" I started to say the manuscript might help prove who may have killed Xavier but that still wouldn't necessarily exonerate Pete. "Never mind." My mind raced. "I left our door open when Maverick and I went for our walk. Someone could've entered there and come through the adjoining door, but they would have had to have known the layout of her house."

"Everyone in town knows. The original floor plan of this old house is on display in the historical center. The Clemashevski family tree has deep roots in the community, and the exhibit is open to everyone. I know the apartment division is new, but not much from the original plan has changed." Dad let Ida's displeased look roll off his back. "Just saying."

Amanda rubbed her hands up and down over her face. "I've got to get some shut eye. I'll talk to you later, Ida.

Meanwhile, make sure your doors remain locked."

Ida turned back to Amanda and searched her face. "You'll look for Meghann," Ida pleaded. "Maybe she came back for the manuscript. She brought it to us in the first place so if she took it, and the door was open, there wasn't really a break-in. In any case, I'd like to know what happened."

"We'll watch for Meghann, but she's a grown woman, free to do as she pleases, mostly. However, your request is going to have to take a back seat. We've had a more urgent tragedy strike last night."

"Is there anything we can do? Any way we can help?"

Amanda looked awful. Her glazed eyes sank in sockets rimmed in a tired gray and her hollow cheeks gave her a skeletal look.

She thought for a moment. "Could you visit the pediatric wing in the hospital? Rachel's had a tough night and needs some spritely visitors."

"Of course, Amanda." Ida sat up straighter. "What happened?"

"We arrested a parent for trying to administer unprescribed medication to her daughter, which could have caused her to get very sick. The mother is undergoing psychiatric assessment to determine if she suffers from a factitious disorder imposed on another."

Dad asked, "I don't understand."

"Sorry. I've been stretched to the limit." Amanda yawned and scoured her face again. "Munchausen by proxy. It looks like the mother purposely made her daughter ill to get attention for them both. She denies it, of course, but Dr. Erickson had Rachel watch them very carefully and she caught the mother administering a dropper of something into a pitcher of water on the child's bedstand. The lab analysis showed eye drops in the pitcher and the dropper and it was clearly not medication listed on her chart. Enough of that and there could've been a fatal outcome." She shook her head. "Pete used his one call to alert Rachel to possible complications with his patient. It's the only thing he was concerned with while awaiting his arraignment."

"You can't still believe he's capable of murder, can you?"

"You and Ida are two of his staunchest advocates, but I go by the book and follow the evidence." She inhaled. "I'm sure, if he's innocent, we'll be able to prove it." *If?* I swallowed a scream. She stopped, gathered her thoughts, and turned to me. "Katie, that fishing contest starts today, doesn't it?"

My right eyebrow flew to my hairline. "Yes."

"I'm going to get a bit of shut eye, but I still want to make myself accessible to my constituency and I think the tournament would be one way I could insert myself into the fabric of my new community. I'll meet you at two."

Incredulous!

"It may be the only way to get close to someone else who knows something about Xavier's death. That in turn may provide more evidence."

"To help Pete?" I struggled to calm my racing heart. I would help her.

She nodded.

"Brock will be thrilled. Alone, I don't quite raise his average age to twenty-four, but adding both of us, his team should fit the bill."

She nodded and shook her head. "Text me the info.

Now if you'll excuse me."

And she was gone.

It certainly sounded like she intended to keep her Columbia position, permanently.

CHAPTER TWENTY-FIVE

The clock chimed twelve and for the next six minutes the rhythmic ticking of Ida's clock sounded like a ball-peen hammer striking a nail head. Ida's knitting needles clacked in chorus and the newspaper pages rattled in Dad's hand.

"That's it, I guess. He's not coming." I rose from the couch and stretched, gathering the materials I'd prepared for Dillon. Maverick pulled himself to his paws and rattled his tags. "What do we have planned today?"

The needles continued to weave the skein of yarn into a glorious cascade of color, and she said, "Today is a day of rest."

"But you told ..." Her grin finished my sentence. "We don't really have anything planned for today, but you wanted him to be prompt. It didn't work, so what do you want to do?"

"Let me finish this row and we can go to the hospital and entertain Rachel's kids before you have to join the tournament crew. Brock left the violin so your dad can play a few songs and I have piano tunes they might like. What will you do?"

She caught me off guard. I thought for a second. "I'll call Lorelei, Carlee, and Kindra and see if they'd like to join me. We can read to the younger kids."

She beamed. "Pack your gear so you're ready to go. You and the girls can read first, and, when you have to leave, your dad and I will take over with the musical entertainment. I think Rachel said there were seven children in the hospital today. You'll have a little time to spend with each of them. Your dad can join you a little later." She secured the end of her needle and stashed her work in the soft-sided organizer at her feet. She rocked forward twice, and I grabbed her hand. I dragged her sturdy body out of the sofa, and we chuckled. "I've got to go on a diet. It'll be my New Year's resolution." She smirked. "Again."

Maverick barked at the door. Then we heard the bell.

"We're leaving at one minute after one," Ida said, her stern voice lowered to give her words gravity.

I opened the door and Dillon stood on the top step, his eyes glued to his shuffling sneakers. Gone were the fancy boots. His straight blond hair stood out in all directions. He hunched his shoulders around his ears and thrust his hands deeper into his pockets.

"Sorry I'm late," he muttered, his teeth chattering. "Could I still work on the make-up until one?"

"I have a prior commitment and need to be out of here by one minute after one."

Dad snorted behind me.

Dillon nodded. I stepped back, and he lumbered inside. Melting snow puddled around his shoes and he kicked them off on the rug, and tried to hide one foot behind the other, concealing the fact he wore one black and one blue sock in dire need of darning. He barreled through the room and headed for Ida's dining table. The legs on the chair screeched as he pulled it out. He dropped onto the seat, and picked up a pencil, waiting for me to deliver the packet.

"Are you okay?" I asked, flipping past the finished pages.

"Yeah. Fine. Let's get this over with," he said with a returning attitude, and added, "Please. Oh, and here."

He handed me an envelope.

My name was written in a flowery scrawl. I opened the envelope. A gift card and a handmade note card fell out. Mrs. Maxwell had sent a thank you.

He furiously jotted solutions but was careful to write the final answers so I could read them. With six minutes remaining on the clock, he put the pencil down and leaned back in the chair. "I'm done."

I'd been monitoring his effort and except for completing the unit exams, he had done exemplary work. "We can finish the tests tomorrow, but Dillon, you don't seem yourself. What's wrong?"

He glared at me, then rolled his eyes, shook his head, and stood. "See you tomorrow. And good luck in the tournament." He scoffed. Having the smart-alecky Dillon back was almost a relief. "Me and my dad are going to wipe Isaacson's team off the ice."

His swagger reappeared and he shoved his feet into

his shoes. He gripped the doorknob but turned around before opening it. "Thanks. Sometimes ... Just thanks." He turned and left.

Ida tapped her tiny toe to make me move faster. I flew around the apartment and collected a travel mug filled with hot tea, a bag of pretzel sticks, a white cardboard box of Ida's sumptuous cookies, an extra pair of mittens, a long, knitted scarf, and my fishing license.

Dad rode with Ida in her purple muscle car, and I followed in the Focus. We parked in the garage and walked through the hospital to the elevators. Rachel waited with a big smile.

"I'm so glad you're here. Some of the kids had a traumatic night; police crawling all over and searching the entire floor doesn't bode well for a calming atmosphere. I know Chief West tried to keep the investigation under wraps, however, Ronnie Christianson can be like a bull in a china shop." I followed her eyes down the hall where Officer Rodgers stood at attention in front of a closed door. "It's been rough. But you're here now. Katie, the books are on the bookcase in the nook. The children will let you know which stories they'd like. Ida and your dad and I will organize the snack table and arrange a little concert area around the piano. Ready?" She raised her chin and ordered, "Smile."

The girls and I took our selection of books and read to small groups. Two fidgety boys, dueling with permanent markers, finally calmed down and sat next to me, captivated by the book Amanda had donated, *Thoroughbred Christmas*. They thanked me before racing to the snack table, snatching cookies and milk, and sitting quietly in front of the piano, completely awestruck by my dad tuning the violin.

While I waited for the girls to turn the final pages of their books, I absentmindedly computed our average age for the tournament. Chief West didn't look ten years older than me, let alone the seventeen we needed to balance the years among us. I felt I'd somehow let Brock down.

Rachel startled me, whispering at my ear. "Why such a serious face? They're having a great time."

"You need noisier shoes." Her mischievous eyes hinted she'd known exactly what she'd done. "You shouldn't sneak up on people like that."

The shine in her eyes dimmed a bit as she glanced down the hall. "Sometimes it's absolutely necessary."

"Chief West told us what happened. Will your patient be okay?"

"She will be, physically. I worry about the family. Her mom's in the psych ward for an evaluation. The little girl was born prematurely and exhibited a few developmental difficulties early on. She seemed to come through it well, but recent records show numerous visits to the ER by the girl and her helicopter mom, sometimes with dad and sometimes without. They're checking those reports for irregularities. When I caught her mom putting drops in the pitcher last night, she told an unbelievable story that when she came back from the cafeteria, she found a note under the bottle with instructions to add two drops to her daughter's water every hour, but she couldn't find the note."

The door to the room opened and two men stepped out, deep in conversation. I recognized one man from our caroling night. His daughter must be the little girl from the ER, Quinn. The other man caught me staring and winked. I was a sucker for his eyes. Eyes were my kryptonite and

Pete's eyes never failed to bring a wobble to my knees.

"I'm so glad the judge released him on bond this morning in time to take care of her. Between Dr. Erickson and Dr. Coltraine, they'll have her right as rain in no time."

Pete was no longer in custody. I waved.

I helped Lorelei shelve an armful of books, and we settled the listeners who ignored our goodbyes, mesmerized by two animated, larger-than-life senior-hams. Carlee punched the buttons on the elevator and my worry level rose as we dropped to the lobby. I hoped Brock had a plan.

"I can't fish today. Good luck," Kindra said. "Catch some big ones. I want to hear all about it later."

CHAPTER TWENTY-SIX

Amanda joined us on shore, and we circled our fearless team leader, Brock, to hear the rules and regulations delivered by the grizzly, bearded octogenarian behind the bullhorn.

"The entrance fee …" The crowed grumbled when the megaphone screeched with feedback. In charge of opening the tournament, he began again. "Your entrance fee goes toward our Let's Get Fishing junior program. Registered teams set up and catch fish during the afternoon hours from three until six. The catch for day one is walleyes; day two is northern; and the day three category is open. Deliver the choice of your catches to the command booth for measuring and counting until seven o'clock each evening. At the closing ceremony, barring any unforeseen events, our mayor will award prizes in too many categories to enumerate here. Know that we consider you all winners, but let's get the fish biting." He tapped his cane on the podium. "Three. Two. One …"

Unprepared for the deafening blare from his air horn, Maverick flinched and yelped. I ducked. What a way to start!

I hunted for the new location of Brock's royal-blue, portable cubicle but his mischievous eyes lit up and I knew he'd been waiting to spring his latest and greatest surprise. His dad decided to join the Isaacson team and had proudly replaced the soft-sided pop-up with a welcome steel-sided trailer.

"Nice to see you again, Ms. Wilk. Thanks for joining us, Mr. Wilk," Mr. Isaacson said. "And pleased as punch to meet you, Chief West." He shook her hand, pumping it like a jack handle.

He opened the fish house door and ushered us inside. Strutting and grinning from ear to ear, he listed the amenities and my mouth dropped: a four-person dinette, a two-burner stovetop, a small oven, a fireplace, a TV screen, a refrigerator, a microwave, two bunks, a rack of jig sticks and spools, tip-ups or something, and five holes fitted with rattle reels—whatever they were. He called it his wheelhouse.

"My boy tells me you like to fish, Chief. Today looks like a great day." He manipulated zip ties from around a bundle of wood and arranged the fuel in the fireplace. He lit a conic fire starter and sat back when it blazed.

Amanda blushed. "Since moving to Minnesota, I've picked up a few good habits."

"Where are you from originally?" asked Mr. Isaacson.

"I came from Arizona."

"I imagine that was quite a culture shock."

She chuckled. "I still remember my first exposure to Minnesota-ice nice. I was a rookie cop working New Year's Eve and we got a flustered appeal from a young OnStar navigation agent, working somewhere in the South, who'd gotten a panicked call from a customer requesting assistance." She took off her gloves, grabbed a spool of green filament, and wound it with a practiced hand. "But when the agent pulled up his map, the car showed up in the middle of a huge lake. As the closest rescue team, my partner and I followed the directions and, I'll admit, I was a little queasy driving on the ice with our cruiser. We found the owner of the truck and I met my first ice fishermen. The tipsy seventy-year-old laughed at having pulled one over on the agent. While I wrote out the warning, he hauled in the most beautiful twenty-four-inch walleye I'd ever seen. We stayed for another half an hour, and I had my first of many lessons from a true sportsman."

Brock rubbed his hands together and snapped the straps on his bib overalls. "Hey, watch this. I've been practicing." He picked up one of the zip ties and laced it around his wrists, pulling it tight with his teeth. He held his wrists above his head and with the whoop of a warrior, he swung his arms down toward his hips and his elbows up and back. The zip tie tore in two and he held up both arms in a sign of victory. "I'm Houdini. Anybody else want to try?"

Amanda gave him a curious look.

He blushed crimson. "Right. Let's get going then. The more fish we catch, the better chance we have of winning. I'm using my Rattle Master."

"Your what?" Lorelei said. "You know you're going to

have to explain everything twice, right?"

Brock shook the triple hooks at the end of a noisy yellow and green lure with glassy orange eyes. "It's been my big winner this week." He pinched a minnow and drove a hook through its tail, then dropped the bait in a hole in the floor. He fed the line through his fingers until it picked up some slack, then he reeled it back a foot and fixed it in place.

Carlee grabbed some gear and followed his lead, but Lorelei turned up her nose and leaned away.

He chortled. "I have plastic bloodworms and barbless hooks for you, Lorelei." She relaxed.

I sat on the edge of one of the recliners but before I could settle in, Amanda said, "I'll help you get started, Katie. We'll use spikes."

I'd hoped to be an age-averaging observer, but it looked like I'd be required to pull in fish too. I copied Amanda, uncapping a hole, and repositioning the nearest hinged arm of an apparatus. She grabbed a hook in one hand and reached into a plastic carton with the other. I did the same but recoiled and tossed back the slimy, squirming yellow maggots.

"Ew." I wriggled, my goosebumps crawling up and down my back, doing a good imitation of the slick critters.

Amanda chortled.

The mechanism next to Carlee spun and rattled. Brock said in a teaching voice, "Reel it in slowly for a bit and then jerk to set the hook." Carlee did as she was told. "Now, with steady pressure, keep pulling in the line as quick as you can." The cigar-shaped walleye wriggled through the opening, but from the look on Carlee's face, it was a monster. Brock secured the fish and gently pulled the hook from its mouth. The fins spread and he displayed the catch next to a beaming Carlee for a photo op.

"Release this one?" Carlee nodded. Brock wiggled its tail like revving its engine and released it back into the ten-inch opening.

Maverick paced around Carlee's successful hole, patiently waiting for another fish. He gave a short woof and sat. A loud rap interrupted Amanda's throaty laugh and the door banged open.

"Amanda?" Officer Christianson scanned the room and when their eyes connected, he said, "Chief, come quick."

Amanda grabbed her coat and cap and dashed after him. Maverick and I followed, racing through a lane of the fancy fish shanties, and stopped in front of the blue-and-gold cougar.

Mayor Maxwell stomped back and forth, his hands gesturing out of control. He blustered and yelled at Officer Rodgers, "What do you mean we'll have to suspend the contest today? Today is the first day and the first day is always the best day. Can't we continue later?" The rules announcer patted him on the back and Maxwell shrugged him off.

"I'm sorry, Mr. Mayor," said Officer Rodgers. "This is one of the circumstances that bar continuation of the tournament. We'll have to investigate before you'll be allowed to resume the fishing tournament tomorrow."

"May I help?" Amanda said. Relief flooded Officer Rodgers' features.

"This way, Chief." He led her inside the monster fish house, Mayor Maxwell tramping behind them.

A dozen disgruntled fishermen and women circled the eighty-year-old announcer still dragging the bullhorn, bombarding him with questions. He put them off, siccing them on Ronnie who looked none too happy to be the center of attention.

"There's nothing to tell. Chief West will make a statement when she's ready. I don't know precisely why they are postponing the tournament for a day, but the postponement wouldn't be done lightly. It's a big money maker for Columbia. Consider today a warmup. We'll move everything back a day."

Maverick tugged me to the far side of the shelter. He stuck his nose under the hood worn by a person sitting on the ice. The hood fell back, revealing Dillon. He shoved Maverick away, but my determined dog went in for a second try. Dillon ruffled Maverick's fur and buried his head against Maverick's neck. I dropped onto the ice on the other side of Maverick.

"What's going on?" I asked. Dillon turned his pale face and puffy eyes to glare at me, but it was much less belligerent than I expected. He shook his head.

The three of us sat quietly until a truck roared up on the ice.

Dillon jumped to his feet and dusted off his backside, as if embarrassed to be caught sitting down or maybe embarrassed to be caught sitting next to me. He joined Mayor Maxwell's cronies, hollering incomprehensible instructions to the truck driver to position the hitch, and line up the trailer. The mayor huffed and paced, gritting his teeth while Ronnie supervised the loading of the trailer and its minor movement fifteen feet to the north.

Amanda asked two fishermen to cut into the ice, enlarging the opening where the trailer had been. Before they'd completed their task, two policemen working with Officer Rodgers roped off the area with caution tape. It

resembled the section of the lake where Brock had gone
through the ice and where we had found Xavier. The cold
wasn't the only thing sending chills down my back.

Maverick snuggled closer to me. He sat and his
melancholy howl reverberated between the houses. I knelt
and scratched behind his ear.

"You," growled Maxwell. "That mutt is scaring the
fish." He towered over us. If his thought was to intimidate,
it worked.

"Look at that," Ronnie said, peering over Amanda's
shoulder at a small screen sitting on the ice.

Amanda scowled. "Quiet."

Maxwell turned to Ronnie. "I told you what we saw, and
you didn't believe me. That's a state-of-the-art underwater
camera and it left no doubt we'd caught something. What I
don't get is how it ended up under my fish house."

Officer Rodgers held fast to the arching line snagged
on something beneath the surface and shoved the chunk
of ice away from the cut out with his boot. He gently
tugged the filament and when the catch broke the surface,
he grabbed it and hauled it out of the icy water.

"It's a body," Ronnie said, and someone gasped.

Amanda glared at him. She put her phone to her ear
and paced as she spoke.

Another police officer forced the growing throng of
onlookers yards beyond the caution tape.

Officer Rodgers rolled the bundle. The wet fabric
clung to her, exaggerating her bony frame, and Meghann's
open eyes stared at me. The agitation and fear I'd seen last
night had been replaced with peace.

Maverick howled again.

CHAPTER TWENTY-SEVEN

I filled a pot with Ida's French onion soup and set it to simmer on the stove. "I hope it's okay I invited Amanda for leftovers. She should be here soon," I said, trying to engage Ida.

Dad opened a bag of premixed greens, threw the salad fixings in a bowl, and tossed it with tongs. He set the table, eyeing Ida with concern.

"I should have gone after her last night." Ida stirred a steaming cup of milk. "What could have happened?"

"Amanda requested an autopsy, so she'll find out how Meghann died. Officer Rodgers checked out the hole Brock fell through, and the thin ice and sludge covering it wouldn't have held much weight. It might have looked solid but if she'd stepped on it, she could have gone in." I stirred the pot. "It was the only visible semi-open water."

"What was she doing there?" Ida shook her head. "How did they find her?"

I shuddered. "One of the fisherman's hooks had pierced Meghann's vest and caught there. As he reeled in the line, Maxwell saw the large floating shape on his underwater camera. He ordered Ronnie to find Chief West so he could protest about the trash thrown in the lake and he wanted to fine the perpetrator besmirching Lake Monongalia's clean water status." I sighed. "He withdrew his complaint after they pulled out Meghann's body."

Maverick barked. Ida set her cup on the end table, rocked twice, and hauled her solid frame out of the chair before the bell rang. Ida straightened her skirt and shook her head of wiry hair. She marched to the door and whipped it open.

"Amanda." She clucked. "Come in."

Amanda stepped through the door, carrying a brown paper parcel. She hung her jacket on the coatrack and kicked off her boots, then got a robust squeeze from Ida, while Dad retrieved the package.

"Something smells delicious. Thanks for the invitation. I'm starved."

"Give me two minutes and supper will be ready," I said. Something clattered behind me. All eyes turned and caught my dog lapping up spilt milk on the floor next to Ida's cup. "Maverick." I shook my head, regretting our lapse in training over the holiday. We'd have to get back to it.

Dad unwrapped the package, and my mouth watered at the aroma of the warm rye bread. "Is there anything you can't do, Chief?" he asked, coaxing a tiny smile.

Before Amanda could reply, Ida began her interrogation.

"How could Meghann have gone onto the ice unnoticed? There are so many people on the lake at Fuller Park Landing this time of year. I've heard the fishing has been great. Did you talk to everyone? Do you think Meghann was so bereft by the loss of Xavier she killed herself? Did you find the manuscript? Or do you think she knew something else, and someone killed her? Do you have any suspects?"

Amanda blinked rapidly. In a matter of seconds, Ida proposed an accident, suicide, and murder.

"Ida," Dad said gently, tugging her sleeve toward the dining table and seating her at the head. "I think Amanda needs a breather. Let's eat, shall we? And maybe Amanda will have some news to share after our Boxing Day repast."

Ida turned crimson. Her fingers commanded all her attention for a full ten seconds. "Oh, dear. I'm sorry. I don't know what I was thinking. All my words just spewed out of my big mouth. But thank goodness Pete was in jail, so he can't be suspected of any wrongdoing in Meghann's death." She watched Amanda closely. "Right?"

Amanda kept her reaction closed. Pete was out on bond, and she took a long moment to choose her words. "Dr. Erickson could not have contributed to her going through the ice."

Ida blew out a sigh. "For what we are about to receive let us be truly thankful." She slid her chair closer to the table. "Let's eat."

Trivial conversation came to a halt when our spoons scraped the bottoms of the bowls. I cleared the table and retrieved the remains of Ida's *Bûche de Noël*.

"That looks delicious. I shouldn't," said Amanda. But we all did.

We retired to the living room and Dad added fuel to

the fire. I rummaged under the tree and found my gift for Amanda.

"Nothing much, I'm afraid, but Merry Christmas."

She picked the tape from the paper and peeled away the wrapping. Before she opened the box, she lined up the edges and folded the paper into a neat rectangle, savoring the process, and my knee bobbed up and down in anxious anticipation. Ida reached over and stilled my knee jerks with her hand. Amanda smiled at my discomfort and slowly, with exaggerated deliberation, lifted the lid. She pulled out a bar of goat milk soap and lifted it to her nose, inhaling orange and anise. She rooted around the crinkled filler paper for another bar scented with cranberry spice and she hummed. I also included a handmade candle with the scent of fresh cut evergreens. And then her hand alighted on the pièce de résistance.

She stared at the lump of coal in her hand. Ida wheezed and Dad cocked his head.

"You should see the look on your faces. You know, it's not just any lump of coal. It's from the *Titanic*." I handed her a certificate of authenticity. "One small piece from the six thousand six hundred eleven tons it carried on the journey."

Dad let out a breath.

Ida swallowed hard and said, "Amanda."

Saved by the bell, Amanda's phone chimed. "One second, Ida. I have to take this." She sought a little privacy, just out of earshot.

When she returned from the dining room, she made straight for the front door. Grabbing her coat she said, "Katie, you and Maverick need to suit up. We have a missing kid and it's going to be a cold night." She tugged on her boots. "Can you contact Drew and CJ and meet me at Fuller Park Landing? We need all the help we can get."

Maverick heard his name and he followed at my heels. My fingers swept across my phone screen, sending a group message. I flew through my apartment, grabbing my outer gear and locating my search-and-rescue go bag. Maverick and I were out the door in under three minutes. CJ's reply was, 'ready,' and we picked him up before speeding out to Lake Monongalia.

The small assembly of searchers, including some familiar canines and their handlers, milled about in quiet groups, awaiting instructions. Maverick and I had been accepted as a probationary search-and-rescue team because CJ believed in us. He continued to train us, honing our finding skills, and as we stood, Maverick and I looked to CJ for clues as to what might be expected of us.

Amanda and Officer Rodgers stepped onto the ice. Her clear voice carried the heartbreaking message without the benefit of a megaphone. "Dillon Maxwell has not been seen since this afternoon and his phone is turned off." I gasped. "His parents are concerned, and because of the events of the last two days and the predicted brutal overnight temperatures, it's imperative he be found without delay. Officer Rodgers will distribute county maps with allocated search areas outlined in an attempt to locate him."

Drew and Jane stepped next to me. I knew I could rely on them. I treasured their friendship and clasped the arm Jane threaded through mine. "We've got this," she said. "We'll find him." She patted my hand.

"Be watchful," Amanda continued. "With the cloudy sky and light snow, it's dark and difficult to see well but if you come across any sign of him or have any questions, call 911."

A metal door slammed. I turned and Pete Erickson trotted next to Drew.

"We're all here." Jane whispered. She followed my bewildered eyes to Pete. "What's wrong? You sent a group text." I searched her face for more of an explanation. "To Drew, CJ, me, and Pete."

I hadn't intended to include him, and my stomach would have fluttered, but at that moment, CJ returned with two maps and one plastic bag with a knitted, long blue-and-gold cap inside. He handed one map to Jane and Drew.

"If anything causes you to believe you need a good nose, call me. We've been directed to have Maverick search the encampment under the bridge. Pete, I'd like you to go with us. I think Maverick has the best chance of finding the young man if he's there." With that, we dispersed.

Maverick clambered into the rear seat next to Pete. Self-conscious of my driving with two oversized men crowding the space, I forced myself to think of Dillon. What had prompted his disappearance and where might he be?

About a quarter of a mile left to go to the parking lot, the Focus rolled to a stop. I turned the key. It clicked. I turned it again, but nothing happened. I pounded the steering wheel. CJ tapped on his phone as he leapt from the dead auto, not willing to wait, and pulled the cap from the bag. Pete opened the rear door, and Maverick jumped over him. I raced to Maverick's side, watching him sniff the cap. I put my hand on his head, looked into his eyes, and said, "Find Dillon." He ran.

Our flashlights cut jagged, jerking lines, pursuing my dog as he exploded into the absolute darkness to the abandoned homeless encampment. A light snow shrouded the yellow streetlamp. The fires were out, and nobody roamed the area. One of our beams alighted on a large, neon-yellow sign tacked to the shelter. 'Closed until further notice, by order of Mayor Maxwell.'

Maverick's tail wagged, bounding from one stinky smell to another, but he never slowed and neither did Pete. He glided over the rugged ground, out of sight. The hitch in CJ's gait was noticeable if someone was looking, but I still struggled to keep up with him until he stood next to what remained of the tent shelters of Xavier and Meghann.

Maverick made short work of his search and plopped next to Dillon. *Oh, thank God.*

The young man sifted a pile of ash through his bare fingers, removing a wire and setting it to the side. He continued separating the remains of the fire. When he plucked part of a blackened scroll from the gray powder he said, in a scratchy voice, "Dad and Mom fight a lot." He didn't look at us. "Last night, I heard my dad fighting with someone else too." He turned sad eyes to CJ. "I don't know what to do."

I removed the thermal blanket from my go bag and handed it to Pete. He wrapped it around Dillon and led him to the parking lot where I was surprised to find Drew's car, idling. Pete settled Dillon in the rear seat. CJ made a call and after his brief conversation, he squeezed into the passenger seat next to Maverick and I slid into the seat next to Dillon.

"Dillon," Pete said kindly. "After I check you out, Chief West would like to have a word with you if you feel up to it."

Dillon's head dropped to his chest.

CHAPTER TWENTY-EIGHT

You haven't been given permission to see patients yet, Dr. Erickson. Your hospital privileges have been suspended. You can't just waltz back in, acting as if nothing has happened until after your peer review. I took charge of your patient load and I'll take care of this patient too. You are not welcome behind the desk as per protocol. You will remain in the waiting room, or better yet, go home." Pete clenched his jaw.

Dr. Coltraine laid her hand on his forearm and said more gently. "I believe you." She straightened his collar. "It's just the way it has to be right now, Pete. I know you aren't guilty, but we must follow the rules. If there's anything I can do for you, just ask. I know you've just lost your fiancée, and I'm sure it feels like the world is collapsing around you, but everything will work out for the best. You'll see." She spun on her spiky shoes and pointed to the nurse who ushered Dillon into the ER suites. Just before the door closed, he turned his head and the desperation in his eyes made my heart ache for him.

Pete sank into a red Naugahyde chair next to me and dropped his head into his hands. He combed through his dark locks, and I wanted to reach out and tuck the unruly curls into place. I started to tell him everything would be okay when the front doors whooshed.

He bolted upright. "Susie, I knew I could count on you. How's Quinn?"

"Rachel and I have been monitoring her and she'll be okay, but I can't say the same for her family. Her dad's a wreck and her mom, Ryn, is still in the psych unit." She blew a long strand of chestnut hair off her face. "What is it you want now?"

"Dr. Coltraine has Dillon Maxwell back there and I've never had to leave a patient. He's okay physically but could you check on him? The kid needs a friend and Coltraine can be—"

"Not so fast, Pete. I'm not doing anything to rile Dr. Coltraine. She's in charge. I don't plan to antagonize her. I don't know how but I've just moved back into her good graces, and I think I've already given up plenty for you."

"I'm sorry, Susie." He took a step toward her, and she stepped back.

"Too little, too late." She tossed her hair and lightly touched her stomach.

"I really am sorry."

She looked at the clock. "I'll do my job," she said. "I'll check on him." She disappeared behind the ER doors.

He slumped back into the chair. "Dillon's healthy and

safe now, but he's scared."

"Did he tell you why he ran away? Why he turned off his phone?"

"He was torn up inside thinking his parents might split up."

I shrugged. "Everyone fights. It's not the end of the world. They may not get along at times, but have you heard of any legal action taken by either Mr. or Mrs. Maxwell?"

"No." Pete inhaled. "But Dillon also thinks he heard his dad fighting with Meghann Popovich."

I sat straighter in the chair. "Is he certain? I suppose that could be something, unless Dillon wants to get back at his dad for some parental infraction, which happens all too often with teenagers. I sure would like to talk to the mayor."

"Talk to the mayor about what?" Mayor and Mrs. Maxwell stood between the glass doors. "Where's our son?" he asked, taking long strides toward us.

Mrs. Maxwell stepped in front of him. "Thank you. Thank you for bringing him home safely."

"He's being examined. He's not hurt, but he's worried about you two." The Maxwells glanced at each other. "He heard you fighting, and he heard you, Mayor, arguing with Miss Popovich sometime during the night. How did you know her?"

"That trollop has been a thorn in my side for over twenty years." I winced at Mrs. Maxwell's high-pitched voice. "When she didn't get her way, she wiggled her hips and some poor unsuspecting soul, usually a naive male, invariably came to her rescue."

Mayor Maxwell laid his hand on her arm. She took a deep breath. "I'm sorry. I should show compassion for her death but …" Her deep emotion ramped up again. "She could be insufferable."

"She was a client of mine," the mayor said. "One of the few clients I had when I was a music agent."

"A client?" Pete asked.

"A former client. I cut her loose years ago. When she disappeared, I thought she'd gone on to bigger and better things." Maxwell went on. "She was a difficult personality. When she wasn't happy, Popovich tried to disrupt the lives of those around her and make them as miserable as she was. Unfortunately, she was particularly enamored with Xavier."

Mrs. Maxwell took over the storytelling. "She hated that he was married to a woman he truly loved." That didn't quite jibe with what Ida had heard, but who knew. "I don't think Popovich's husband was particularly keen with the schedule she had to keep, but we never even met him, so it was hard to say. It was as if he never existed. Meghann told Xavier's wife that we'd had an affair." Mrs. Maxwell sniffed. "As if. Xavier may have played a pretty violin, and he partied with the best of them, but he was an egocentric boor. Everything was always all about him. And he never changed."

Maxwell cleared his throat and said, "He loved deeply, but not well. He was a temperamental but exceptional musician and his continued success put good food on our table and a fancy roof over our heads."

Mrs. Maxwell nodded, and her tone softened. "Erica called Xavier out on the supposed affair the night of the accident."

A cart rolled into the waiting area and interrupted his story. Pete stood abruptly; his eyes were dull, and his face was drawn and pale. My heart went out to him. He joined Jim and disappeared down a corridor.

"That poor boy," said Mrs. Maxwell. "I'm sorry. I should have shown more concern."

"I'd almost forgotten he lost his mother," said Maxwell.

"Maxie stood by me," Mrs. Maxwell said. "He corroborated my story and explained Meghann's incessant need to insinuate herself between spouses. And that put Meghann's job on the line. Xavier had had enough, and after that final lie he'd called the orchestral board. He told Meghann if she didn't turn herself around, she'd played her last concert. The Notrecalis wanted to get away from her as quickly as possible. Erica was twelve years older than Xavier and slightly more responsible. She had less to drink and thought she was sober enough to drive but …"

"Erica died in the fatal accident that also killed Pete's mom," I said. I heard the ticking of the ancient clock on the wall.

The mayor shifted uncomfortably. "Popovich died under suspicious circumstances," he said with rancor. "Chief West grilled me for forty-five minutes after we found her."

It's a good thing I didn't gasp. They might not have continued to share.

"Nothing about the deaths of either one of them would surprise me," said Mrs. Maxwell. "She and Xavier were more alike than different. They were mutually toxic."

"Then why was she still following him after all these years? They must have had very little liking for each other." According to Brock, she'd hung around all the time, but always at a distance.

"They had a symbiotic relationship. There's a fine line

between love and hate. Xavier held her responsible for the accident that killed Erica and she held him responsible for her nosedive in the industry. He used the talent of his musicians and if they were strong enough, they used his celebrity to step into another venue with great credentials. Twenty-five years ago, Meghann played cello beautifully, almost better than Xavier played violin. He probably led her to believe they might have had a future, but not the one she would have imagined. Maybe he felt culpable for blackballing her, her banishment from the life she wanted and deserved. She went through much the same life as Xavier. Had she not been so unreliable and held Xavier in such high esteem—"

"And not tried to sabotage his relationships—"

"She might have made the big leagues. She was good enough, just not confident enough."

Mayor Maxwell took Mrs. Maxwell's hand. "Last night Popovich came to me with an outlandish tale about a new piece Xavier had penned, and if I wanted to publish it, she needed a cello, a performance gig, and a share of the royalties. Although a new composition intrigued me, I was never going to promise her a job. I don't have connections any longer and even if I did, I wouldn't foist her on someone else. I told her so." His hand went to his chest.

"Maxie, are you all right?"

He took a few deep breaths and nodded. "She pleaded with me to at least get her a new cello and when I asked what she'd done with her old cello, she got nasty and told me she'd get my son in trouble. I told her to get lost."

Mrs. Maxwell inhaled sharply and withdrew her hand. "You didn't tell me she'd threatened Dillon. Were you worried about him, or how his trouble would affect you?"

"I was angry, but I didn't kill Meghann," said Maxwell.

The door behind the registration desk opened, and Dillon stomped out in front of Dr. Coltraine.

"Mom?" he croaked. "What are you doing here?" He crossed the room and stood next to her. She reached up, maybe to put her arm around Dillon, but let it drop. He scowled at his dad, and I saw a resemblance strong enough for Meghann to confuse Dillon with the Maxwell she remembered.

The doors opened again, and Amanda walked in. "Just the folks I'd like to talk to. I have some more questions."

Mayor Maxwell lifted his chin. "Talk to my attorney, Chief West."

"Can we go home now?" Dillon asked his mother.

Mrs. Maxwell gave Amanda a withering look and steered her son and her husband out the double doors, like a mother bear protecting her family.

"What was that all about?" Amanda said.

"The Maxwells knew Meghann and Xavier, and didn't much like either one," I said.

Amanda's head tilted. "I asked you to stay out of it, Katie."

I shrugged. "They were parents, talking while they waited for their son."

"That kid's not squeaky clean. One of the fishermen told us to check with his two friends and figure out why they harassed Xavier. By the way, the towing company will drop off your car here in about fifteen minutes."

"Why does a towing company have my car?"

"CJ called them so they could determine why your vehicle stopped." She almost laughed. "You ran out of gas."

Heat crept up my face. "Thanks."

"I've got to run but, Katie, stay out of it. Both deaths are hinky and I can't have you get in the way of our investigation."

I nodded. My thoughts surely couldn't get in the way, could they?

CHAPTER TWENTY-NINE

Fifteen minutes of quiet would give me time to contemplate both deaths. Could Xavier have accidentally taken too much of the medication, died at the water's edge, and tripped? Could he have purposely taken an overdose of the drug himself and fallen in? If he died somewhere else, who put him in the lake? And if he was killed and dumped, who were possible suspects and what were their motives?

Everyone heard about his difficulty with alcohol, but he wasn't as crazy as everyone thought, and he said he knew things.

He had a long, rocky history with the Maxwells. Mrs. Maxwell was thankful for Xavier's talent but not too broken up about his death. And as trustee of Xavier's trust,

Maxwell wielded a lot of control over Xavier and his family. Maybe Xavier was going to put an end to that trusteeship. And what about the family? Did anyone know where the children were? Could they have hastened Xavier's death for a shot at their inheritance? Meghann's ties to Xavier had been her downfall. His irascible personality rubbed many people the wrong way. Maybe she killed him.

I gulped.

The night Brock had gone through the ice, while they tried to drag Xavier out of the ER, he had clearly said, "Don't give her more. Just don't." Now it sounded like he had known Quinn's mom had been giving her something to make her ill. But how? Would that have been motive enough for Quinn's mom to kill him? And Xavier almost accused the custodian of stealing toys from the collection carton. Did he? What else did Xavier know?

I walked to the window and searched the street for the tow truck and the Focus.

Nothing explained Meghann's death. If Maxwell could have gotten his hands on a new manuscript composed by Xavier, and if it turned out to be the caliber of his early work, it could have been worth a lot of money, and he might not have wanted to share the profits. He also could have been angry when Meghann dangled the possibility of the composition but didn't produce it. But if she'd taken the manuscript from Ida, wouldn't she have provided proof? Maybe Maxwell stole it from Ida's. Where was the manuscript?

Revenge could be a powerful motive. Either Mrs. Maxwell loved her husband, and she harbored anger that Meghann had tried to break them up years earlier, or the accusation was true, and she didn't want it dredged up again. That felt superficial. But what if Meghann had something on Dillon? That could have inflamed the mother bear—a force to be reckoned with.

And what could Meghann have had on a seventeen-year-old basketball player? I knew Dillon wasn't the best student. He'd had his share of difficulties. And if he had been the one to slam the garbage can lid down on Xavier, as Kindra suspected, I wondered why. He wasn't the nicest kid, but could he be a suspect in either murder?

My phone buzzed. "Hi, Jane."

"Hey girlfriend, where are you? It's late and Ida's a little worried."

"I'm still at the hospital. They're supposed to deliver my car soon."

"I'll tell Ida. You sure you're okay waiting by yourself?"

"I'm sure. When are you flying home to Georgia?"

She hummed. "Drew has tickets for Wednesday. Dad sounded so happy we'll be able to get there, even if only for a short jaunt. Check with you tomorrow?" She ended the call. Her contagious happiness reached through the phone line, and I smiled at her good fortune—finding Drew.

That prompted a memory of something else Maxwell had said. Meghann was married. Where was her husband? "Oh, Meghann," I sighed.

"She was some piece of work." Pete's voice startled me. "But Meghann didn't deserve to die."

"Are you okay?" I asked.

"I will be. I'm not the only suspect in Xavier's death anymore. I'm not off the hook, but to be fair, Dad respects Chief West. When I was in custody, her interrogation was by the book. I can't say the same for Ronnie; he's not a happy person. But I'm worried about Dillon. He punches a lot of buttons for the chief, and he might be in a lot of trouble." His eyes combed the street for a glimpse of the tow truck.

He shuffled his feet and cleared his throat. "How've you been? Feels like we haven't spoken in forever."

I couldn't catch my breath. When we were seeing each other, he'd listened when I had something to say. He looked for the good in people, even when he'd seen some of them at their worst. I had trusted him with my dreams and then time and space got between us. But now he was no longer engaged. A free agent. My lip curled up on one side, and then fell. It was too soon. But I could wait for his broken heart to mend.

"I'm sorry I listened to … other sources. I know CJ is a good friend. He's my friend too. But everything pointed to his meaning more to you than just a friend and I didn't want to get in the way of your happiness."

Is this where I ask him who led him to believe CJ and I were more than friends, as if I didn't know?

A door opened behind us. "Dr. Erickson." Dr. Coltraine stood behind the desk with her arms crossed over her chest, tapping her toe. "A word?"

"Excuse me, Katie." Pete turned away from the window and followed Dr. Coltraine into the ER suites.

No sooner had the door clicked than I heard raised voices but couldn't make out the words. I heard an intense but muffled discussion which only ended when the door flew open, and Pete followed Susie out.

"What did you tell her?" Pete asked.

"I told her the truth." Susie turned to face him. "I told her you wanted me to check on your patient. She countered with 'a murder suspect will not be hanging around the ER.'"

"What else?"

"I told her I would never allow a murderer near my baby."

Baby?

"Susie, I didn't kill anyone."

BABY?

I shook my head to clear my senses. I'd misunderstood Susie. How could she and Pete be having a baby? Well, I knew *how* but I didn't want to believe what I'd heard.

The tow truck pulled into the circle drive, and I dashed out the door, their garbled conversation fading behind me.

I fumed on my drive home, ignoring the blips of incoming text messages on my phone.

Baby?

I stormed into the apartment, slamming the door. Dad and Ida looked up from their mugs and quietly watched me stomp up the stairs.

I turned off my phone and threw myself on my bed.

I wouldn't get in the way of a baby.

CHAPTER THIRTY

Sunshine poured through my windows and warmed my face and my disposition. But if the sun was already streaming, I could be late again. I squinted to read the numbers on the clock. We had scheduled Dillon's last two exams to occur after basketball practice and I flopped back onto my pillow. I had ninety minutes.

Dillon had done well enough and unless he earned a zero, I could honestly tell Coach Michaels, Mr. Ganka, and Mrs. McEntee he'd caught up and earned the right to play in the holiday tournament. One could hope he wouldn't revert to his obstinate ways.

I pulled on a fleece warm-up and jeans and replayed the conversation I'd heard last night in the ER. What had I expected? I vigorously brushed my hair, mad at myself for letting my feelings get the better of me. I had good friends. No, I corrected, *great* friends, and although I never counted Susie among them, Pete was. I hoped they could mend their rift before the baby came, and I was determined to wish them well.

I bounded down the stairs, intending to make the most of my first full week of winter break, and inhaled the cinnamon sweet aroma of warm, freshly made doughnuts. I hadn't needed the tented 'Help yourself' cardboard note in front of the covered plate. I couldn't have survived the temptation and would have taken one anyway.

I licked the last remnants of crumbs and gooey glaze from my fingers before Maverick could do it for me and put on my warmest cold weather clothes. After a quick walk and the meeting with Dillon, the rest of my day would be open.

I packaged four doughnuts, just in case, scratched Maverick's belly, and slowly drove the slick streets to the high school.

Mrs. McEntee couldn't resist the pastry. She smacked her lips and sipped her pale coffee concoction while catching up on her daily tasks.

Dillon rushed in from practice, pushed his damp hair back from his face, and sat, tapping the pencil in his hand on the desktop. I thought he should begin with one of Ida's doughnuts, so I set it in front of him and I handed him a calculator and the test pages. He inhaled the sweet pastry and set to work, feverishly scribbling solutions.

Fifteen minutes later, Lorelei and Brock stepped through the door and made a beeline straight toward me.

"Ms. Wilk, can we stop by when you've finished here and check out the violin?" Lorelei spoke in a whisper.

"Brock would like to take a look at the case and that note again, see if Xavier left any other instructions, before we head over to the fishing tournament."

The unexpected jangle of Mrs. McEntee's phone caused Dillon to stop writing and the four of us watched her answer. Her perky greeting turned serious in a matter of seconds. She hung up and her concerned eyes swept over the counter and across the commons area, stopping when Chief West and Officer Christianson tramped through the front doors, straight to the office.

Amanda's eyes met mine and I saw sadness in them, and then resolve. She marched up to Brock and stood next to him. "Brock, did you know Xavier Notrecali and Meghann Popovich?"

"Yes. Why?"

"We'd like you to come down to the station."

Brock?

"Right now?" Brock said.

"We have some questions we need you to answer. We've already talked to your dad and his attorney will meet you there."

Brock's eyebrows shot up. I saw a mix of emotions: confusion, misery, disbelief, determination, and fear. He smiled and said, "What do you need Chief West? The tournament restarts today at three and I've got to be there."

"This is a bit more important than a fishing tournament. You need to come with us now."

"It's okay, Brock." I knew that wasn't necessarily true, but I had to toss him a lifeline. What could Amanda be doing? "Your dad knows where you'll be."

Brock stepped between Chief West and Officer Christianson. He towered over both.

Lorelei glanced at Brock, Chief West, Ronnie Christianson, Mrs. McEntee, and me, each in turn, and panicked. When she started to follow, Ronnie said, "You can't go with him."

"You and Ms. Wilk have to catch the big ones today or we'll never win. Promise me," Brock said, pasting a fake smile on his face.

Lorelei's shoulders drooped but she said, "I promise. I won't let you down. Neither will Ms. Wilk. We'll see you there."

They paraded him out the front door.

"Mrs. McEntee, what's that all about?"

She briskly rubbed her hands together and took a deep breath. "Chief West asked if Brock Isaacson was here, and I said yes, and she said thank you."

My heart pounded against my ribs. My ears steamed. I wouldn't believe Brock could do anything anymore than I believed Pete had, and just when Pete seemed to be safe from prosecution Brock needed my help. Brock did not kill anyone.

Don't say anything, Brock.

I'm not sure she really meant to encourage me to investigate the allegations, but Mrs. McEntee believed in kids, first, last, and always, and I agreed with her.

"Someone needs to find the real killer," she said.

Could I do that?

CHAPTER THIRTY-ONE

A moping Ida was not a pretty sight. The yellow scarf clashed with her frizzy, red-dyed hair and couldn't hold back her tangled bob. The dark lipstick belonged on a Halloween mannequin. She wore blue jeans and a faded orange sweatshirt. I'd lived in her rear apartment for almost five months and never knew she owned a sweatshirt. And she paced. She walked into my kitchen, then walked out, and a few minutes later, she tiptoed back in. I didn't think I could bring up Brock's difficulty and add to her apparent distress.

"I could have eaten a dozen of your doughnuts this morning. They were delicious," I said brightly. "Thank you for sharing. Can I make you a cup of tea?"

"No." She was gone again, and the room was quiet.

Maverick rose and stretched, then went in search of her.

I listened for the creak of the floorboards or the click of his nails to herald their return and that's when I heard the drip. Avoiding the obvious, I checked the faucet and fixtures in the bathroom. I opened the dishwasher and finally stuck my head under the sink. It wasn't much, but the next plink landed in my eye.

"Ida?" I called. "Ida."

I slid out from under the sink and gasped when I found her standing right next to me. When I caught my breath, I said, "It's dripping again."

She spoke sternly and quickly into her phone and marched into her apartment. She returned wearing a purple peasant blouse and a bright green swishy skirt held together by a shiny black belt. Silver hoop earrings dangled below freshly brushed hair. She dabbed her lips with a tissue and tossed it in the trash. The listless Ida had vanished, and her animated face gave her an ageless quality. I'd have bet she'd applied her flawless makeup with Steve in mind as her plumber and potential beau material, but I would have lost that bet.

The doorbell rang. Maverick raised his head, looked at Ida, and lowered it back on his paws. How did my dog pick and choose whose arrival to announce?

"Thanks for coming so quickly."

"I'm here for you, Mrs. C."

"We should have called you in the first place, Gene, but my tenants called in a rookie, thinking they were helping." I shrank under her stare. "It's a trickle now, but last week we set off the monitor, so I know it could soon be catastrophic."

Gene glided under the sink, fiddled with some knobs,

and slithered out. "Looks like a do-it-yourself job. And these fixtures have been here longer than you have." He chuckled and ducked under her feigned swat. "I might need to charge extra if I have to undo and redo much."

"No problem. I'll pass along the charges. I'll leave you to it." She headed for the adjoining door. "Katie, come."

My militant landlady had returned, and I didn't know if that was good or bad. I followed her like a puppy.

She started the tea kettle, and said, "What's going on?" She plated four shortbread cookies.

"That's what I was going to ask you."

"*Moi*? Every year I suffer from Christmas withdrawal and allow myself to wallow in the blues until I'm needed. You certainly took your time needing me." She handed me a tray with two teacups, a teapot, and a plate of cookies, and I carried it to her living room.

"I noticed you didn't call Steve to fix the leak."

"He's just another pretty face, isn't he? His first fix didn't last a week. I wonder what he really does because he certainly isn't a tradesman." She gave me a sidelong glance as she sat. "What's bothering you?" When nothing came out of my mouth, she said, "Sit."

I plopped onto the sofa and took a sip of the hot tea. I also grabbed a cookie and took a bite and swallowed hard. "Amanda picked up Brock as a person of interest in the murders of Meghann and Xavier. His dad's attorney was supposed to be waiting at the station." My words came faster. "Who investigates a kid? And Mrs. McEntee thinks someone should work out who the real murderer is, but I'm worried Amanda has set her sights on Brock, and he's going to be a dad." There. I said it.

Ida squeezed her eyes closed. She opened them and

shook her head to clear it. "Brock?"

"Brock what?"

"Brock's going to be a dad?" She stood and began her pacing again.

"No. Pete." She halted and squinted at me. I looked down at Maverick. "Pete's going to be a dad."

The laugh detonated with so much force, she snorted. She laughed so hard a tear wormed its way down one cheek. She swiped it away. "No, really."

What could I say? Her smile became a frown and she flopped onto the piano bench. She made a *hmmm* noise and grimaced. "It just can't be." She wriggled, trying to get comfortable. It didn't work. She opened the lid and a handful of pages spilled onto the floor. She picked them up, perused the top few, and stared at me.

"Xavier's music."

"I thought it had been stolen."

"I was so flabbergasted by the missing music I forgot about the pages I crammed under the bench lid. We're still missing the bulk of the manuscript, but maybe we can make something of this now."

She straightened the pages and lined up the corners. She spun on the seat, cracked her knuckles, turned on the lamp over the keys, and played.

I closed my eyes and cringed. Even to my unsophisticated ears, the dissonant notes collided with no reprieve, no resolution, no hummable melody, no motif to recreate in variations. "It's no better now than it was the first time you played it. Is it as awful as I think or is it just too innovative or avant-garde for my simple taste?"

Ida hunched. "It's not just you. I don't understand the musicality. Xavier wrote beautiful, lyrical pieces played by professional musicians around the globe. This doesn't make any sense." She turned to a new page and continued to tap the keys. The next song felt different, brighter, quicker, but no better. "I don't think I could have written anything this bad on purpose. I can't imagine what he wanted to create."

Gene called from my kitchen and Ida hastened to his summons. I took her place at the piano and plucked a line from the music. The notes didn't follow a key and the melody line fought with the accompaniment.

A thought came to me.

I grabbed my coat and keys and waved at Ida and Gene as I sprinted out the door. The slick roads kept me from racing, but I had to see if my memory served me well. I thought I'd seen something like it before and hurried to satisfy my curiosity.

I slammed the Focus into park near the entrance of my school and mounted the steps two at a time. I yanked on the door and my hand slipped from the handle.

The door was locked.

CHAPTER THIRTY-TWO

I glanced at my watch. Twelve fifteen. Lunchtime for the skeleton crew managing office hours. I leaned against the glass, peering into the dark recesses of the commons area to catch someone walking through. We had to request a master key if we entered after hours, and I hadn't thought I'd need it. I rapped until my knuckles ached, and I saw movement in the office.

Mr. Ganka plodded to the door, stuffing a last bit of something in his mouth when he saw me. He furrowed his brow and his double chin tripled behind a pudge of concern. He chewed and swallowed and then pushed on the door. "Ms. Wilk? What's up?"

"Thanks, Mr. Ganka. Sorry to have disturbed your lunch." I squirmed through the doorway past him, calling over my shoulder as I hurried to the math department. "I really need to get some papers from my office. I'll just be a minute. I'll check out with you when I leave."

With remonstrations of 'No running in the halls' circling in my head, I half power-walked, half trotted down the dim corridor, stopping in front of the math office, and pulling out my key. I turned it over in my hand.

What if I was wrong?

Charles liked to quote Einstein, and one of his favorites was 'A person who never made a mistake, never tried anything new.'

I inserted the key, opened the door, and flipped the light switch.

I crossed the department common area through a clean, light lemon scent to the shared math office where the teacher desks stood in straight lines, chairs pushed in, tops cleared, and for the first time since I'd started teaching at Columbia, everything was in its place, ready for the new year.

I turned to face my own little corner, appreciating my small, professional domain. I removed the thick file from the shelf and shoved the bookend shaped like the back half of the *Titanic* to close the gaping hole I'd left between 'B' and 'D.'

I popped into the office to bid Mrs. McEntee a great day and check out, but I couldn't promise her I was finished for the day.

Anxious to study the possible key to the puzzle made the ride home seem much longer than it should have been. My phone buzzed. I barked my greeting. "What?"

"They're holding Brock," the voice said, hitching.

I hadn't known who belonged to the number on my screen, but the moment she spoke in her shaky voice, I understood her emotion.

She snuffled loudly. "I don't know what to do. They accused him of stealing Xavier's violin and that could be a reason to kill him. They also said he might have killed Meghann because, as Xavier's protégé she probably knew the truth. You have to save him."

"Mrs. Isaacson, Brock has a lawyer looking out for his interests, doesn't he?"

"Yes, but as bright as Donald is, he told us he wasn't a criminal attorney."

"Then I have a recommendation for you. Dorene Dvorak is one of the best criminal defense attorneys in the area. I'll text you her number, and please mention my name. I can't say it will help, but it won't hurt."

My friend, Dorene, had gone to bat when CJ needed a defense attorney and she had a soft spot for kids. She read her clients well and only took cases where her involvement forwarded the cause of justice. I knew Brock was innocent and she would prove it—I hoped.

Mrs. Isaacson clicked off as I maneuvered into my garage stall. I texted Dorene's name and number. I crossed my fingers, then raced inside.

"Ida?" I yelled. "Dad? Anybody?" Maverick padded into the kitchen, bouncing from one paw to the other. I rustled behind his ears, and he leaned into my scratches. "Where is everyone, boy?" I said, urging him to the piano. The stand was bare. Xavier's pieces were missing. I dialed Ida and her phone went to voicemail. Dad's ringtone jangled from his room, and as he wasn't here, he'd forgotten it again.

Seated at my kitchen table, I opened my fat 'C' file, peeled away the last few pages, and lined them up in front of me to study. Musical cryptography took many forms over the centuries and provided an inscrutable means of sending secret messages. The most common encryption assigned letters to different notes of music, hiding communications in plain sight or, rather, sound. Modified systems designated intervals or duration to replace specific letters. Sometimes the music sounded correct and sometimes the untrained ear ignored the series of pitches written merely to convey a message.

I redialed Ida a few times as I scanned the page.

Ingenious musicians employed the encryption to transfer essential messages to 'save the king,' for example. Brahms pined a lost love by encrypting her name in his music. Others penned artistic exercises. Notes in scores intentionally spelled out signature motifs for master musicians Bach, Schumann, Berg, and others, and succeeded with better camouflage and much better sounding results overall.

Perhaps Xavier had thought he could do the same, but his attempt came with disastrous results.

My phone buzzed and I read the display. "Hi, Ida."

"What's so important you called me nine times. I'm at the grocery store."

"Do you still have Xavier's pages? I think I know what to do to read his composition."

The line was silent.

"Ida?"

"I called Amanda, and she asked me to drop them off, but I'll stop home first, and you can tell me what it is you think we can do. I'll be there in ten minutes."

I read more about the process and hoped he hadn't employed some of the more elaborate methods of codifying. In one example, each of twelve distinct pitches could be used for at least two different letters of our alphabet. In another example, twenty-six different tones replaced one letter apiece. My shoulders slumped. Without a key, our decryption process could take time. And maybe I was wrong.

The door banged, and Ida stormed into her kitchen. I heard paper rattling, doors opening and closing, and drawers slamming. She burst through the doorway, clasping the ragged pages in front of her.

"Out with it."

"I think the pitches dictate a message." I showed her the examples of musical cryptography.

Doubtful, she said, "Who, but you, would have the slightest chance of having this information?"

My hand covered the precious pages I'd collected while studying cryptanalysis in London. "Charles ..." I smiled with a memory of a cherished wink. "Charles loved all methods of secret messaging, and I just couldn't throw his collection away."

She sat next to me and spread the musical staves in front of us.

After an hour of going nowhere, Ida said, without conviction, "You might be right, but how will you ever figure this out? Xavier would never leave it to chance for someone to accidently discover his greatness. There must be a hint, a key so eventually someone could decipher his message and then applaud his huge intellect in conjuring such an obscure code. Where do you begin?"

"I know you promised to bring the music to Amanda, but could I duplicate them first?" She nodded and I made copies.

I tried to untangle the web of notes, diligently sorting

elements I thought might construct a word by using different sample techniques, but closed my eyes when nothing revealed itself. If it was an encoded message, the key remained hidden from me. I was losing my touch if I ever had it.

CHAPTER THIRTY-THREE

My entire body convulsed, submerged in an ice-cold Lake Monongalia, and I woke with a start to someone gently tapping my shoulder.

"Dad," I said, blinking. I shuddered. I'd fallen asleep at the table. My fingers tingled and my shoulders ached.

"You were crying out, darlin'. Were you dreaming?

"Not sure," I could fabricate a story with the best of them. I stretched and yawned.

"What are you doing?" He rotated a page, and his finger flew across the lines of music.

"Ida found the pages she buried under the piano lid and I'm trying to see if Xavier left a message in his weird composition. Nothing seems to work, and I'm overwhelmed with the possibilities." I shook my head and laughed. It sounded absurd when I said it out loud again.

"Like Messiaen's *langage communicable* in *Méditations*."

"Like what? My *Meditation*? What are you talking about?"

"Not Massenet but Messiaen's organ piece. In the foreword, Messiaen reiterated a distinctive set of pitches with specific notation to represent the twenty-six letters of the alphabet." Dad handed me a cup of tea and grabbed his coat from its hook by the door. "If anyone can find the message, you can, darlin'. You have a knack for the peculiar and sensational."

I gave him my most dubious glare; I wasn't sure if his remark was meant to be reassuring or disapproving.

He finished buttoning his coat and wrapped his new scarf around his neck. "I just got back from the library; there wasn't much there about Xavier. And now I'm meeting Ida at the community center, but we'll be back in time for supper. She's got something that smells delicious in the slow cooker." He breathed in the aroma and sighed.

I typed the information Dad gave me into my laptop and pulled up an obscure scholarly paper on the code encryption built into Messiaen's composition, and never heard the door close behind him.

My first note-letter pairing of one page of the manuscript yielded gibberish, probably an introduction of the piece. I sighed and Maverick nudged my hand for a scratch. However, matching enough information on the next sample produced words from the opening bars of a juvenile song from my youth, "snmsittinginatreekissingfirs." Maybe Dad had provided the ticket to a solution, but when I searched the five remaining pages for one beginning with 't', which was the next letter in the song—the continuation of the words in the lyrics—nothing fit. The page might have been among those stolen. And to whom did 'snm' refer?

I decrypted two pages written in the key of A# and numbered pages four through six—'n'tdrivingtheca" and "ovetoldmetoprotecth.'

Maverick barked and then came the irksome knock. As more letters morphed into words, I didn't want to be bothered and I ignored the rapping.

My phone dinged with a text from Jane.

I can see you.

I opened the door and Jane marched in with three long clear garment bags draped over her arms.

"Take these."

I transferred the slippery bags to the back of the chair. "What are they?"

"I'm sure you don't have a dress for the New Year's Eve Party—"

"What New Year's Eve Party?"

"The Columbia Community New Year's Eve Party at the community center. Ida's co-chair of the event. They're closing in on the amount needed to earn a matching grant for the homeless shelters. Your dad is in charge of lights." I started to protest, but she was right; I didn't have a formal gown, but I didn't want to attend a New Year's Eve Party anyway. She continued, "And yes, you have to go. These dresses may be a little short, and they'll be a bit loose, but they'll work out just fine." She scrutinized my work at the table. "What's this?"

"Ida invited Meghann—"

"The dead woman they found in Lake Monongalia?"

"Yes. Ida invited her to join us Christmas night after you and Drew left and she brought along pages of a composition belonging to Xavier, and I think it might be full of messages."

Jane lifted the page with my first deciphered message, glared at me, rolled her eyes at Maverick, and said, "Sounds like a taunt, someone caught kissing. Well, we'd better finish before Drew gets here." She looked at her watch "We have seventeen minutes, and if he sees you working on this, he'll blow a gasket because it looks like you're investigating, and we told Chief Erickson—"

"I think Pete is off the hook."

"Well, then, why are you still looking into this?"

"Brock Isaacson is now a person of interest."

She snorted. "He couldn't kill anyone. Where'd they get that idea?"

I shoved my chair away from the table. Jane followed me and watched as I pulled the violin case out from under Ida's tree and opened it.

"That's a beauty." She strummed the strings, and the warm tones filled the room. "What does this have to do with Brock being a person of interest?"

"Dad said this violin, if properly authenticated, could be worth a lot of money. Xavier gave it to Brock to guard, but Amanda insinuated that Brock may have stolen it from Xavier and then she hinted he may be involved in the murder of Meghann as well because he knew her."

The legs screeched as Jane yanked the chair away from the table and sat with a pencil in her hand. "Let's get to it."

Two people worked much faster and from the music on the next two pages we deciphered 'avemorecommonsensethanhispuddinheadedfat.'

"What does that mean?" Jane asked.

"The communications read like diary entries and if

we extrapolate pre- or post-letters, maybe we can decipher something to help Brock." *If we could help Brock.*

Jane pointed to the first line of decrypted text and said, "This could be 'wasn't driving the car when.' When what?"

"Xavier's wife, Erica, supposedly drove the car that killed Pete's mother. Maybe this meant she wasn't driving the car."

Maverick woofed encouragement and we mulled over the possibilities.

"Do you think Xavier was driving?" Jane couldn't look at me. "That would have given Pete or his dad a motive—"

"Nope. Didn't happen." I knew. "But maybe someone *else* was driving?"

"But who? All the evidence pointed to Erica behind the wheel."

"Let's try another line."

Within a few seconds, Jane looked at me with her huge brown eyes. "If I add what first comes to my mind, this line could read 'my love told me I have to protect her or him.' It could still refer to Xavier's wife but maybe there was someone else. How do we find out?"

I read the letters of the next entry. "Could this be 'he'll have more common sense than his puddin'-headed father ever had'?"

"That's My Boy, Bill, the *Soliloquy* from *Carousel*. It looks like it fits. If he's using familiar song lyrics, maybe he couldn't concoct his own. Katie, this could be nothing but an exercise, not a composition."

"Then why was he killed? Xavier had a son and a stepdaughter. Maybe he was writing about his own children. If it didn't mean anything, why was Meghann killed? And why was the rest of the manuscript stolen?"

My head dropped to my chest.

"What rest of the manuscript?"

I raised my head partway to see if she really didn't know. Then I sat tall and gave her the short version.

"It would have taken a concentrated effort to encode all those pages if Xavier didn't have an ulterior motive. I tend to think you're right; Xavier was hiding information in plain sight. But for what purpose," Jane said. "Was it blackmail worthy, making it murder worthy?"

CHAPTER THIRTY-FOUR

Drew caught Jane and me pondering the missing parts of the messages we'd revealed and demanded an explanation. It took time but he still shook his head at our nonsensical stab at decoding the manuscript. If only we could figure out what it meant.

Maverick and I made it to the ice at two fifty.

By tournament start time, Brock had not been released, and his mom and dad were at the police station waiting for information from Dorene. We assumed Amanda wouldn't attend today, so Lorelei enlisted the help of Kindra, Carlee, and Galen. Jane had promised her decorating skills to Ida and couldn't participate, but Drew figured if I'd requested Jane's presence, we needed all the help we could get, and he was a welcome addition. However, if CJ had not decided to chaperone his daughter and if he hadn't looked so distinguished, our age-average would have disqualified our daily take. I presumed it was close but if anyone would've asked for identification and done the math, I didn't know if the numbers would have met the criterion. CJ's formidable presence precluded anyone asking and Maverick wouldn't have been too happy either.

Lorelei cringed and scowled when Drew and CJ hooked their minnows, and, although she only had one nibble, she preferred the use of her plastic bloodworms. Our haul consisted of seven fish and if Galen hadn't thought to use Lorelei's can of sweet corn, my preference for bait, we might have only caught one, and had CJ not been there to give the correct cue, I wouldn't have been able to rescue that first thrashing fish from Maverick's jaws.

Carlee clutched Galen's hand as we stood in front of the tournament placement post. Two of our fish made the top ten for the tournament first day's take in length, and one made the top ten in weight. Lorelei texted Brock's mother with the news. If Brock had been with us, we'd have celebrated, but instead, subdued, we waited for a response.

When Mrs. Isaacson's text came through, Lorelei thrust the phone into Carlee's hand. "You read it, please. I can't." Tears formed at the corners of her eyes.

"Mrs. Isaacson says they're releasing him, and Brock and his dad will be here tomorrow unless something else happens. Congratulations on the catches." Carlee returned the phone, and Lorelei snuffled.

"If we need you, can we depend on you for tomorrow?" Lorelei asked Drew, preparing our team for day two.

"The plan is for Ms. Mackey and me to be on our way to Atlanta, so I'll have to bow out," said Drew. "You've got great equipment here. The Isaacson team should do well."

"Wrestling practice is from two until four. I can call you and see if you need me then," said Galen.

"And I can be here until five," Kindra said. "The pep band is playing the second round of the holiday basketball tournament, and I already promised I'd attend. But Patricia might be able to take my place fishing."

Lorelei dutifully wrote the notes then chewed on the end of her pencil. "Ms. Wilk? Carlee? Dr. Bluestone?" We nodded. "We'll touch base tomorrow. Thanks for helping. This means so much to Brock."

"Why is it so important?" I asked as gently as I could.

"This is the twenty-fifth year of the tournament, and Brock wants to win in honor of the man who started it all. His grandfather made a huge impact on his life and what better way to remember him than to win."

Maverick and I left the ice, hopeful.

* * *

Maverick bounded from the car and up the steps. I owed him an extra-long walk.

I poured the kibble into his dish and walked through the house. Apparently, advanced decorating took more time than ice fishing, but the aroma of Ida's comfort food permeated the air and drew me like a magnet. I set the table, anticipating eating soon.

While I waited for Ida and Dad, I expanded the search parameters around Xavier and Meghann. I reread some of the articles that popped up, but with the addition of Meghann's death, the number of articles tripled.

Meghann grew up in Toledo, and graduated magna

cum laude from the McNally Smith College of Music in St. Paul, Minnesota. She played cello in Minneapolis, New York, Los Angeles, and Chicago where she met Xavier and joined sundry string ensembles he'd led. The photos showed a petite blonde with porcelain features and a bright smile, but if I didn't know better, from the besotted look in her eyes, I would have assumed, like Ida, something amorous passed between them.

Scrolling to the earlier, more obscure articles, Meghann had been a successful musician in her own right. The reviews of her soloing with orchestras around the world glowed, with accolades similar to Xavier's. Why she tethered herself to him, I couldn't fathom.

I clicked on a video of Meghann, clad in a black sequined gown, confidently sitting with the Jacksonville String Quartet, playing Pachelbel's *Canon in D*. It brought tears to my eyes. The song was my solitary concession to Charles' music selection for our wedding.

Farther down on the page, I read a teaser heading and clicked on a wedding announcement. My computer employed the rotating circle of death, and I never knew how much time would be needed for the file to load, so I slapped on my cap, shoved my feet in Mukluks and my arms in coat sleeves and lifted the leash off the hook.

"Let's make this quick, Maverick. It's freezing."

We walked, slipped, jogged, and slid two blocks north, into the territory my dad called no man's land, where trees and houses blocked connectivity. The path continued three more blocks we could traverse in less than thirty minutes. When we exited no man's land, my phone pinged seven times with an urgency I couldn't ignore.

I read the first line of the latest message and tugged

Maverick down our street. "Let's go, boy."

I had two text messages from Coach Michaels, one from the mayor, and two from Mr. Ganka. I'd neglected to give them a status report on Dillon. I texted he'd caught up and he should be allowed to play.

My phone rang from an unknown number. I debated answering, but not long. "Hello."

"Ms. Wilk? This is Dillon Maxwell." The echo of balls striking the gym floor, ref whistles, shoes slapping a staccato rhythm, and riotous cheering overpowered the sound of his voice. He spoke more loudly. "You cut it close, but thanks for giving the go-ahead for me to play. I hope you come watch. Our game starts at seven. We're going to crush them." He ended the call.

I had thirteen minutes.

Much to Maverick's discontent, I finished our walk, pulling him with all my might. And as much as I wanted to tuck into the fabulous smelling Asian chicken dish, I brushed my staticky hair, exchanged my fur-lined bomber hat for a stocking cap, and dug the car keys out of the basket.

My hand hovered above the laptop cover, preparing to close it, when a photo from the wedding file caught my eye. Meghann wore an elegant, sleek, fitted bridal gown. She carried a single orchid and she gazed into a familiar face.

CHAPTER THIRTY-FIVE

Even with the twenty-plus intervening years, I recognized Steve White. What brought him back to Columbia? Certainly not plumbing. Why would he pretend not to know his wife? Maybe he didn't. The photos of her as a young professional looked nothing like the destitute, homeless, paranoid woman we'd met on Christmas. But with her name and face plastered all over the news, he would have found out.

Which meant he probably knew Xavier too. It couldn't be coincidental. Maybe he'd come back for her. Words popped into my head. 'Steve and Meghann sitting in a tree, k-i-s-s-i-n-g.' S. N. M.

I checked the time and still had a few minutes, so I forwarded a text message to Amanda. It couldn't hurt

Brock. My phone rang seconds later and before I could say hello, Amanda lit into me. "What are you doing, Katie? Why are you sending me wedding photos?"

"Did you read the caption, Amanda? The bride in the photo was Meghann Popovich and her groom was—"

"That's Steve White." I heard Amanda's deep breathing. "I've got to go." And she hung up.

I tossed Maverick a dental chew and hustled to my car. I wouldn't have chosen to attend the basketball game but at least I understood the rules and knew when to cheer. I wasn't as well-acquainted with the scoring and practices of soccer, wrestling, and hockey, but teaching had its fringe benefits, and we could attend the games at a reduced fee.

The cacophony of the gym nearly drove me home, but the close score of the first quarter kept me rooted to the bleachers until half-time. As much as I hated to admit it, Dillon was fun to watch. He appropriated the opponent's ball with lightning speed, dribbled to the basket, and put the ball up in a jump shot for three points too often to count. The Columbia Cougars led by twelve points at half-time and my hunger pangs began growling almost as loud as the crowd. I collected my gear and snaked through the masses toward the doors where I collided with Ida and Steve White.

A pounding heart replaced my growling stomach, and as I stood in front of them, I couldn't think of one word I could say without giving away what I knew. Yet, I couldn't let my lovely landlady be alone with him. He could be a killer.

"Katie? Did you try the sesame chicken and rice? What did you think?"

I blinked.

"Katie." Ida tugged on my arm. "Katie?"

I had to think of a way to get her away from him. "No, I haven't eaten yet, but I'll give it a try when I get home and I'm ready to go now."

"Good game, huh?" Steve said. "Say, Ida's going back to the community center to pick up your dad and she was going to give me a ride but I'm the other direction. Could I catch a ride?"

No, no, no, no, no. Wait. If he was with me, he wouldn't be with her, and I could grill him.

"Sure. Where are you staying?"

"The Monongalia Bed and Breakfast," he said.

"I promised Harry I'd be back, and we could finish setting up the lights and check that off the to-do list. I'll see you at home, Katie. And can you make sure the slow cooker is turned off?" Ida lifted her hand and wiggled her fingers in front of a big grin.

Was she infatuated with a killer?

"Ta-ta, Stevie." She scurried through the crowd.

Stevie?

Talking about Ida's food, my stomach reverted to rumbling, and I wanted to delay being alone with him until I could manage my thoughts, so I took my place behind two students in the concession line. "I'm going to get a box of popcorn. I'm expected to support the …" I read the sponsor from the marquee. "The Honor Society. I love their popcorn." I filed away *concessions* as a possible fundraiser for my science club and mock trial team. I never knew when Mrs. McEntee's petty cash stash would run dry. "Would you like anything?"

Steve shook his head.

I handed over the money and picked up the box. I

poured a handful of popcorn into my hand and shoveled it into my mouth and immediately deleted the fundraising idea from the short list.

We left the building and headed in the direction I thought I'd parked my car.

Let the grilling begin.

"I'm a little protective, but exactly what are your intentions with my lovely landlady?" I asked as lightheartedly as I could. To keep up the pretense, I chewed one over-salty, stale kernel at a time and wished I'd purchased a soda to accompany the pale imitation of airy goodness.

Steve didn't answer.

I couldn't remember exactly where I'd parked the car, so I pulled out the key fob and pressed the lock button. The car's horn beeped, and the lights flashed two cars to our right.

"Loaner car," I said as we threaded our way between autos. "I can't always remember what it looks like." I slid into the driver seat and Steve took the passenger's side. "Soooo?"

"I think she's swell."

Who says swell?

I drove to the end of the parking lot. I felt safe, knowing where we were going, but I let Steve lead us. He pointed to the right. Under cover of night, he said, "She's a wonderful person but I don't have designs on Ida ... yet." I thought I could detect a smile at the end of those words, and I flinched. "At the light, turn left."

We drove in silence until he pointed again, and I pulled into the circle drive in front of the familiar Monongalia Bed and Breakfast. He released his seatbelt and it flapped into place.

"Thanks for the ride."

He yanked on the handle but before he could drag himself from the car, I blurted out, "I know Meghann was your wife." I kept my eyes forward.

"Then you also know she had issues. I lost touch after our divorce, but I received a Christmas card right after Thanksgiving indicating she'd come back to Columbia but was doing poorly. I hoped we could reconcile our differences, and I could help her. But she didn't even recognize me." Our conversation ended with the thud of the door.

Steve didn't sound like a killer, but I'd been fooled before.

I drove onto the street and parked at the end of the block. I waited long enough for him to exit the lobby and make his way to his room. Then I jogged inside.

"Katie," sang the voice behind the desk, hanging up the phone receiver. Mr. Walsh and I had become friends during my stay at the bed and breakfast while I searched for a place to call home. After a career as an engineer, he'd taken a job as a custodian at my high school, but his wife passed away and he had too much time on his hands, so he sometimes picked up a night shift and manned the registration desk. "What are you doing here? Is that popcorn from the high school?" He gave a hand-it-over gesture.

I hadn't realized I'd grabbed the box of airy nothingness, and unenthusiastically set it on the counter. Like a connoisseur, he looked, he sniffed, he plucked one kernel from the pile, he nibbled. "Honor Society?"

My eyes widened. "How did you know?"

"Their advisor uses his own store of ancient kernels he's had for-e-ver. I wish I could find it and dispose of it.

Alas, I think he takes it home with him." He shook his head and tossed the box in the trash. A bright smile replaced his annoyance. "What can I do for you?"

"When you watched Maverick—"

"When Maverick watched me. Go on."

"You always knew when I returned and brought him up within minutes. How did you do that?"

"The hotel software keeps track of entries and exits using the keycard."

"Then you know when the rooms are occupied and unoccupied?"

"That's the idea. Why?" His forehead crinkled and his bald head creased. "What are you looking into now?"

"I'm wondering if one of your guests left in the overnight hours of Christmas. Steve White."

If Mr. Walsh was surprised, he didn't show it. "I happen to be studying that data right now. I can't tell you when the occupant was here or gone. Confidentiality and all that." My shoulders sagged. "But it won't hurt to tell you when the cleaning staff might have been able to do their jobs." He turned the screen for me to read.

My shoulders sagged even more. The staff couldn't have cleaned the room until almost eleven the morning before Meghann's body was found and Dillon had said she and his dad had words at some time that night, so Steve wouldn't have had the opportunity. "It's almost foolproof."

"Almost?"

"The highest balconies are on the second floor, and they are not monitored under the keycard access, so theoretically, a patron could leave and return via the balcony. "

"Thanks, Mr. Walsh." I turned to leave but something

troubled me. "Why were you accessing those records …"
The sound of a siren grew louder, and I exited in a hurry.

Reflected in my rearview mirror, I watched Amanda
escort Steve White to her patrol car. She hadn't wasted
any time. I didn't see handcuffs so they weren't ready to
arrest him, and I doubted they ever would. Steve could
have jumped from the balcony but to return, unnoticed,
he would've needed a very long ladder. There were no
handholds, no trellis, no trees, no crumbling siding, no way
to climb up.

I pulled up his wedding photo again. The bride and
groom gazed into each other's eyes, oblivious to the antics
of the laughing wedding party. All, but one, made funny
faces and mimed cheers. And I recognized that serious
face.

CHAPTER THIRTY-SIX

The name below the photo read Jim Jaeger. The hospital maintenance man knew Meghann and Steve as well.

My phone pinged with a text from Ida.

Your dad and I are headed to the pediatric ward. Rachel could use our help. Join us?

I'll be right there.

I met Dad and Ida in the lot and kept my eyes open for Jim as we entered the quiet hospital and rode the elevator to the children's wing. A subdued calm replaced the usual bustle of activity among Rachel's patients during daytime hours, but her eyes lit up when she saw me.

"I'm glad you're here. Fortunately, my census is down. I do so hate when kids have to stay here. That being said, because my census is down, they've cut back the staff. It's so quiet it's almost creepy and I don't want to broadcast that vibe to my kids or their parents. Visiting hours are over in twenty minutes so ..." She handed us volunteer ID tags clipped onto lanyards. "If you want to hustle down the hall and see if anyone needs anything, that would be awesome."

We each took a different hallway. I passed open doors and empty beds until I came upon a room with a woman curled up on a chair, covered in a thin gray blanket. A young boy lay on his bed tethered to an IV stand. He put a finger to his lips and mouthed the words, "My mom finally fell asleep."

I whispered, "Do you want anything?" I glanced at the name on the white board. "Eddie?"

His big blue eyes twinkled, and he shook his head. He lifted the television remote and edged up the volume on a superhero cartoon. He closed his fist and flexed his right arm before he silently giggled.

Quinn sat in the bed next door, playing chess. The dark, wary eyes of her opponent looked up from the board and drilled into me. "What do you want?" he said.

"I came by to see if I can get anything for you."

Quinn folded her hands across her lap. "I'd like some apple juice, please, but I want to open it myself. And I'd like to see my mom."

The man's head fell forward, and his curly black hair covered his face. When he raised his chin, grim lines formed at the corners of his mouth. I winced at the familiar expression. "Honey, mommy can't see you yet. She's sick, and they're taking care of her."

"But I'm good now. I can help her," Quinn insisted. "Daddy, when can we see Dr. Pete? He always knows what to do."

I sucked in a breath but hid it by clearing my throat. Coltraine wouldn't take kindly to Pete's caring for this child.

Her dad took her hand and without looking at me said, "I'll take a cup of coffee too, if it's not too much trouble." I didn't envy her dad his job of explaining.

I followed voices to the small room with a coffee machine, a fridge, a microwave, and a table covered by a large tray of cookies wrapped in cellophane. Dad snared four bottles of water. I grabbed a trolley and arranged two plates of prepackaged treats and beverages. I dropped off two humongous chocolate chip cookies and juice boxes for the boy and his mom and steered the cart to Quinn's room. The door must have closed behind me when I left. It creaked when I opened it. I gasped.

Pete hovered over Quinn with a stethoscope, listening. "You're looking good, Quinn." He caught my eye and winked. "I think you should try to get her released tomorrow, Paul. Do you have help at home?"

"No. But I'll find some."

"I think she'd do better there." Paul nodded. Pete added with enthusiasm, "And look what my friend, Katie, has brought. Cookies and juice."

"And coffee for Daddy."

"Katie, can you sit with Quinn for a minute? I'd like to talk to her dad."

They left the room, and I took Paul's seat at the chess board. It only took a moment for me to see he was doomed. "You know you have your dad at checkmate."

"Yes, in three moves, but he tries so hard to play. I always pretend he's going to win until the very last move. Don't tell him." The eyes sparkled.

"I wouldn't dream of it." I watched her take a bite of

cookie. "How are you feeling?"

She swallowed and thought about what she might share. "Promise not to tell …"

I crossed my heart. "I promise I'll try not to tell."

She seemed to gauge how well I would do. "I stopped taking the medicine they give me here. It made me feel funny and I feel fine now. But no one will tell me what's going on with my mom. I always know when Daddy's hiding something. Once, we were supposed to draw our family tree for school, and he acted the same way until he told me he was adopted."

"Dr. Pete said you're doing well. With the two of them watching over you, you should be fine at home." She nodded and moved her bishop.

"You're a pretty smart little girl, aren't you?"

She beamed.

Her dad reentered and the pleasant chime noted the end of visiting hours.

"Goodnight, Quinn," I said. "Goodnight, Mr. …"

"Karlman."

Pete waited in the hall.

"May I walk with you?" I nodded. What else could I say? "She really likes you, Katie, and she usually takes quite a while to warm up to someone. She was born nine weeks early and her mom was distrustful of new places, new things, and new people. She's seen Dr. Coltraine whenever I was unavailable, and she still shrinks away when they get together." Our footfalls echoed in the empty corridor. "Would you mind not broadcasting I was here? I've been worried about Quinn. Paul called and I came. Quinn needs to feel safe."

"You were visiting." Time for another truth. "I

promised to try not to tell, but Quinn's not taking her medication anymore."

He nodded. "I halted all meds."

"She said she's not taking the meds they give her *here*."

Pete stopped. "She shouldn't be on any medication." I think he would have turned around and gone back to Quinn's room, but the elevator door opened and Dr. Coltraine soared into the ward and up to the nurses' station. He ducked into an empty room.

I stopped at the desk. "Rachel, is there anything I can do before I check out?"

Dr. Coltraine frowned and said, "Visiting hours are over."

"Thanks, I heard the announcement. I was visiting my friend, Eddie, but his mother was asleep, and I didn't want to wake her. Rachel, could you please tell her I was in." Thank heavens I'd read the notes on the wall.

Dr. Coltraine's eyes narrowed. She squinted as she perused the short list of patients. Her face relaxed, and I figured she'd seen Eddie's name. "Have a good evening," she said. She marched down the corridor and into Quinn's room.

Pete sauntered out of his hideaway straight to the elevator, joining Dad, Ida, and me. The doors closed and the metal box began its descent. Ida turned to Pete. Her red face matched her red hair and she said, "I have always considered you to be like a son to me. But you have been banned from practicing until the committee can resolve the issue raised by you being a suspect in a murder investigation." She shook her finger at him. "What are you thinking being here?"

"Ida." He clutched her hand and brought it to his chest.

"You know I love you. You've always been there for me. Since my mother died, I've tried to do what she would've wanted, the right thing when someone needs me. My life's mission is to help those in need. I may do so at my own peril, but that's on me."

He released her hand. "Quinn could've died if she'd had any of that contaminated water. If I can save that little girl, I don't care what they do to me. Something is happening. She's been a guinea pig for some horrific experiment." His voice rose. He was ferocious when a child's health and safety were threatened. "There is nothing medically wrong with her not inflicted by some outside element and although the evidence points to her mother, I'm not sure it was her. Paul said his wife would die before harming Quinn. There must be another explanation."

Ida reached up and brushed a wayward curl behind his ear. "Your mom would be so proud of you." She swiped at her eyes, sniffed, and swatted at him. "But that doesn't mean you should tank your career. You have people who will help." Her look encompassed Dad and me, and we both nodded. "What do you need us to do?"

"I want Paul to take Quinn home tomorrow. It's the safest place for her as long as she is under constant surveillance. She is a very smart young lady and knows to look for tampering but Paul has to go back to work or he'll lose his job, and right now he is worried about health care benefits. He hasn't said anything, but even with his wife's income, I think they were living on the edge. If we can schedule someone to be with Quinn during the day, that would go a long way to protect her."

"How do we keep her from being poisoned?" Dad asked. He lowered his voice. "How do you know it isn't her father?"

"In answer to your first question, she knows she needs to open everything herself, all her own beverages and packaged foods, and we're going to have meals delivered. We may have whoever is staying with her share her food or test it. As awful as it sounds, she won't have anything homemade or delivered by anyone but Officer Rodgers. He is the only one who will know where the food is coming from. And he'll stay through the meals. As for her dad, he's been on the road most times Quinn's been brought into the ER."

"Where does Paul work?" I asked.

Pete huffed. "He works for the city. Maxwell got him a job driving a sanitation truck."

CHAPTER THIRTY-SEVEN

Dad thought a dog would be a welcome diversion for Quinn, so Maverick and I took the early morning shift.

"Take real good care of her," said Paul. "I took her out AMA—"

"AMA?"

"Against medical advice. Dr. Coltraine wasn't very happy. If anything happens to Quinn, I don't know what …" Paul exhaled, and his shoulders slumped. He scratched behind Maverick's ears and pasted on a grin. He kissed Quinn on the top of her head. "Have a good day, honey. I'll be back before you know it," he said.

"And we'll see mommy?"

"We'll try to see mommy," he said, and sped out the door.

She sat at the kitchen table, licking big globs of Café Lot oatmeal from her spoon—my favorite, studded with raisins and walnuts and topped with a touch of brown sugar. Maverick nudged her with his cold, wet nose, and she squealed.

"What do you want to do today, Quinn?"

"Does your dog need a walk? I want to go outside. Maybe we can make a snow monkey."

"That I'd like to see."

She zipped her coat, tied her hood tight, and wrapped an extra scarf around her neck. She tugged on her boots and mittens and waited while I hurried to put on my outside clothes before she overheated.

If we didn't move, the brisk temperature crept beneath our layers. She tossed a tennis ball for Maverick, built a small fort, hit me with five snowballs, and admired the sun dogs—a bright pair of halos formed by the ice crystals surrounding the sun. We made snow angels and when I worried her cheeks were too pink, she reluctantly followed me inside.

She opened a juice box. "Wanna make cookies?"

"We can, but you know you can't eat them. Dr. Pete is trying to make sure you don't get anything that can hurt you. There may be a contaminant."

"What's a con-tam-i …"

"A contaminant is something that might be mixed in where it shouldn't be and may harm you." She pouted. "Any other ideas?"

Her shoulders rose to her ears. She giggled and pointed to a worn and battered chess board with unique pieces, carved to look like Tenniel's characters in Lewis Carroll's stories. Alice held the most prominent spot with the king at her side. A perfectly round Tweedledee and Tweedledum stood at attention in place of the rooks. Two unbalanced, awkward White Knights sat astride fat horses and two Mad-Hatters flanked the royal couple. Eight White Rabbits dangled pocket watches from their tiny paws and faced a terrifying Queen of Hearts and her cowering underlings.

"Where did you get this chess set?"

"It came with Daddy." Her eyes lit up.

I picked up the Red Queen. I rubbed the jagged edge at the end of her right arm where the hand holding the royal scepter bearing a heart topper should have been. I texted Pete.

Quinn beat me three times while we waited for him. If I'd have been paying attention, I might have given her a run for her money, but probably not.

Maverick barked and then, of course, the doorbell rang. I tore open the door and leaned away in surprise. Dr. Coltraine stood on the top step, poised to ring the bell again. Her eyebrows rose and crawled into a scowl.

"What are you doing here?" she asked.

"I'm staying with Quinn this morning while her dad is at work. What can I do for you Dr. Coltraine?"

"I knew releasing her was a bad idea." She raised her chin. "I'd like to see my patient now." She barreled past me, tearing tan leather gloves from her hands, and stuffing them in her pocket. She unwound a soft woolen scarf and set it over the back of a kitchen chair. She composed her features and said, "Where is she?"

I scanned the room. Quinn and Maverick had disappeared.

I didn't know where they were, but I couldn't tell her that. I smiled and said, "She's resting. Come back when her dad's home. He'll be better able to answer your questions."

"Please take me to look in on her. I made this trip to make certain she's being well cared for. Rachel has her doubts and so do I."

Rachel supported Pete's decision to get Quinn home, but I didn't know what she thought of Paul going back to work and Ida, Dad, and me babysitting.

Dr. Coltraine surveyed the room and her eyes alighted on the chess set. She stopped and sniffed, and her nose curled as if she smelled something unpleasant. "You can't have a dog in here. She's allergic to dogs." For just a moment, I feared Maverick might send Quinn into a tailspin until I remembered her dad had known I brought my dog. If he didn't think Maverick would pose a problem, why should I? Before I could step in front of her and cut her off, Dr. Coltraine quickly advanced down the hall leading to the rest of the small house. Her coat flapped behind her as she headed for the closed door of Quinn's room, knocked sharply, and pushed inside.

No Quinn.

But I caught the swish of a black tail, sweeping dust bunnies and fluttering the bed skirt and hurriedly turned to follow Dr. Coltraine to the next room where Quinn lay tangled under a pile of quilted fabric, snoring softly in an academy award-winning performance. Dr. Coltraine stepped to the head of the bed, stopped next to Quinn, and lightly shook her shoulder. Quinn sighed and feigned a slow wakening. She stretched and yawned, and I thought I saw her slide the edge of a phone under the pillow next to her hand. She opened her eyes and blinked a few times. "Hi."

"You remember me, Quinn. I'm Dr. Coltraine. I came

all this way to see if you are doing well this morning." She turned to look at me. "If you don't mind, we'd like a little privacy, wouldn't we Quinn?"

Quinn's eyes grew round, and she sobbed. "I want my mommy."

"Dr. Coltraine, I'm afraid I'm going to have to ask you to leave. Come back when Paul's home."

"Not until I finish my examination. I will not let anything happen to this little girl. We don't know what's hurting her."

Quinn sucked in a breath, and I think she might've been ready to defend her dad, but the doorbell rang, and Maverick barked. Dr. Coltraine turned her head toward the unexpected yelp. She turned back, and her angry I-knew-it eyes dared me to stay with Quinn.

Ida called, in a lovely and welcoming lilt, "Quinn, where are you, dear? Granny Ida's here and I brought company."

Quinn scrambled off the bed and ran out the door, down the hall, and into Ida's waiting arms. She buried her head in Ida's ample bosom. Behind her, Officer Rodgers stamped snow from his boots on the rug in the entryway.

"Lunch time," he said. He jiggled the handles of two large paper bags and handed them to Ida. "I hope you like chicken legs, fries, and frozen yogurt." He didn't act surprised at the number of mouths he might have to feed. "I brought plenty," he said, looking from Ida to Dr. Coltraine and back to me.

"Dr. Coltraine, it's grand you're making house calls. That doesn't happen often." Ida could charm the stripes off a chipmunk. Dr. Coltraine never knew what hit her.

"Not usually, but I hate sending a child home without a diagnosis or a care plan and Quinn's case is troubling."

"You haven't found a definitive cause for her illness yet, have you?"

Dr. Coltraine shook her head.

"I know her dad is worried, and he will not be leaving her alone. We have coverage for her every minute he's at work and, as you can see, we also have Officer Rodgers checking in on her, bringing meals. Two pediatric nurses are sharing the overnight duties. And her mother is still in the psych unit." Ida smiled. "You've done so many tests. Hopefully, you'll be able to pinpoint the source of her difficulty soon and it'll be something you can take care of."

Dr. Coltraine picked up her scarf and said, "I should be getting back to the hospital. Please tell Mr. Karlman I'll stop by later to check on Quinn." She tugged on her gloves. "May I speak to you, Officer Rodgers?" He nodded but didn't move. "Alone?" He followed her out the door, closing it tightly.

Ida gave Quinn another squeeze. "Great thinking, honey. After you texted me, I called Officer Rodgers and told him what was happening. But you do know, Dr. Coltraine is looking out for you, right?"

Quinn nodded but her eyes told a different story. She started to sniff. "I really do want my mommy."

The door opened and Officer Rodgers walked in. He removed his boots and jacket and washed his hands. The table was set for four and he joined us. "Dr. Coltraine is concerned that there is an allergen they have not yet detected which might be making Quinn ill. Or that one of her p-a-r-e-n-t-s could be giving her something."

"They are not." Quinn's jaw jutted out and she crossed her skinny arms in front of her.

He tapped the top of her head and nodded. "I told

her my job was to deliver food and wait to see if she has a reaction. I have an epi-pen and Benadryl, but if it's a poison, I just don't know."

Quinn huffed and uncrossed her arms and scooped a large spoonful of creamy yogurt onto her plate.

"Me first." Officer Rodgers smiled, stuck his spoon in the plastic container and took a bite. He closed his eyes and hummed. "You won't like this one bit." Then we all took a big scoop.

My phone buzzed.

Is she gone?

CHAPTER THIRTY-EIGHT

Pete talked to Quinn under the supervision of Officer Rodgers and Ida. He followed me home and I shared my suspicion.

"What do you think?" I held the Queen of Hearts in my hand, rotated the broken crockery piece in the other until they fit together, and held them until the glue set. I waited for Pete to say something.

He shook his head. "Xavier seldom spoke to me and what he did say never made much sense. I don't know why you found the Queen's hand in Xavier's tent nor why it fits Paul's chess piece, but I'll ask him when I go back this evening."

I handed him the repaired and haughty Queen of Hearts. "Please return this. I promised Quinn I'd get it back to her today and I'll be fishing in the tournament until six."

Pete chuckled. "Fishing again, eh?"

Dad chuckled too. "Not really," he said. "She's just there to make everyone look old."

"Brock needed me on the team to raise the average age." I blushed. It made me sound ancient. "But Dad's an antique and when he shows up, they don't need me at all." The cuckoo clock chimed the one forty-five. I got up from the table and grabbed Maverick's leash and my outer gear. "It's almost two and I promised I'd be early to set up. Dad, what time do you take over for Ida?" I clipped the leash on Maverick, and he acted as if he knew where we were headed, bouncing back and forth from paw to paw.

"I plan to haul in winners until four thirty," Dad said. "Ida told me to come for supper. And Paul is usually home shortly after seven."

"Harry, can you text me when Paul gets home? I have the completed test results and I'd like to discuss what's next," Pete said.

"Are you going to catch another basketball game tonight, darlin'?" Dad asked, sliding his feet into his boots, and lifting his coat from the hook by the door.

"I think I'd better. I have a vested interest in one of the players," I said, locking the door behind us.

From the top of the steps, I pointed and pressed the key fob and the car locks clicked. Dad lugged the cooler across the frosty sidewalk to the Focus and hefted it into the rear seat then slid into the passenger seat.

Pete walked with me, the silence strained between us. "Katie," he said.

My phone rang. "Let me know what Paul tells you about the chess piece," I said as I continued walking and answered the call brightly. "Hi, Jane. You made it?"

"Say hi." Pete mouthed the words and lumbered to his car, his hands shoved deep into his pockets. He was going to make a great dad. If only Susie could see that.

"Pete says hi. How's your dad?" I asked.

"He's great and wishes everyone a happy holiday."

Jane gave me the lowdown on their Georgia plans until our arrival at Fuller Park Landing cut short our conversation.

* * *

Dad did as he promised and hauled in fish, left and right. His lighthearted banter together with Maverick's antics, chasing and yelping at the flopping fish, helped ease some of the tension in the fish house. Brock tried not to show it, but he jumped whenever someone knocked on the door and it happened with some regularity. Brock's dad sat on an overturned plastic bucket with a jig stick, keeping his eyes on his son but I wasn't certain he'd attached bait of any kind; he couldn't even get a nibble. We talked of everything except the trouble Brock might have.

I caught one tiny northern and Dad insisted I include it in the cache of fish we took to the judges' table.

"You just never know," Dad said.

He and Kindra left when Galen showed up, so our age average fluctuated but when the head judge made a surprise visit, I could honestly say our average was above twenty-four.

Lorelei's fake bait didn't draw any prospects, so she removed a small, orange plastic box from her backpack and began to string tiny glass beads onto an eighteen-inch piece of fishing line. She knotted the ends together and wound it around her wrist. Her speedy fingers created two more and she offered a royal-blue, gold, and white one to me.

By the end of the evening, we'd caught, weighed, measured, and released three different kinds of fish. Before I left for the day, Lorelei gave me two more from the handful of wraparound bracelets she'd finished, one for Jane and one for Quinn.

Returning to a quiet, dark, looming house in the dead of winter was depressing and I had no idea when to expect Dad or Ida. Maverick circled four times, collapsed onto his cushion, and promptly closed his eyes. I swept the floor and vacuumed the living room rug. Restless, I searched for something else to do. I picked up my book, *The Code Girls*, but when I reread the same page for the third time, I put it back. I wouldn't have schoolwork for days and I wasn't used to being idle.

Although I knew she was with Dad, I still knocked on Ida's door before entering and made my way to her cookie jar. The gingerbread men looked up at me with their frosting smiles, looking totally unappetizing. I wandered to the piano, plopped onto the bench, and flicked on the lamp. The beam illuminated sheet music written for solo cello and orchestra, resting on the music rack. I plunked out the solo line and played the first few measures of the strangely haunting melody. I peered more closely and found some of the notes written in crimson, like corrections or embellishments in the score, interspersed and handwritten within the bars.

Something clicked.

I pulled up Messiaen's encryption key and matched the letters of the alphabet to the symbols: 'duierica'.

My stomach dropped. DUI Erica. I confirmed the pairings. Could it be correct? Had Erica been driving the night of the fatal accident? Or had he let his dead wife take the blame and this was to help him remember? Had he killed Pete's mom? Did the message even refer to that night?

I looked back at the score, and more red notes jumped out at me. I continued decoding: 'sdaughter'. I scoured the music for additional information but didn't find any.

DUI Erica's daughter.

Erica's daughter would have been old enough to drive the night of the accident. Was she behind the wheel? How did that happen? Was she under the influence? Where was she now? And where would I find the answers?

I poured kibble into Maverick's dish, and he rose from his cushion, shook, and rattled his tags. He devoured his supper, padded to my side, and rested his chin on my knee.

I raised my phone and punched in the numbers.

CHAPTER THIRTY-NINE

Amanda answered on the fifth ring.

"I was going to leave a message. You must be busy." I ran my hand over Maverick's head and under his collar.

"What can I do for you, Ms. Wilk?"

Either she was in the middle of work among colleagues and wanted this to sound like a professional call or she was angry with me. "I think Xavier and/or Meghann wrote secret messages in their music. I found a legend and transcribed some of the notes into letters of the alphabet."

"Encoded messages? Can you bring them to the station?" I lit up, anxious to unload my conclusions. Voices rose in the background and she added, "Tomorrow at ten?" My mood deflated.

"Do you know where Dr. Erickson is? He isn't answering his phone."

The clock read seven thirty and Paul could be home, but I wouldn't speculate as to Pete's whereabouts. "No, I don't."

I heard voices shouting in the background. "… seen at the county park." "How'd she get away?" "Who could have helped …" "… snow could accumulate."

"I've got to run." Amanda sounded distracted. "Tomorrow," she repeated and hung up.

I dialed Pete's number. It rang until voicemail kicked in.

"Amanda has been trying to call you and I'm wondering how Quinn is doing. And I found an interesting message encoded in a cello piece." I also wondered what Paul had said about the Queen of Hearts.

The basketball game began at seven thirty, so I'd only missed a few minutes. The Cougars played well again. Dillon made several steals, succeeding at more than half of his jump shots. After the pep band half-time performance, I caught Kindra's eye and gave her a thumb's up on the fine musical addition to the evening's event. At the beginning of the fourth quarter, with a commanding lead, I expected the Cougars would win and go on to play in the championship game, so I collected my jacket, hat, and gloves. I looked into the stands and caught Mrs. Maxwell glaring at me. I fluttered an embarrassed wave as I marched in front of the stands.

I reached the gym doors and a perky whistle shrieked behind me. The game action stopped. I'd missed the infraction for which Dillon Maxwell earned a technical foul. One more foul and he'd be out of the game. He stomped off the court and collapsed into his seat.

My thoughts drifted on my drive home. Minnesota winters are magical: sipping hot chocolate, cuddled in fluffy blankets, and warmed by crackling fireplaces, ice skating, fishing, looking out frosty windows at pristine snow blanketing the world, until it isn't. Winters are also brutal: freezing rain, sheets of ice, sleet, and bodies rising to the surface of Lake Monongalia. My wipers brushed lacey flakes off my windshield, and I hoped the weather wouldn't get worse.

Dad and Ida stood around a card table in her living room, twisting and turning pieces of her Christmas jigsaw puzzle.

"Who won?" she asked.

"They were still playing when I left, but the Cougars were ahead by twelve. How's Quinn?"

"Very well. Pete can't find anything left in her system so either it's been flushed or what was happening was temporary."

"Did he get my message about Amanda?"

Dad gave Ida a congratulatory knuckle bump as he slid two pieces into the frame.

"Pete tried calling, but Chief West didn't pick up. Officer Rodgers didn't stay long after dinner either, which leads me to believe something happened." He yawned. "I'm beat. I'm going to bed. See you in the morning. I'll take the first shift with Quinn tomorrow." He planted a kiss on my forehead and Maverick wiggled between us. Dad headed to his room and Maverick prodded me toward the puzzle table. His nose caught my bracelet and when he backed away, it came apart and beads flew everywhere.

Time to clean again.

I rolled the vacuum across the floor, sucking up the

tiny, noisy glass beads, and Ida crossed her arms in front of her, watching. She chewed on her lower lip.

I flipped the switch to off. "What's wrong, Ida? You said Quinn was alright." She nodded. "What is it then? You look like you have something to say but you don't know how."

"Katie," Ida said, her eyes glued to my face. "Susie is pregnant."

I sighed. I didn't want to talk about Susie and Pete. "I told *you* that."

"But Pete's not the father."

I opened the debris reservoir to dump the mound of dog hair, crumbs, and little bits of whatever I'd collected and missed the garbage can altogether.

"What do you mean?" I scooped the hair with one hand and grabbed a damp paper towel to handle the remains, my hands shaking.

She raised an eyebrow as if she couldn't believe I needed her to repeat her message. "Pete is not the father."

"But I heard Susie say—"

"Pete was always Susie's mother's choice. 'Marry Dr. Erickson,' she said. 'He's perfect.' They dated for a while." Ida shook her head. "But Susie's first love is a classmate of hers who guides hunters in Canada. The last time Gregory came home, she got pregnant. He went back into the wilds before she knew, and when he didn't respond and she couldn't get hold of him, she was afraid he'd given up on her or something happened to him. She told Pete she was expecting, and he said he'd help her however he could."

"How do you know this?"

She ignored my question. "Understand where Pete is coming from. His best friend through high school was raised by a wonderful single mom. But no one understood the difficulties and bullying he experienced until it was too late. We all missed the huge obstacles life dished out and he got in with the wrong crowd. He got caught stealing and was sent to a juvenile detention facility. Eventually he just disappeared. Because of that, Pete vowed he'd help any child the best way he could. He was just trying to do the right thing, but Pete's not the dad.

"When Susie wrote Gregory in Canada and told him she was expecting, he'd written back, ecstatic about the baby, but he never heard from her. He thought she'd moved on or found someone else, but he came home to help with the fishing contest and went to see her." Ida gave me a hug, smiled, and turned to go upstairs. "Susie's mom complained to her friends that all her work to influence her daughter's choice in husbands by intercepting the letters was for nothing."

My head swam with dizzying thoughts I couldn't put in any order. Pete wasn't the baby's father. Susie wasn't marrying Pete. I entered our apartment and closed the door between them. Why was Amanda curt? What made Quinn unwell? What did Paul say about the Queen of Hearts? I poured a tall glass of cold water. What was the score of the basketball game? Who killed Xavier and Meghann? Was Pete still interested in me?

My exhaustion muddled my mind. A text from Pete pinged on my phone.

Spoke to Chief West. She's been busy. Some idiot thought he could win the fishing tournament by stuffing his fish with lead weights. She almost had a riot on her hands.

My fingers weren't fast enough to return a text.

Paul's wife snuck out of the psych unit. They're looking for

her. Paul's had the chess set for as long as he can remember. Queen's hand always missing.

I texted back.

If Xavier had the Queen's hand, could he have had it the entire time? Paul is adopted. Could he be Xavier's son?

Dots indicating typing appeared and disappeared, appeared, and disappeared again.

The phone rang in my hand. "Pete?"

"If Paul is Xavier's son, he's due his inheritance and so is his sister. We have to find someone who would know."

"Mayor Maxwell should know."

"Why would Maxwell know?"

"He was Xavier's agent and remains the trustee of the trust. Maxwell must have some way to determine familial lines and disperse the funds. The Maxwells were at the basketball game tonight, watching Dillon, but they should be home soon. I left at the beginning of the fourth quarter."

"I'm going over there. Face-to-face will make answering my questions more imperative. I'll pick you up in five minutes."

I'd been trying to finagle a way to go with him and I almost missed the invitation. "I'll be ready."

CHAPTER FORTY

We were both lost in thought and silent until we stopped in front of Maxwell's home. Headlights came toward us and when they turned into the driveway, they highlighted the determination on Pete's face. The garage door rose, and we exited Pete's truck. Rather than continue into the garage, the Maxwells got out of their Mercedes and waited for us on the driveway.

Maxwell tilted his head and glowered. "What do you want, Dr. Erickson?" He eyed me with suspicion. "We won, by the way, Ms. Wilk, in case you were wondering."

"I had no doubt," I said.

"We have a few questions about Xavier's estate," Pete said, jumping in with both feet.

"What in blazes—"

Mrs. Maxwell raised her forefinger and silenced him. "Please, come in," she said.

We sat at the kitchen table behind four cups of tea.

"It's time." Mrs. Maxwell raised her chin. "Tell them."

Maxwell gazed into his cup. "Let me start by saying Xavier was a phenomenal musician. After the accident, he fell apart. His family fell apart. And I tried to help the only way I could, limited as I was by the terms of his trust."

"Do you know where Xavier's children are?" Pete asked.

"I know where his son is. I'm still looking for his stepdaughter."

"Paul Karlman is Xavier's son."

Mrs. Maxwell gasped, making Maxwell's poker face moot, and he said, "Xavier always knew where his son was. He watched from a distance, not willing to chance screwing up his son's life. Xavier was intuitive but could be toxic." Maxwell's head dropped. Mrs. Maxwell took his hand. When he looked up again, he said, "He was like a brother to me and knowing him could also be invigorating. He gave me my start."

Mrs. Maxwell threaded her arm into his.

"What happens now?"

"With Xavier's death," Maxwell said, "Paul will inherit a goodly sum—"

"They've been struggling financially, and any amount will go a long way to help that family." I sat back in my chair.

"You didn't let me finish." I closed my lips. "The morals clause disqualifies family members from inheriting if they cause someone harm and Ryn is accused of poisoning their daughter. If they can tie Paul to the poisoning or prove he didn't do all he could to prevent it, he'll not receive a penny. That's at my discretion."

"But that's backwards. The money would assist ..." My eyes went wide. "Oh, my goodness. Quinn is Xavier's granddaughter. How could he watch them struggle when he had the wherewithal to help them?"

"Katie," Pete put a calming hand on my shoulder and said gently, "Xavier didn't always have the presence of mind to understand everything going on around him."

"He knew he'd set up a good thing with his trust. Everyone told him so at the time and he didn't want to mess it up," said Maxwell.

"We just have to find Ryn and prove she didn't harm Quinn."

"Find her?" Mrs. Maxwell said.

"She's missing from the psych unit. They're searching for her."

"If Meghann would have gotten help, none of this might have happened. Meghann saw herself as Xavier's soulmate and muse. As long as she made good music, he did nothing to dissuade her. But when she tried to separate him from his beloved wife, he put his foot down. That was the night of the accident." Maxwell looked directly at Pete. "He never forgave her but held himself equally responsible and he punished them both until he died."

"Where were you the night Xavier died?" Pete asked.

One corner of Maxwell's lip curled. "We attended an event at the Depot until after midnight and stayed at the Marriot. I have three hundred witnesses and receipts."

A car revved out front and a door slammed. Dillon bounded into the kitchen. "Great game, huh?" He beamed, glancing around the table.

Maxwell grunted. "You got a technical."

Dillon's smiled faded. His shoulders sagged as he waited for an affirmation of a job well done. It didn't come.

"How did you figure out Paul is Xavier's son?" said Maxwell, ignoring Dillon. "That chess set?"

Dillon's face transformed from expectant to resigned, and Mrs. Maxwell watched.

Her gaze returned to her husband and she blurted. "He gave both children the same stupid chess set and broke the hand off one of the pieces of each as a token, a remembrance of his family." She turned burning eyes to her husband. "You can honor Xavier's wishes now and execute the trust."

"Not yet. The morals clause. And I haven't located Xavier's stepdaughter."

"Keep her assets in the trust, protect them for her, but use your discretion." Mrs. Maxwell's voice rose. "This is it. He's had you in his thrall our entire life, dictating your moves. I won't take anymore. Dillon has been waiting for you to be a dad for the same length of time. If you can't figure this out, Dillon and I are ..." She turned her fiery eyes to Dillon, but he was gone.

Her chair scraped against the tile floor, and she raced upstairs. "Dillon?"

Her footsteps pounded across the upstairs and she called out.

Heaving, she stumbled into the kitchen.

"He's not here."

She dashed out the door. We followed. Their truck was missing. Mrs. Maxwell craned her neck, searching the streets. She burst into tears and rushed inside. Maxwell trailed her.

We walked to Pete's truck. He started the engine and made a call.

"Hey, Chief. I'm with Katie and you're on speakerphone. Dillon Maxwell took another runner."

"I can't help with that right now."

"Can we do anything for you?"

"Ryn Karlman is still missing. Ronnie and his team scoured the fishing village, and they're talking to Ryn's friends and visiting the churches for any sign of her. Katie, could you and Maverick check once more at Fuller Park Landing and the encampment site? And Pete, she might go back to the hospital to look for Quinn, or she may go home. That would be in your purview. She knows you.

"The precipitation is tapering off, but the temps are plummeting. I'm not sure how long she can survive out in the cold."

"On it."

* * *

I collected my gear, clipping the leash to Maverick, and shared the information I had with Ida and Dad. They headed to Karlman's, intending to do all they could to protect Quinn.

I pulled into the lot at Fuller Park Landing. I opened my door and Maverick barreled over me across the parking lot onto the ice. I chased him, shivering at the gale that tore through channels between the dark fish houses.

"Maverick!" As the sky cleared, with the new moon, the stars sparkled brightly, but the howl of the wind covered any other sounds.

Maverick stopped yards from where I'd found Xavier's

body and barked with his entire being, his tail thwacking in a rhythm to his yelps.

"What is it, boy?" I knelt and scratched under his collar. He sat and bayed. Between breaths, I heard a huffing. "Shh, Maverick," I said softly.

The 'help' was so quiet I thought I'd imagined it. I flashed a beam of light toward the sound and a dark ripple coalesced into a shape hunched over on the ice.

"Hello? Do you need help? What can I do?" I took tentative steps, closing the gap between us, careful to watch for aberrations in the ice.

"Help," I heard again.

The lessons I'd learned from Xavier stuck with me. I spotted the ladder hanging from the firetruck and yanked it free. I dragged it over the ice, gingerly stepping closer, shoving the ladder in front of me. When the end was close to the figure on the ice, I called to Maverick. He sat on the last rung, and I pleaded, "Stay." I stretched out and crawled across the wooden slats, under the caution tape, and ended up next to Dillon Maxwell. He strained against a load and heaved, out of breath and out of time.

"Help." The ice creaked. "We've got to get her out of there."

Water inched its way onto the ice, lapping around my knees and crawling up my thighs. Dillon's teeth chattered and his body shuddered. I gripped one arm of the figure and pulled. We hefted the body out of the water.

I held tight.

I recognized her pale, gaunt face, and watched Dillon slither away from the lip of thin ice. I wondered if he'd leave us, but I heard his voice behind me. "Nice doggy." He'd crept the longer, safer way around. "Here, doggy."

Maverick stepped off his perch, and the end dipped

precipitously into the water. Water sloshed my face and hands. I held tight to Ryn. Dillon grabbed the other end of the ladder and whisked us away from the opening. I felt like I was on a toboggan, slipping and sliding away from the water's edge.

He hoisted me to standing.

"Help me get her to my car," I said. Before I could tighten my grip on Ryn's side, Dillon lifted Quinn's mom as if she weighed nothing and carried her across the ice. I raced ahead and opened the doors. Maverick hopped in beside me. I started the car and Dillon laid her inside, crawled in after, and slammed the door.

I could've collected several speeding tickets and jerked to a stop in front of the ER. Dillon slid Ryn across the seat and rushed her through the doors where he was met by Susie and Dr. Coltraine. One look at me, and Susie shook her head in disbelief, but as a consummate nurse, she performed her duties to perfection. I made a call as Dillon laid Ryn on a gurney. Dr. Coltraine and Susie wheeled Quinn's mom through the ER doors. Dillon was breathing rapidly, realizing death lay just beyond.

"You did great," I said. Dillon stared at the floor.

When the sirens and lights stopped behind my car in the drive, Amanda stormed through the sliding doors first. "Katie, where did you find her?"

I pointed to Dillon. "He found her out on the ice at Lake Monongalia and probably saved her life."

"Good job, kid. Katie, we'll touch base tomorrow." She and Officer Rodgers disappeared through the doors.

"Are you okay, Dillon?"

He nodded as we walked through the exit.

"Where's the truck?"

"I ditched it downtown."

"Can I give you a ride home?"

"Can we go back to the lake?"

Maverick vaulted into the rear seat and curled up. Dillon sat in front.

"Dillon, why did you harass Xavier?"

My attempts to get him to talk seemed to fail but before the uncomfortable ride ended at the parking lot, he said, "His name came up a lot in the fights my parents had."

I parked. He didn't move, but said, "Can I show you something?"

I turned off the car. Maverick stayed contentedly curled up. I followed Dillon to the lake shore, to the overflowing trash receptacle where *someone* had slammed a lid on Xavier. Dillon dug in one can, tossing garbage on the ground. When it appeared he hadn't found what he was looking for, his manic movements shifted to the next bin, and I picked up what he'd thrown out. Then he attacked the third. "Dillon, what are you hunting for."

"It's not here."

"What's not here?"

He plopped onto the snow. "I heard my mom and dad fighting over a chess set. I come here to think, and I saw one. I thought if I could get my parents that game, they wouldn't be so mad at each other. I swear it was here. I found it right before I heard the lady screaming. But it's not here now. Who would have taken it?"

"You found a chess set? Are you sure?"

He pulled something from his pocket. "It's all I had time to grab."

He held a red caterpillar sitting on a mushroom, just like the one in Paul's Alice in Wonderland set.

CHAPTER FORTY-ONE

Dillon shuffled to the door held open by his mother and they exchanged a few words. She peered at his open fist. She recognized the chess piece. She dragged him into a bear hug. He didn't pull away and he didn't look back, but Mrs. Maxwell nodded to me, and I returned the acknowledgment.

My heavy eyelids closed when I pulled into my garage stall, but only until Maverick licked my ear and I shrieked. He pulled me up the stoop and through the door.

"We heard you found Quinn's mom," Ida said.

"Dillon found her. I only helped bring her to the ER." I covered a huge yawn with my hand. "Amanda wants me to stop by tomorrow and give her the information I've gleaned, but do you think my interpretation is viable?"

Another yawn escaped. "Sorry. I haven't even shown you how it works." I started toward my notes.

"Go to bed, Katie," said Ida. "We'll talk in the morning."

Dad pointed me toward the stairs and gave the tiniest shove. "To bed," he said.

I didn't remember anything until my phone pinged. A weird yellow hue from the streetlights sliced around the window shade; it was still dark outside. I groped for my phone and struggled to read the message.

I just finished my shift. Do you think we could talk? I have some things that need to be said but I don't want to be overheard. Susie

I blinked away the fog and responded.

On my way.

Meet you by the vending machines near the cafeteria.

I pulled on my Cougar sweatshirt, jeans, and my warmest socks, tied my hair into a ponytail, and threw my phone in my jacket pocket. Maverick's eyes followed me as I tiptoed down the stairs, but he remained snuggled cozily on his fluffy cushion. Maverick breakfasted at six, and as he saw no hope of food at twelve thirty, he never moved.

I turned the key three times before the Focus growled to a start. Cold air blew through the vents and forced me fully awake. I thought about everything Susie could want to talk to me about.

How was Ryn? Did she have anything to do with Xavier's death? He'd been a larger-than-life and not always well-liked personality. It was difficult to find someone with much good to say about Xavier and yet he'd saved Brock's life. Maybe Jim had tried to frame Xavier for stealing toys meant for the children and pry Meghann away from him. Maybe Susie could prove who stole the toys. Could Paul know he was Xavier's son? Xavier charged Maxwell to execute the terms of his trust, but the morals clause could preclude Paul from claiming his inheritance if his wife was found guilty of trying to hurt their daughter and he is not completely exonerated. Xavier claimed to see things and Quinn's mom had been confined again. Maybe Susie obtained some answers from her.

Or would our conversation revolve around Pete?

Every thought ended in a yawn. I determined I couldn't handle more than one winter break a year.

I decided not to dwell on Susie. I had no idea what she wanted to talk about. Instead, I thought about the secret messages in the musical scores. They could tell a story if we had more of the notes and knew the players. I'd share my truncated transcription with Amanda, and she might understand what the words meant. If the DUI referred to Xavier's stepdaughter, how could she have been driving the night of the accident, and where was she now? The mixed-up cellist had her difficulties. I wondered what Steve had thought. He couldn't have killed Meghann because he couldn't have left his room. Jim had known Meghann and Steve since their wedding but maybe now he wanted Meghann out of Steve's life. But then why send him a card and bring Steve back at all. Who else would have wanted her dead? I had too many questions.

I had my choice of spaces in the empty lot. I breezed by the unmanned welcome desk, passed the elevators, down the stairs, and into the lifeless cafeteria. My Mukluks slapped the linoleum, making the only sounds.

"Hello? Susie?" I called. "Anyone here?"

A cart with squeaky wheels rolled around the corner. Jim blinked bloodshot eyes and scratched a bristly chin before he recognized me. "Visiting hours are over."

"I know. I'm meeting …" Susie didn't want anyone to overhear. "Someone." Curiosity always got the better of me. "Jim, how well did you know Meghann?"

"Too well. You know, she could have been something, that one. When she showed up here again, I hoped seeing Steve would turn her around, so I sent him a card. It didn't work, and now she's gone." He smothered a yawn. "I'm about done in. Do you need anything?"

"You didn't like Xavier much, did you?"

"No. I really didn't." His dark eyes bored into me. "But if you're going to ask where I was the night he died, I worked two shifts. I don't have family here so I'm their go-to person when they need someone over a holiday."

"Sorry."

He shrugged, rolled the cart a few feet, stopped, and said, "I'd ask me too." He rounded the corner out of sight.

Heels clattered from the other end of the corridor and Dr. Coltraine materialized from the dark hallway. She disentangled a chain securing a pair of glasses around her neck from her stethoscope.

"Ms. Wilk? Susie was just finishing with a patient. I was on my way down and she asked if I'd let you know she'll be here shortly."

"Thanks." I glanced around the dimly lit room. "It's sure quiet here."

"The cafeteria closes at eight, but I can get you a cup of coffee or tea. Follow me," she said. I walked next to her as she backtracked the way she'd come. She cleared her throat. "The patient you brought in is currently in the ICU under guard."

Tears clouded my vision for a moment. "I hope she'll

be okay."

What looked like a sneer flitted across her face. Dr. Coltraine opened the door to a large office and invited me in. "Let me text Susie that you've arrived."

I admired an abstract painting hanging over a tall bookcase filled with thick tomes bearing scientific titles. Awards, diplomas, and photos covered two walls. The photo display spanned a career: Dr. Coltraine in cap and gown, in a long silky dress, shaking hands with various dignitaries, wearing skis on a snowy slope, slyly winking over the tops of round glasses.

"You can wait for Susie here."

"Do you know anything more about Quinn?" I asked.

Dr. Coltraine shook her head. "It's sad, really. Every time Quinn's mother brought her to the ER, someone commented on what a great mother she was, how watchful and caring. When Quinn grew out of her maladies, it seems her mother invented occasions where Quinn might need assistance and, as a mom, she would receive a pat on the back for a job well done, until the last time. She tried to trick her daughter into drinking water laced with tetrahydrozoline, but Quinn is very intuitive, just like her grandpa, and she didn't drink it.

"Some women are just not cut out to be mothers. Take Kelton for example. But it's all straightened out and I can't wait to reinstate Dr. Erickson, get him back on board. We make a great team." She glowed. "He's understanding and patient and not too hard on the eyes. I can see why so many females are attracted to him."

I couldn't help but smile.

"You too?" I might have been mistaken but for a moment it looked like a few sparks flared from her eyes.

"Would you like a cup of herbal tea?" I nodded. She placed a cup beneath the spigot of a machine and pushed a button. She indicated I take a seat. I slid out of my jacket and hung it over the chair back.

I sat, returning my gaze to the art hanging above the bookcase. "What a curious piece." The more I stared at it, the more the forms in the piece took shape. "It's Alice falling down the rabbit hole, isn't it? Ida would love it. She's an artist, you know."

When the whirring sounds quieted, she handed me a fragrant, warm cup and I took a greedy sip. She made a second cup for herself. Her steel gray eyes watched me through the steam above her cup.

"Karlman didn't look well when they brought her in. She's suffering from acute hypothermia, and anything could happen." She sipped her tea. "It's quite sad. But if Quinn uses her talents and her intellect, she'll break away from her family and do well," she said with an edge to her voice.

I yawned and blinked rapidly, my smile fading. *Intuitive.* Maxwell described Xavier with that word. *Like her grandpa?* Who knew that? I scratched my scalp and rubbed my face. What did I know about tetrahydrozoline? I tried to keep my eyes open and spilled a bit of tea.

"Let me take that." She removed the cup from my stiff fingers. "I know I've said too much."

I glanced at the picture on the wall of her wearing glasses and remembered similar frames in the photo taken at the scene of the accident that killed Pete's mom. Coltraine's cold eyes met mine.

I slurred my words and thought I said, "It was you. But why?" My fingers tingled.

"You heard him in the ER. Papa threatened to expose me. I've waited too long and couldn't have him give everything to his darling baby boy. After all I did for him, all those years ago, he cut me loose to fend for myself and I worked my fingers to the bone to get where I am today. His mind was nearly gone, his paranoia taking over, and I had my baby brother where I wanted him. I led his overprotective wife down the rabbit hole." She barked a brittle laugh. "She readily gave Quinn the meds I prescribed, thinking they were keeping her healthy. I never meant for Quinn to be harmed, just uncomfortable. Everything was going as planned until Dr. Erickson started to care for Papa and the rest of the lowlife losers out at the encampment. I tried to make him persona non grata, unacceptable, labeled a thief. But Papa was going to ruin it all."

"With the music?" I muttered.

"During one of our talks, Papa told me he'd written down everything. I made several pro bono health visits to the village. Mayor Maxwell lapped that up. I searched while I was there but couldn't find anything. I didn't realize he'd written it out in a composition. I didn't even know he still could write music. Popovich came to see me after his ... death, in tears. She taunted me with, 'Don't I know you?' and I couldn't believe she didn't remember everything." Coltraine laughed. "All she wanted was a new cello. Hers went up in smoke. From the fire I started. She told me she had a secret manuscript, and that's when I understood everything. She was obstinate, I'll give her that. Just before she died, she told me that little red-haired lady had it."

Ida.

"And you stole it?"

"Burned what I found but it seems I was too hasty. I

missed some pages. I doubted Popovich could decipher its meaning, but I couldn't leave that to chance. You, on the other hand … When you called about the possible messages in the music, you caught Chief West and her team investigating Ryn's disappearance." Her face softened and she almost smiled. "Officer Christianson had a lot to say about your interference and methods of problem solving. And you kept showing up."

"Erica's daughter was driving. That was you."

She faltered in her telling. "Xavier and my mother were lushes, and who do you think they called to pick them up so they wouldn't get into legal issues? Me. Everything depended on me. And my allowance was dependent on my taking care of them, staying in their good graces. At the drop of a hat, I was expected to be wherever they needed me. The one time he promised he had business to attend to and they absolutely would not be partaking, I went to a party."

"You were driving …" I fumbled for the next words I wanted to say. "Under the influence?"

"No more than my worthless parents, but there is no statute of limitations for a crime involving the death of another. Papa adored my mother and her dying words were—"

"Protect her," I mumbled. "Your name, an anagram? Coltraine—Notrecali."

"Check," she sneered.

Words formed in my mind and fought past my thick tongue. "Brock?"

Vindication darted across her face. "He was in the wrong place at the right time. That's what he gets for taking my dad's antique violin."

I stood too rapidly and crumpled to the floor. I screamed, grabbed my shoulder. and heard Coltraine say victoriously, "Checkmate."

Then my world went dark.

CHAPTER FORTY-TWO

Long, sharp spikes of pain drilled into my shoulder, and I winced. Tape covered my lips and I struggled for every shaggy breath, fighting the constriction in my chest. I gagged at the overbearing smell of fish. My nose, ears, and fingertips were icy, but beads of sweat rolled down my back. Zip ties around my wrists locked my hands behind me and curtailed any expansive movements. My cheek brushed against a stiff, scratchy floor covering.

The thrum of tires pounded in my head. We were on the move, but to where? One eye opened. I squinted at the space around me. My eye adjusted to the shadows, and I dragged open the second eye. A tiny crack in the ceiling let in a lot of cold and a little light. The small space came into focus. I could touch one wall of the small trailer with my knees and one with my back. I sat up. When the spinning in my head receded, I braced myself and ratcheted my body to a standing position. I leaned against the wall until my breathing became more regular.

We hit a bump, and my knee thudded against the inner fender covering the wheel well. Tiny stones clinked along the metal lining. I groaned.

Coltraine was Xavier's stepdaughter. She'd been the one driving drunk when the cars collided, and two loving mothers died. She was selfish and angry and had killed her stepdad and Meghann to protect her secret and inheritance. I was only one more impediment. My head throbbed. I thought about what I had to do to help Paul, Ryn, and Quinn.

But first, I had to get out of this closet-like place.

I closed my eyes and pictured Brock ripping apart the plastic bindings for fun. My hands were secured behind me. If my mouth could move, I would've smiled. Jane put me through a lot of pain twice a week, stretching every which way, and I hoped her penchant for creative movement made me flexible enough to get my hands in front of me. I bent at the waist and promptly tipped over, striking my forehead on one wall, and unceremoniously tumbling to the floor. I curled into a ball and shifted my hands around my feet. The shooting pain in my shoulder brought tears to my eyes, and I screamed behind the tape. I didn't know if I could raise my arms over my head, but if I didn't try and Coltraine returned, I might never feel pain again. I peeled the tape from my lips and breathed deeply.

I fumbled my way into a standing position again and took three breaths. I cleared the area in front of me. It had to happen synchronously, and, with the injury to my shoulder, I'd probably only have one shot. I took three more breaths and carefully raised my arms. I pressed my lips together to swallow my scream. In one swift motion, I brought my hands down, and yanked my elbows back.

The plastic broke. My wrists ached and fire tore from my shoulder. I was still sluggish but free.

I felt along the wall for a knob or a handle, but only located an indented section, a plausible opening. I ran my fingers along the edge, looking for a little leeway. We hit a bump that slammed me to the ground.

And we stopped.

I scrambled awkwardly to the floor by the door, slapping the tape over my mouth and clasping my hands together behind me. If I could fool her so she'd get close enough, I might catch her off guard. Maybe.

I waited. Nothing happened.

The motor started up again and the rocking movement on the uneven surface threw me off balance, knocking me into the walls. We stopped and reversed. I pitched forward. One end of the box rose and crashed to the ground. One side jerked down in increments as if lowered by a jack, then the same thing happened on the other side. Losing my sense of balance, I toppled and the rug beneath me slid, revealing a hinged rectangle, a trap door with a metal circle at one end. I ripped the tape from my mouth, stood, and pulled up on the ring.

I tapped slush with my toe and icy water bubbled to the surface. Coltraine had successfully parked the trailer over an opening in the water. And she'd probably done it before.

A section of the trailer wall tore loose, crackling like adhesive. I had no time to react. The golden rays of daylight, cresting over the treetops, poked through the entry. I'd certainly missed my meeting with Amanda. I'd been unconscious for longer than I thought.

Coltraine stuck her head inside. "I was hoping you'd still be out. But you must be feeling woozy at the very least. Very resourceful, aren't you? But don't you see, it's just a matter of time. You've no place to go."

"Where are we?"

"We're in one of many fish houses on Lake Monongalia, but the fish never seem to bite here, so we are very much alone, far away from anyone else, where you'll never be heard."

"Why are you doing this?"

"I have the perfect life, and when my poor brother's crazy wife is sent to prison, he'll be denied his birthright. I'll come forward." She stepped inside and opened her hand, revealing an Alice chess figure missing its hand. "I'll be duly crushed, of course." She put on a very long face. "All the tragedy in my family." Her hands covered her mouth and her eyes widened. "And so surprised. How would I have known about the significant inheritance?" She dropped the façade. "And I'll be quite a catch for a young, unattached ER doctor."

I heard the distant rumble of engines and the familiar bark of a dog, and I felt the inkling of hope.

"How will you explain my disappearance?"

"Me? I won't have to explain anything. I barely know you, but I've overheard all kinds of chatter about the loss of your young husband and your despondency." Unbidden tears filled my eyes. "There, you see. You're still so easily saddened, so I might drop a hint that after encountering so much death you took your life into your own hands. The ice is more than a foot deep. No one will find you until the spring thaw if they find you at all. The depth just off the point is close to one hundred feet." She extracted a syringe from her pocket. "Would you like to glide easily into the water, unaware of the cold, or would you like to go kicking and screaming, because …" She removed the cap, flicked the base, and squirted a drop through the needle on top. "You. Will. Go."

Her menacing voice added goosebumps to my goosebumps. My eyes darted from one wall to the other, and then to the ring in my hand. I stooped to set the trap door back in its frame and my knees buckled.

"Much better," Coltraine said.

My head dropped, accepting defeat, watching until she stepped over the hollow-sounding metal. I wrenched the trap door with every ounce of strength I had left.

She stumbled backward.

I scuttled to the opening in the wall.

Coltraine's iron grip encircled my ankle. I lurched, kicking at her hand. I grabbed the frame and pulled myself to the edge of the exit, screaming. She wrested my hands free and hauled me inside, flipping me onto my back and mashing my shoulder into the floor. I howled. She loomed over me, her face red and splotchy. Meghann's gold cello charm swung from her neck. The syringe sliced cold air out of its way toward its mark—me, and halted.

A deep growl, like far off thunder, rumbled and I wriggled to glimpse its source.

Maverick.

Coltraine retreated and regrouped. She bellowed as she went for my dog.

Nobody hurts my dog.

I snared a boot and she tripped. The syringe flew from

her hand, and we grappled for it. Maverick yapped and snarled, taking one stalking step and another, baring sharp, white fangs. Coltraine backed away.

I stood and wavered, the doorway going in and out of focus. Maverick continued to bark, his yowls undulating. I thought I was going to black out but forced my feet forward. Just when I thought I'd be out of the dank shanty, I came face to face with a black-suited, helmeted creature.

Caught between the enemy who wanted me dead and an entity I did not know, I decided to take my chances and, with the cry of an attack, charged forward.

CHAPTER FORTY-THREE

Strong arms encircled me, and no amount of thrashing loosened the grip.

"Katie," a gentle voice said. "I've got you."

The voice belonged to Pete and the capture turned into a hug. My arms wrapped around him, and I buried my head in his chest.

"You're shivering." The tinted visor flipped up, and he took off his jacket and draped it over my shoulders.

Maverick leaped from the doorway. His tail batted back and forth, brushing the space wider between us.

A feeble voice called from the trailer, "Help me. She tried to kill me."

I glanced inside. The syringe protruded from the back of Coltraine's hand, and her eyes fluttered closed.

"No. No. No." I shook my head. "I didn't …"

"I know," Pete said. His hands released me. He hauled himself into the trailer and returned, carrying an unconscious Coltraine to the snowmobile.

"I'll send someone," he yelled over the loud noise. "You'll be okay?"

I nodded.

He mounted the sled and cradled Coltraine's ragdoll-like form in front of him. The engine caterwauled and stuttered, then kicked into high gear and they took off over the ice.

I dropped down next to Maverick, nose to nose, and, despite the calamity, his rough tongue tickled as he lapped my tears and I giggled. "What now, my friend?" I quivered and headed back inside for some protection against the cold when a second snowmobile slid to a stop.

"Need a lift?" asked Dillon. "No strings." A helmet dangled from his hand.

The three of us raced toward the crowd on the shore, and Dillon slashed snow as he slid to a stop in front of Ronnie Christianson.

"Thanks," I said, my teeth chattering, my knees knocking, and my hands burning from the cold, and I stumbled from the back.

He nodded and caught his dad waving from the door of his cougar fishing lair. The proud smile stretched from ear to ear and Dillon zoomed in that direction.

"You again," Officer Christianson said in a huff. I took two steps away from him before he said, "Where do you think you're going? Stay right there."

I stopped. Maverick sat next to me, looking from Christianson to me. Shivering, I ran my hand up and down, trying to ignore the excruciating pain in my arm, creating very little friction. He had to notice I'd started to shudder. "Arrest me and take me to jail if you must, but I'm freezing and I'm going to get out of the cold, one way or the other."

A large, crinkly cape fell over my shoulders and Officer Rodgers said, "Let's get you someplace warm."

Lorelei opened the door of the Isaacson fish house and dragged me inside, settling me in front of the blazing stove. Mr. Isaacson smiled shyly, cupping my fingers around a warm mug of hot chocolate. Maverick gulped the dog biscuit thrown his way.

"The board wanted to suspend the tournament until you were located, but Officer Christianson led the complaint that you might be orchestrating your disappearance to insure we won. We were ahead in the point totals, but did anyone even see your fish?" Mr. Isaacson laughed. "Like you would make or break the victory. Oh, sorry."

But I suspected he wasn't really sorry.

"I thought fishing would keep you out of trouble," Lorelei said.

"How did anyone know to look for me?"

Lorelei looked at Brock and he nodded. "The scuttlebutt was that Maverick missed breakfast and went berserk, and your dad couldn't find you. Mrs. Clemashevski pulled some strings and called in law enforcement ahead of the missing person wait time. Ms. Kelton came forward this morning and said she saw you leaving in the middle of the night with Dr. Coltraine. Chief West discovered Coltraine is really Xavier's stepdaughter. Looks like she not only let Pete take some heat, but Brock and you too."

"How did they find us?"

Lorelei nodded out the window. "They'd already checked with the fishermen on this side, and no one had seen you, but fishermen watch each other and park where the fish are biting. That lone fish house stood out like a sore thumb. Dillon pointed the trailer out to Chief West and told her fishing was never any good out there. You know the rest."

Someone rapped at the door and Brock answered it.

The chief said, "Are you up to talking, Katie?"

"The sooner the better."

The kids and Mr. Isaacson rose to leave, but Amanda said, "Please stay. This affects you as well. Coltraine didn't care who got blamed, Brock, as long as it wasn't her. You just happened to be in the right place. When Officer Christianson originally interviewed her at the hospital, she said Xavier had asked you to hold onto an extremely valuable violin and maybe you didn't want to return it. It seemed plausible. She suggested you had parked your pop-up near the hole you already prepared for Xavier's demise to keep casual passersby from locating it or stumbling in until you needed it, and you accidentally fell in. I think she'd planned to get rid of Xavier and prepared the ice ahead of a visit with him, but he must have sensed her intentions." *His intuitiveness.* "She killed him anyway and dumped his body in the hole."

Brock's eyes popped. "Huh?"

"What do you have for me, Katie?"

I repeated everything Coltraine had told me. I asked, "How is Ryn Karlman?"

"She's going to be fine and so is Quinn. No charges with be filed for mistreatment of a child. That was all Coltraine—what an aunt." I almost snorted at Amanda's sour expression. "You should probably go to the ER and get checked out."

I'm not sure what crossed my face, but the ER was the last place I wanted to be, and they all laughed.

Amanda said, "I guess not right now. But you should go home and have your family take care of you."

"Is Coltraine going to make it?"

"Yes."

I edged forward then cocked my head. "Today is the final day of the tournament. I've got fishing to do," I said and, keeping my squeamishness in check, I reached into the bait carton.

We made a good haul and after we turned in our day's catch, I made a quick trip to urgent care.

CHAPTER FORTY-FOUR

I tightened the Velcro holding my arm in place, put my feet up, and tried to rest without much success. Everyone and their grandmother visited, bringing holiday greetings and goodies Ida dutifully delivered to the churches hosting the displaced families, thus in need of foodstuffs.

A manilla envelope showed up in our mailbox with my name on it. I think Ida and Dad watched me open it, hoping it held the message from Maverick's kennel veterinarian, but when my gradebook and two biographies from my cryptanalyst file dropped out, they both pretended to ignore me. Typed on a notecard clipped to the cover was the word, 'Found.' I'd never really know, but I had my suspicions.

After supper, I caught Dad and smiled sweetly. "Daddy?"

"I haven't heard that in a lifetime. I'm in for it now, aren't I, darlin'?"

"Can you warm up the Focus and take me to see Quinn? I'm not supposed to drive yet. I have a little something for her and I want to see how she's doing."

"Me too, darlin'."

Minutes later we parked in front of the Karlman home.

Ryn answered the door. "You're the one."

Afraid to admit to anything, I waited.

"Thank you for everything. Please, come in." She called over her shoulder, "Quinn. Paul. It's Ms. Wilk and her dad."

Quinn ran at me with open arms but slid to a stop. Her wide eyes took in my sling, and she said, "Does it hurt?"

"A little, but it'll be fine in no time." She hugged my side and I hugged her back. "You're looking great."

"I *am* great. I'm Ta Great Quinn," she said, emoting. Oh, dear Quinn. If you'd only known your grandfather. She hugged Dad too.

She opened my gift, a stuffed rabbit, and thanked me politely but she tore into the Alice in Wonderland five-hundred-piece puzzle Dad gave her. Paul took Ryn's face in his hands and gently kissed her. They gazed at each other for a moment then turned and watched Quinn and Dad choose their pieces, turn them every which way, and fit them together.

The doorbell rang. "Now who?" said Ryn.

Paul returned with Maxwell in tow. "It's true? He *was* my father?" he said angrily.

Maxwell nodded. "He was an eccentric who built a fortress around his head and heart for fear he'd hurt those he'd promised to protect. He loved you and your stepsister the only way he knew how, and with his death you will be able to take even better care of your family. Can you meet at the law offices of Tupy, Dvorak, and Sticha on Monday morning to go over the terms of the estate?"

Paul stammered. "Don't I have my job anymore?"

Maxwell grinned. "That, Mr. Karlman, is totally up to you." He handed an envelope to Paul and bade us a goodnight.

We watched Dad and Quinn work on the puzzle together and Ryn said, "You're all invited to her birthday party on January 15th. I hope you can make it."

After they'd joined border pieces, Dad said, "It's time for me to take my girl home, Quinn."

Quinn and her dad followed us outside. He wrapped his arms around her and as she gazed at the night sky, her face lit up. "Daddy, a shooting star."

Her eyes closed and when she opened them, he asked, "Did you make a wish?"

"I wished that all the children living where Grandpa used to live get a home for the new year."

He gave her a hug and they waved as Dad and I pulled from the curb.

"That's a brave little girl," I said, sniffing.

"I think I know another," my dad said, smiling at me.

* * *

More of the same happened Friday, and all I wanted was to read my book, rest, and heal. Dad and Ida understood when I declined to go with them to the Columbia New Year's Bash.

But guilt was a powerful motivator.

I parked the Focus at the end of the long line of cars near the community center and trudged through the snow to where Ida said they'd be viewing the New Year's Eve fireworks display over the lake. I'd had enough of my family and friends checking on me, making sure I didn't need anything so I found a quiet place next to a huge cedar tree, close enough to see all my cherished people through the large plate glass window overlooking the lake and count my many blessings. I had to work up my courage before I could join them. I straightened the strap of the sling behind my neck to make it more comfortable, and someone crunched through the snow next to me.

"Does it hurt much? Do you need a little prick from a local?"

My eyes moved first, and I glanced sideways. He couldn't remember those were some of the first words he ever said to me when I'd sat in the ER getting stitches. Could he? My head turned next. Pete's eyes focused on the spectacle in front of us and the exploding reds and whites and blues of the open salvo of fireworks reflected off his smiling face. The shadows played on his features, but I found comfort in the deep dimple. I sensed he could.

He turned toward me. He removed his black leather glove and extended his right hand. "Hi. I'm Pete Erickson."

I removed my mitten and clasped his hand. "Just Katie" I answered.

"Think I might need a do over."

A large, noisy contingent from the community center emptied onto the deck in front of us.

Dorene Dvorak saw us first and stomped to where I stood with a look on her face I couldn't decipher.

"Thanks for the referral but you really don't ever have

to send a kid my way again."

I grinned. She was the best and, if anyone I knew ever needed an attorney, she'd be the one I'd call.

"Happy New Year, Katie."

A hulk of a man caught sight of Pete and marched toward us, clenching and unclenching his fists. Susie hustled behind, tugging at the sleeve of his jacket. He towered over Pete and furrowed his brow, but Pete stood his ground and swallowed hard, his Adam's apple riding up and down his neck. He gritted his teeth, prepared to take whatever blow came his way. But the giant wrapped his arms around Pete and lifted him in a bear hug. "Thanks, Bro."

Arms grabbed me from behind and we nearly toppled. "Girlfriend!"

I winced.

Jane spun me around. "What happened to you?" She took a disapproving look at my attire and raised an eyebrow. "This time."

"I'll tell you later. What are you doing here?" I asked.

"We came back to celebrate New Year's Eve with you, and I brought my dad's new favorite bubbly."

I squinted to read the label on the bottle she held up: Jones von Drehle "Blanc de Blanc."

A new burst of color shimmered across her face. "Come," she said.

Arm-in-arm we crossed over the snow to join my Columbia family.

CHAPTER FORTY-FIVE

I'm so proud of Brock. After Paul assured him the violin was his, Dorene helped Brock secure a buyer. He's keeping half of the proceeds to buy his own beginner violin and put some money away for college," I said.

"But the donation he made put our funds over the top," Ida said. "We'll have those families into shelters in no time." She unplugged the tree lights and wrapped them around a cardboard tube.

In the middle of stowing decorations, the water alarm went off again and Dad and I rushed into the kitchen with armloads of towels to sop up the puddle of water dribbling from under the sink onto the floor.

Ida stepped in. "We're going to have to watch it. Gene said it was a temporary fix while he waited for parts, but

I called him, and because of the super-freeze, water pipes all over Columbia are in need of repair. He's backed up for three days. He can't find any help with experience."

"Ida, I know a real plumber." She rolled her eyes. "He's been down on his luck and out of work, but could we put them in contact with each other and see if he can be of service?" I rummaged through my coat pockets and came up with the resumé of the dad whose family I'd driven to the church the night of the fire. Ida made the calls.

She hung up and said, "I can't wait for next December." She sighed, flicking dried needles from the branches. "We're lucky the city picks up Christmas trees and grinds them into mulch, but they have to be out on the corner by six tomorrow morning."

Dad stifled a snort, and holding the last glass ornament by its hook, he deposited it in Ida's outstretched hand. She wrapped it in light green tissue paper and nestled it into the clear plastic tote next to the rest of the treasures. He removed the star from the top of the tree and held it in his hand for a long time.

"What are you thinking about, Dad?" I asked. I folded the tree skirt and slid it into a plastic sleeve.

"I'm wondering where I'm going to put your trophy."

I blushed and read the words on the base of the five-inch-tall award, 'Third Smallest Northern.' Any fish caught might claim a prize; unfortunately, only the current year's chair knew the bizarre trophy categories.

Dad held the tree trunk stationary. I turned the knobs on the stand securing the Frasier fir and held the base. Dad rocked it back and forth to encourage the sap to release the stand. A few drops of water sloshed onto my hand before the sticky goo let loose. Ida opened a huge bag to cover the tree and keep the needles from falling everywhere in the house while we carried it out the door.

I inhaled the fragrant pine one last time and Dad and I marched to the corner, removed the bag, and set our bundle atop three others. I took one last look at our tree and something shiny and silver winked from the uppermost branches. I extended my hand, weaving through the tree limbs, and pinched the hook securing the ornament. I cupped it in my hand to protect it on its way out. A heart-shaped mirror reflected the sunlight

I held it to Dad, wondering if he knew its origin. He shrugged.

Ida welcomed us back inside with two steaming mugs, and I didn't much care what was in it. "Do you know where this ornament came from?"

She winked and settled into the living room chair. "Perhaps."

"Are you going to tell me?"

"Maybe another day."

Dad took a sip from his mug and set it on the table. He fished out a vacuum to finish our cleanup. I slurped the warm creamy goodness, set down my mug, and wiped the melted marshmallow from my lips. I bundled the plastic sheet protecting the floor under our tree. Maverick rooted around, swishing his thick, black tail, snuffling close to the wall. The tail stopped moving and he backed up, slobbering all over a fat envelope.

I stopped moving.

"What do you have there, big fella?" Ida asked, one eyebrow raised above her impish green eyes.

The plastic slipped from my arm, and I dropped to the floor. I swatted my thigh. "Here, Maverick." He padded to my side and dropped the envelope in my lap. I picked it up with shaking hands and sucked in a breath. "This is it."

HOT BUTTERED RUM BATTER

1 quart of vanilla ice cream (softened)
1 lb. brown sugar
½ lb. butter (softened)
cinnamon
nutmeg
cloves

Mix first three ingredients well and freeze batter. When ready to use, thaw for thirty minutes. Put 2 T in a mug with 1 scant shot of rum (or not). Fill with hot milk. Sprinkle with cinnamon, nutmeg, and/or cloves.

Mary has always loved a good mystery, a brain teaser, or a challenge. As a former mathematics teacher, she ties numbers and logic to the mayhem game. The Katie Wilk mysteries allow her to share those stories, as well as puzzles, riddles, and a few taste-tested recipes.

When she's not writing, she's making wonderful memories with family, walking her dog whose only speed is faster, dabbling in needlecrafts, and pretending to cook. Mary is a member of Mystery Writers of America, Sisters in Crime, American Cryptogram Association, Dog Writers of America, and PEO.

Thank you for taking the time to read *Fishing, Festivities, & Fatalities*. If you enjoyed it please tell your friends, and I would be so grateful if you would consider posting a review. Word of mouth is an author's best friend, and very much appreciated.

Thank you,

Mary Seifert

* * *

WHAT'S NEXT FOR KATIE AND MAVERICK?

Katie Wilk and Susie Kelton have been at odds since the moment they met, but when a new math teacher begins to insinuate herself between Katie and her students, colleagues, and friends, Susie is the only one to see through the façade and read the signals correctly. Unbelievably, she's on Katie's side. Then Maverick finds a body, and Susie is accused of killing the jeweler who stole her engagement diamond. Can Katie put aside their differences and come to Susie's aid? Only time will tell.

Get all the books in the Katie & Maverick Series!

Maverick, Movies, & Murder
Rescues, Rogues, & Renegade
Tinsel, Trials, & Traitors
Santa, Snowflakes, & Strychnine
Fishing, Festivities, & Fatalities

**Get a collection of free recipes from Mary—
scan the QR code to find out how!**

Visit Mary's website: MarySeifertAuthor.com/
Facebook: facebook.com/MarySeifertAuthor
Twitter: twitter.com/mary_seifert
Instagram: instagram.com/maryseifert/
Follow Mary on BookBub and Goodreads too!